Band Mates

Megan Becker

Band Mates

Copyright © 2025 by Megan Becker

This book is a work of fiction. People, places, events, and names are products of the author's imagination or are used fictitiously. Any resemblance to real-world people, locations, or events is purely coincidental.

All rights reserved. This book or any portion thereof may not be reproduced or used without the express written permission of the author, except for the use of brief quotations in book reviews.

Printed in the United States of America

Front Cover Artwork by Alexandra Aiken

Lattes & Lovebirds Literature

Print ISBN: 979-8-9898118-1-6

A NOTE FROM THE AUTHOR
Content Information

Thank you for picking up a copy of Band Mates!

This story shares thirty years of Mia's life, told through a series of flashbacks mixed in with her present-day experiences. Throughout these years, Mia experiences waves of joy and pain, just as many of us do.

I hope you'll enjoy her story, but I understand if there are topics that will keep you from doing so. Here are some details of what you can expect, just in case you'd prefer not to read any of the below themes at this time:

- Discussion of a friend's death via car accident

- Pregnancy (intentional and accidental)

- Suicidal ideation

This book also includes brief on-page sex and (slightly less brief) profanity.

There is also a lot of humor, friendship, and love throughout.

♫♩

If you or someone you know is struggling with suicidal thoughts or mental health matters, call or text 988, the Suicide & Crisis Lifeline. Calls are free and confidential.

For Ashley & Shannon
and friendships that feel like coming home.

BAND MATES

MEGAN BECKER

CHAPTER 1

now

I HATE FLYING.

And yet.

Here we are, beginning our descent, and it strikes me how the ground below—carefully laid out in grids and cul-de-sacs and dotted with white-yellow street lights and the red and green glow of traffic lights—resembles Christmas tree lights strung across stretches of land.

I rest my head against the cool glass of the airplane window and feel myself smile. It's beautiful down there, and I'm beyond excited for what awaits: my best friend, vintage Nintendo games, fresh-popped popcorn mixed with a smorgasbord of chocolatey candies, and staying up far too late so we can chat about babies (her), music (me), and life (both of us).

I hate flying.

But I love coming home.

CHAPTER 2

now

JULIE'S PARENTS' BASEMENT IS exactly as I remember it: In one corner, there's a square of hardwood floor and a wall lined with mirrors from her tap dancing days. There's the mountain of carefully labeled red and green bins storing all of her mom's holiday treasures, nearly hiding the washer and dryer tucked into the back corner. Most importantly, front and center, there's the wrap-around couch from the late eighties.

This couch is the most important piece of furniture from my formative years. The countless nights we sat here playing video games and watching artsy movies (for Julie) or classics (for our friend Sydney) or musicals (for me) are embedded in my brain, fused into my DNA.

"You okay over there?" Jules looks at me like I have three heads, then shifts her gaze to the couch, which I now realize I've been staring at since I reached the second-to-last step. Which I'm still standing on.

God. This couch.

"I know," she says, rolling her eyes. "It's older than we are. Sure you don't want to stay at the Springs?"

"I'm sure." I'm eighty percent certain Songbird Springs Bed and Breakfast hasn't been updated in thirty years, and one hundred percent certain it's haunted. I mean, yes, it's beautiful, and it has great ratings, but I prefer not to have ghosts cozy up to me when I'm trying to sleep.

"Well, if you change your mind, I won't be offended. I know this isn't quite the arrangement we'd discussed, but..." She shrugs, then turns to start making up the couch.

"Jules, I can do that myself." When I reach for the sheets and blanket in her arms, she pulls them away.

"I know you can. And this has nothing to do with you being who you are. You're our guest, so I'm going to take care of you like I would any other guest."

I pick up a throw pillow. She glares at me, so I pick up another. "Aren't you technically a guest, too?" I tease.

"More like a squatter, it seems. Though squatting is becoming more of a challenge these days." Her laugh fills the basement as she steadies herself on the side of the couch and attempts a squat, supporting her stomach with her free arm.

"So, so graceful," I tell her. "Are you trying to induce labor with that move?"

She shakes her head and shifts her feet under her. "Are you kidding? No way am I having a baby while living under my parents' roof. I watched El go through that, and you could not pay me enough. Also—" she shifts again and jerks her head, motioning me over. "A little help, maybe?"

I help her up from her squatting position (and make her promise not to try that again without proper supervision... or without someone recording it), and we sink into the couch like it's twenty years ago. "How is El, anyway?" I ask, picking at a thread in a hole in my jeans. Elliott Bailey is the golden child of Songbird Springs. Or, at least, he *was*, until his old girlfriend had to come clean about her very surprise pregnancy and her parents made it their mission to destroy his reputation.

Elliott is two years older than Julie and me, but he's as much a part of my growing up as this couch is.

Julie groans. "Do you know what makes me feel old?" Without waiting for me to answer, she points at her belly and says, "I'm thirty-five and about to have my first kid. And my brother has a freaking *adult child*."

"Which is crazy, by the way, because the last time I saw Zoe she had pigtails and was wearing mismatched socks. But time flies, I guess." She didn't really answer the question about how Elliott's doing now, and I wonder what kind of extravaganza he's got planned for Zoe's big day this summer. He always was the type to go above and beyond and make the people he cared about feel special. Some of us were lucky enough to be in the fallout zone and still be infected with that feel-good energy. But enough about Elliott. I'm here, in a house I spent all my free time in growing up, with my very best friend of thirty years. "Speaking of time, any word on when your place will be ready for you?"

Julie rattles off a list of all the things that have gone wrong during their pre-baby home renovation, from finding a whole host of animal corpses buried in the yard when they simply wanted to dig holes for fence posts, to needing to replace drywall thanks to a careless handyman who was confused about which wall to swing his sledgehammer through (and who was subsequently and quickly fired), and all of that is on top of the work the contractors came to do: redo the kitchen and all the flooring throughout the house, with fresh coats of paint in most rooms, too.

"It's so overwhelming," she says, and I nod like I have any idea what she's talking about. Sleeping on a bus or in a different hotel every night while on tour may not sound attractive, and I don't always love my landlord, but I'll choose either over the trials of home ownership any day of the week. "Anyway, it's maybe another month or two, tops. Jess just feels better if we stay here, away from all the dust and noise and random strangers."

"It sucks, but at least we're together here." I reach forward and take her hand in mine. "I've missed you, Jules. I've missed this."

"Ugh. *Same*. I'm so happy you're back. Even if it's just for a little." She pats her belly again and looks around the room. "I did a terrible job getting everything set up."

"Are you kidding? You picked me up at the airport, *and* you're six months pregnant. I think you're doing great."

She squeezes my hand in hers. "Thanks, Mia." After a yawn, she shakes her head. "Mind if I head up to bed? Will you be okay down here?"

There's no place that feels more like home to me than the Baileys' basement couch. "I'll be one hundred percent fine," I answer.

Jules stands and gives me a giant bear hug, then waddles to the steps. "Sleep well, my friend. I'll see you in the morning." She takes two steps up and stops, leaning back. "And Mia?"

"Hmm?"

"Welcome home."

CHAPTER 3

now

ELLIOTT BAILEY IS STANDING in the kitchen wearing nothing but a pair of pajama pants.

It's nothing I haven't seen before, but his shirtless phase hit its peak back when he was a lanky twelve-year-old. At ten, I thought boys had cooties and I wanted nothing to do with them. I stand very much corrected.

I'm not expecting to see him, which is maybe why I've ventured up from my basement dungeon in a tank top, short shorts, and a pair of knee-high socks, wrapped up in one of the blankets Julie left for me before going to bed.

By the looks of it, he's not all that surprised to see me, and he smirks as he scans my outfit. "Well, well, well," he says. "Looks like the prodigal child has returned."

"That's me," I reply, trying to make my dropped jaw look like a natural yawn. With great effort, I manage to unglue my eyes from his torso. It's well past midnight, and I can't think of a single thing Elliott might be doing in his parents' kitchen at this hour. "Actually, maybe that's you, too."

"Huh," he snorts, before returning to his task of scooping chocolate chip cookie dough ice cream into a massive bowl.

Because their parents always told me to make myself at home and because it's just Elliott, anyway, I shuffle to a cupboard and extract an equally ginormous bowl, then slide it to him. He quirks a brow at me. "Fill 'er up."

He shakes his head and shovels more ice cream into his own bowl before dropping the scooper into the carton. He lifts his spoon for a comically large bite, leaving me to fend for myself. How he and Jules are siblings, I'll never know. "Help yourself," he tells me.

"Wow. Great manners. Bet your mom would be so proud."

Another taunting bite goes in. "Sorry. I just thought you meant it when you sang about not needing a man. But if all your songs are a lie, I guess I can help." He moves to reclaim the scooper, but I grab it first.

"Whatever. I've got it. What are you doing here, anyway?"

He shrugs. "We only had Neapolitan at home."

"I call B.S."

"Fine." He rinses the empty plastic carton and drops it into the recycling bin. "I'm here for Zoe."

"For Zoe?"

"My daughter."

"I know who Zoe is, El."

He smiles, and this whole scene makes me feel like I'm sixteen again: Ice cream in the kitchen with Elliott when Jules and her parents are sound asleep. Slumber party in the basement. Calling him El. El smiling at me. The butterflies in my stomach fluttering to life under his gaze.

"Well, despite my expert parenting and excellent taste in music, it seems my daughter has fallen into a certain subset of teenage girls and rather enjoys listening to a particular band."

"Is that so?" I ask, finishing my ice cream, shivering because now I'm cold inside and out.

"Yeah. And I, always a devoted father, may have given into requests to have a sleepover here so that she can greet you first thing in the morning."

Something I've really had to work on over the last decade is managing my facial expressions. On stage, I need to make sure it looks pretty at all times, even when I'm belting out a note or forming normal vowels. People are always taking pictures, and the worst ones tend to be some people's favorites to post. Unfortunately, I forget all the work I've done in that area, and I roll my eyes.

"I know. It's lame." Elliott retreats and busies himself with wiping down the counter, avoiding my eyes. "We can make sure we're not in your way in the morning and get out of here early, before you emerge from your lair."

"No, it's not that I don't want to see her. It's just that you didn't have to haul her over here for a fake sleepover just to set up a meeting. You could have just asked."

"As soon as Julie heard you were coming home, she warned me not to bother you."

Of course she did. Julie is a protector, always has been. I know she wants me to feel comfortable here, to let Songbird Springs be an escape for me for a few weeks, but sometimes she overdoes it. "I don't know if you know this, but Julie is not my official bodyguard."

"You know how she is though, Mia."

"I do," I nod. "I think we can take her, though. All things considered."

Elliott smiles and so do I, imagining the thought of a waddling Julie trying to chase him down.

"Next time, ignore her. Just text me, okay?"

"Sure," he says, shrugging. "But I don't have your number." His fingers brush against mine when he reaches for my dish, and the butterflies take note. This feels natural, eating ice cream and doing dishes and talking to Elliott. The idea of domesticity is one that I'm not fully comfortable with, yet Elliott makes it feel so easy.

Actually, he makes everyone feel easy and comfortable, and maybe that's why I say, "Well, maybe we should change that" more flirtatiously than I would have preferred.

"Maybe." He extracts the bowl from my fingers and turns, rinsing it before loading it into the dishwasher. With his back to me, I roll my eyes skyward and silently chastise myself for responding to him like I'm trying to pick him up at O'Donnell's Pub.

"I should get going, I guess." I stretch and yawn, more for show than out of necessity, and Elliott calls my bluff.

"Sure, pop star. You're tired at—" he glances at the clock on the microwave and smirks. "Wow. Midnight? Really?"

He's caught me, and I shrug. "There was a time change."

"Yeah, no, it's only nine o'clock out west."

I readjust the blanket around my shoulders, shifting my weight from one foot to the other. Does he think I'm trying to avoid him? Isn't that exactly what I'm doing? "I figured I would get out of your hair and return to my cave."

"Or," he says, leaning against the counter, crossing his arms.

"Or, what?"

"How about a movie?"

This all has the potential to end very, very badly. But it also has the potential to distract me from the fact that I can't sleep, whether it's nine o'clock or midnight or three a.m. "What do you have in mind?"

♫♩

What Elliott has in mind is sitting at opposite ends of the couch, each of us tugging at a blanket that was not meant to cover the expanse between us, and watching *Rear Window*. There's something about a classic thriller in black and white that fills me with the same sense of nostalgia as literally every other moment I've experienced since setting foot back in the Baileys' house.

I've been in this basement plenty of times, watched a thousand movies right here, on this exact cushion, but it's never been just Elliott and me. Not to watch a movie, anyway.

In some ways it feels like a betrayal, doing all of this without Julie, even though "all of this" is simply just fighting insomnia with an old movie. And, obviously, her brother. But that's no big deal, because he's just Elliott. And besides, she's upstairs, most likely snuggled next to her wife, and Elliott and I don't have the luxury of having someone snuggle-worthy in our lives. I don't think, anyway.

"Are you seeing anyone?" I blurt out, and immediately I feel heat rise into my cheeks.

The shake of his head is nearly imperceptible, and he never moves his eyes from the screen. "You?"

I turn back to the TV and try to catch his reaction in my periphery. "Not really."

This makes him turn, and his brows furrow even as a smile spreads on his lips. "'Not really'? What does that mean?"

It means that no one has put in the effort to make things work with me. It means that I haven't found anyone worth putting in effort for, myself. It means no one makes my knees weak or my heart race. It means no one is *him*. But how the hell do I tell him that? *Do* I tell him that? Do I tell him what that translates to in my life? No. I definitely don't. What I do is shrug, barely meeting his eyes before gluing them back to Jimmy Stewart and his telephoto lens. "My lifestyle isn't necessarily the best for maintaining relationships."

"Except with Jules."

"Duh. That's different, though."

"How so?" he asks. "If you can stay friends with her, surely you could figure out how to make things work with a Grammy winner or athlete or whoever it is you'd want to date."

"The difference is, no one puts as much effort into a relationship as your sister. There's no way she'd ever let our friendship fall apart."

CHAPTER 4

thirty years ago

THE FIRST DAY OF kindergarten went by in a flash. Or many flashes, as it was, since Mom could not seem to put down her disposable camera. Not long enough to kiss me goodbye, or long enough to tell me she loved me, or long enough to pack me a snack.

So there I was, seated in a tiny plastic chair at a table with four other kids, all with their hair impeccably gelled or curled or braided, after all the "welcome to kindergarten" introductions, my stomach gurgling as Mrs. Frank invited us to have our snacks while she wheeled in the TV cart.

I tried not to make eye contact with the Goldfish and animal crackers that my tablemates began devouring, their snot-soaked chubby fingers reaching into plastic sandwich baggies to extract their crunchy calories. It only made my stomach protest louder: *Hey Mia, I'm here! I know there's food nearby! Feed me!!!*

Instead I looked away, smoothed the pink and blue floral dress that I hadn't worn since Easter Sunday, and focused in on a scuff on my black patent Mary Janes.

"Your dress is really pretty," a tiny voice said from the seat next to mine. Her hair was in two fat braids, each fastened at the bottom with ponytail holders featuring pastel plastic balls that matched her own lacy dress.

"Thanks," I answered, feeling a little less sad but no less hungry.

"Want some pretzels?" She slid her baggie toward me, like she just knew I was going to say yes. There wasn't a drop of snot on her, so I nodded and took two tiny pretzels, hoping it was okay that I'd taken two, but she *had* said pretzels, plural, so I figured it was fine. But her eyes grew wide as she looked at my hands, and guilt flooded me. Turns out, it was an unnecessary emotion. "You can have more. You sounded really hungry."

That was the beginning of Julie Bailey taking care of me.

First, of course, was taking care of my little body by offering me her sustenance. Then it was her taking care of my heart, when she grabbed my hand and led me to the playground after lunch, a sure sign that she was taking me in. After complimenting my lace-trimmed bobby socks, she guided me around the playground, telling me about the most fun equipment out here, because her brother was in second grade and had already told her about the best things to do at recess at Skyline Elementary.

"He said the jungle gym is just for boys, and the swings are really fun to jump off of, but we'll probably get yelled at if we do it."

"I don't want to get yelled at."

Julie shook her head. "Me neither." She looked around the playground, then back toward the blacktop near the school's entrance. "Want to jump rope?"

There was only one jump rope in the recess bin—an old rope with plastic tubes in red, white, and blue stacked around it—so we took turns teaching each other our favorite jump rope chants: *Miss Mary Mack. Cinderella, dressed in yella. Teddy bear, teddy bear. Mabel, Mabel, set the table.*

I was the stronger jumper, but it didn't matter. Julie's friendship was not conditional on her being superior to me. She celebrated when I logged more jumps and skips than she did, and she celebrated when I was the first one chosen to update the classroom's weather station for a whole week. She even celebrated when I was Student of the Month and when my mom was asked to come in for Career Day instead of hers.

The greatest lesson I learned in kindergarten, beyond skip-counting by five or that I needed to pack my own snacks or that the jungle gym was for *everyone*, was that Julie Bailey was the most supportive, loyal friend a person could ever hope to have.

CHAPTER 5

now

IT'S HIGHLY UNLIKELY THAT a herd of elephants casually strolled in overnight, so the cacophony overhead must be everyone else in the house, awake and roaming, while I wipe the sleep from my eyes and the drool from my cheek. I'd hoped to be awake before the others, but with the time difference and the late night last night, I should've known it wasn't going to happen.

When I finally fell asleep, long before Jimmy Stewart broke a second leg and the credits rolled, Elliott was parked at the opposite end of the couch, his feet tucked up next to him, grazing mine. The heat radiated off of him, and everything felt right.

This morning, without him, there's only the chill of the winter air that creeps into the poorly insulated basement.

I pull on a sweater from my suitcase and make a quick stop in the half bath. Then it's a deep breath in, a slow release, and a climb up the stairs.

The door is open barely two inches when Julie chirps out "Good morning, sleepyhead," and all eyes turn toward me. Including Zoe's, which go wide as saucers as I push the door open farther and step into the eat-in kitchen.

"Morning," I answer, desperate for coffee and my toothbrush. It's after nine, but I'm dead tired.

Mr. Bailey beams at me over a platter of still-steaming pancakes, and the aroma of his signature recipe is the perfect welcome home. Mrs. Bailey rises to wrap her arms around me. "Mia Montgomery, in the flesh," she says. She steps back and holds my face in her hands, examining every pore, it seems. "Let's get you breakfast."

There are three truths about the Bailey household: First, everyone is welcome, no questions asked, no matter what. Second, everyone is expected to show respect and help out. Third, everyone is well fed. This morning is no exception as Jess passes a plate my way with three pancakes and a pile of shredded hash browns, the perfect shade of crispy brown on top.

Julie shifts to her left on the bench at the table, and I lower myself into the spot next to her. Zoe is almost instantly at my side with a cup from the nearby coffee shop. "I hope it's okay," she says, biting her lip, looking equal parts excited and terrified.

I smile up at her and take a sip. It's freaking perfect, despite being lukewarm. "Is this a chocolate-covered strawberry mocha?"

"I saw it was your favorite, in that Indie Artist of the Year interview." She takes her seat at the end of the table. "Sorry it's not super hot. I wanted to make sure it was ready when you woke up."

"It's perfect. Thank you, Zoe."

I eat some of the first home-cooked food I've had in six months and compliment Mr. Bailey on his cooking skills. "Somehow these are even better than I remember them," I say about his pancakes.

"Thanks. I've been using oat milk recently and I think it really adds something to the flavor."

I nod and take another bite, trying not to think too hard about the one obvious absence around the dining room table as everyone else chatters about their lives.

The best part of coming home to the Baileys' house is that here I'm just Mia (minus the subtle fangirling from Zoe). It's the one place I can visit where I can just be myself, because that's exactly what everyone expects from me. I'm not Mia Montgomery: Pop Star. I'm just Mia Montgomery: Quirky Kid, Who Happens To Be A Famous Adult Now.

Once everyone has finished their breakfast, I clear the table and start rinsing dishes. Mrs. Bailey puts a gentle hand on my back and takes the plate from my hand. "I'll get these, dear."

There's a fine line between being respectful and helping to do the dishes and being disrespectful by telling the woman of the house 'no.' Avoiding the line, I simply respond, "I'm happy to do my share."

"And I'll let you," she says. "But why don't you get settled in a bit?"

"A shower would feel great." I think we're both unprepared for the wistful tone in which I say it, because Mrs. Bailey laughs and places the plate in the sink.

"You know where it is," she says.

♫♩

Society is spoiled now, with our en-suite bathrooms and Jack-and-Jill bathrooms and our guest bathrooms in our more modern homes. But these classic brick boxes that were all the rage in the eighties? Nope. Half bath on the living level. One full bath upstairs where all the bedrooms are.

With my arms full and overflowing with everything I need for the shower and after it, I push the bathroom door closed with my butt. I straighten some of my toiletries on the vanity (I'm under strict instructions to leave my things there with everyone else's and make myself at home) and turn the water on as hot as I can. I help myself to one of the fluffy blue towels in the linen closet, then hang it on the hook that's been reserved for me on the back of the door. It might not be nearly as elegant, and I may be responsible for cleaning up after myself, but the hospitality here outshines any of the hotels I've stayed at recently.

Post shower, I turn on music, then wrap myself in the towel while I wash my face and brush my teeth. I'm singing along quietly as I do my makeup, then a little louder as I dry my hair. And let's be honest: there's a difference between singing on stage in front of a crowd that has paid to hear your best and singing along in a bathroom to your favorite boy band from your childhood era.

Maybe that's why, when I leave the bathroom, Elliott Bailey shouts at me from his childhood bedroom. "Do I get a refund for that performance?"

I do a double take as I pass by the room that I've only glimpsed before, always adorned those decades ago with Phillies and Eagles posters and a collection of bobbleheads modeled after his favorite athletes and actors. Now it's a home office and Elliott sits at a large wooden desk, peering over a computer monitor at me.

"I know." He looks around the room, too, then meets my gaze. "Sure, they save Julie's room and erase any proof of my existence." There's a playfulness in his voice, but maybe also a little hurt. I can imagine it would suck to have your sister's room perfectly preserved while yours is overhauled into the most dreaded room of the house.

"They didn't erase *all* the proof," I tease, and I take a large, theatrical sniff of the room. "Yeah, that's definitely Elliott stench."

"Oh yeah? Elliott stench?" He arcs a brow at me.

"Yeah. One half sweaty T-shirt, forty-nine percent Axe body spray, and a dash of midnight snack."

He smiles and rises to his full height, then stretches and pushes in the desk chair. "Okay, kid. If you say so."

"Kid? El. You're only two years older than me."

"Two and a half," he corrects me, and as he passes me I take back everything I said about Elliott stench. He's definitely not the same as the teenager I remember. He smells fresh, like a clean cotton T-shirt and a hint of vanilla. He turns and lowers his voice, dipping his head toward mine. "And I don't recall you minding the midnight snack last night," he says. His eyes lock on mine for a brief, very smoldery moment before he turns and bounds down the stairs.

CHAPTER 6

now

ALL DAY LONG I obsess over Elliott Bailey and his stupid, smirky, handsome face.

Like when Julie and Jess take me out to lunch. Or when we drive to the mega-mall just up the highway. Or when we sit around the table for a late dinner, with Julie to my right and Zoe to my left and Elliott directly across from me like the universe is out to punish me for ever fantasizing about being with him. Which, if we're being honest, is a lot. Was. *Was* a lot. Right?

Dinner is followed by a rowdy game of Farkle, which is then followed by a fresh-brewed pot of decaf and a family movie night. That movie is followed by Zoe's request for another, and that request is followed by some light groans from almost everyone over the age of thirty who declare that it's too late before heading up to bed.

"Please, Dad? One more?" I catch her quick glance in my direction.

"We have an early morning, Z," he answers, and my heart melts a little. I haven't seen him in Dad Mode in such a long time, and even back then it was with a kindergartner who was smitten with him. Easy. Parenting a teen? And having them actually seem to *like* you? That seems so much harder.

"It's not even that late," she says, and if that's the most rebellious thing she does, he's a lucky parent. Or so I assume, anyway, because what do I really know about the topic?

He shoots me a look, like '*you in for one more?*' and I shrug. I've barely been awake twelve hours, so I have no right being tired. Plus, Zoe's sweet, and it's much more fun to hang out with her than hang out in the basement by myself.

Zoe chooses *Titanic* and curls up on the loveseat to watch it. Elliott sinks into a recliner and I take the couch, which is thankfully much newer than the one in the basement.

It's funny to me, this almost full-circle moment. *Titanic* was one of Julie's favorite movies growing up, even though her parents didn't really want her to watch it because of the brief nudity. But that didn't stop her; she'd sneak the VHS down to the basement as soon as her parents went to bed. And now here I am, watching it with her brother and his seventeen-year-old daughter on a streaming service, just above the scene of the crime from our youth.

Maybe it's the slow start to the movie, but Zoe is out before Jack and Rose ever meet. Her gentle snoring gives her away. Being the world's best dad, apparently, El quietly rises, turns off the light, and covers his daughter with the crocheted afghan slung over the back of the couch and drops the volume on the movie to maintain a little white noise while Zoe sleeps.

"I should go," I whisper, rising and straightening the throw pillows.

"You tired already?"

"I didn't say that."

Before I know it, Elliott's on his feet, just a few feet away, his voice deep and hushed. "You avoiding me, Mia? We spend one night together and you can't stand to be in the same room as me?"

I know he's joking. I swear I do. But does he have any idea that I have wanted nothing *but* to be in the same room as him for more than half my life? Does he have any idea that his voice, his nearness... they're on my mind, far more often than is appropriate?

This borderline flirtation from him sends a tingly heat through my limbs, but I force myself to straighten and look him in the eye. If he's going to play, I'm going to, too. "We spend one night together, and *you* can't stand to be *away* from me?"

It's so dark in here, but finally the light from the TV flashes and I can see his eyes—which are trained on my mouth. My chest nearly explodes and I bite my bottom lip instinctively. It's absolutely the wrong thing to do. Elliott raises his eyes to mine and all the playfulness is gone, replaced with an intensity I've only ever seen from him twice before.

"Want to watch a movie?" he asks, holding my gaze. "Downstairs?"

Is there a choice here? I'm going to go down and turn on the TV anyway, so why not have him join me since everyone else is sound asleep and he'd be bored up here?

I shrug and give a (hopefully) casual "Sure." Then I breeze past him and through the dining room, opening the basement door as he riffles through the freezer for more cookie dough ice cream. He finds one pint, grabs two spoons, and follows me down the stairs, closing the door gently behind him.

All of this feels scandalous: sneaking around late at night in my best friend's parents' house, with her brother, eating ice cream straight from the carton (Mrs. Bailey has rules against it), and staying up long after everyone else has gone to bed. I feel pretty confident I could find forgiveness for the ice cream (we're going to demolish this whole container tonight, anyway) and the staying up late thing (I'm an adult, after all), but the whole *best friend's brother* thing might be harder to justify.

"What sounds good?"

His voice snaps me out of my guilt-trip trance.

"I don't know. You pick," I reply. But what I want to say, when he asks what sounds good? *You.* The things I wish I could say. The things I wish I could've said, way back then. Maybe, if I would have, everything would be different.

I open the ice cream carton and dig in while Elliott makes up his mind, and my eyes go wide when he hands me an old video game controller.

"That's not a movie, El."

"I know. I went rogue." He plops down two cushions away from me and gets Mario Kart up and running in record time. "You still like to be Princess Peach?" he asks, and I'm flattered that he remembers my favorite character.

"Of course," I reply. "She's a badass."

The next twenty minutes are hilarious: There's me, trying to remember all the command buttons. There's also me, moving my whole body to execute every turn. There's Elliott, cursing loudly when he falls off Rainbow Road. There's us, laughing in whispered snorts and gasps through all of it.

Then: There's Elliott, on the cushion next to mine. There's Elliott's elbow, jabbing at my ribs. There's Elliott's hand, catching my elbow when I jab back. There's me, trying to pull away, laughing. There's Elliott, falling into me.

There's Elliott's face, inches from mine, his eyes on my lips. His lips on my lips.

God. This couch.

<h1 style="text-align:center">CHAPTER 7</h1>

<h2 style="text-align:center">twenty-six years ago</h2>

FOURTH GRADE WAS OFF to a great start, until it wasn't.

Julie got along with everyone, and I hadn't crossed paths with anyone I strongly disliked, but one day someone quite literally crossed *my* path, and I found myself in the principal's office.

"I told you, Mr. Salazar. It was an accident."

Maybe I seemed too angry or too defiant to make a case for myself as the innocent child who just happened to be doing exactly what she was supposed to be doing when someone else got injured, but Mr. Salazar was not buying what I was selling.

"Mia, regardless of whether it was an accident or not, you are directly responsible for another child's injury. One that requires medical attention."

Sure. Put the blame on me, and not on the person who walked in front of me while I was on the swing set. Actually, no. She didn't walk. She *stood* there. Taunting me. Mocking the poem I'd written for Mrs. Macy's class.

"Go away, Sydney," I told her, over and over and over. I felt the heat of tears sting my eyes, and I was confused. We were never really *friends,* but we weren't enemies, either. I didn't know why she was going out of her way to make fun of me.

And then, out of nowhere, a red playground ball whizzed through the air and smacked Sydney in the back. She lurched forward, just as I swung my feet, and before I knew it she was on the ground, clutching the side of her face as crimson droplets fell to the sleeve of her petal-pink cardigan.

"Mrs. Alto is going to call your parents to come pick you up and take you home for the day. I also would like for you to write an apology letter to Sydney when you get home tonight. You can bring it into school tomorrow and I'll review it before you give it to her."

It didn't seem fair to be punished when I hadn't done anything wrong. I hadn't, right?

Regardless, I sat and waited in the office while our secretary, Mrs. Alto, made numerous calls, all of which went unanswered. She picked up the phone again and after a whispered exchange, Mr. Salazar reemerged in the office.

"Change of plans," he said. "You're going to go back to your classroom for the day. But I do expect that apology letter first thing tomorrow."

"Okay," I said, nodding. I was grateful not to be sent home, but the pitying look on Mrs. Alto's face told me it wasn't because Mr. Salazar had a change of heart. Instead, it was because my parents couldn't be bothered to pick up the phone.

The nurse's office is on the path from the main office back to Mrs. Macy's classroom, and as I walked back I could see Sydney sitting there, an ice pack pressed to her forehead. A familiar voice danced in the air: it was Julie, sitting with Sydney. Providing *comfort* to her. How could she?

I stomped up to my classroom and pouted, near tears, the rest of the day.

♫♩

Mom and Dad had very few questions about the recess incident that night, and I was content not to share any details. I kept my head down, wrote my letter, and moved on.

The next morning, Mr. Salazar approved the letter, told me it read like it had been written by a sixth grader, and sent me on my way to Mrs. Macy's class to hand it off to my frenemy.

I trudged to the storage cubbies and dropped off my lunch bag and backpack, then sauntered across the room to hand Sydney her letter. "Sorry," I said, not really meaning it but feeling a little bit of guilt when I saw the small bandage next to her left eye.

"Me, too," she said, producing her own letter and holding it out for me to take.

"What's this?"

She shrugged, but a smile started to form on her face. I could tell she was holding back; smiling too much would probably hurt near her stitches. We opened our letters at the same time, and I read in her neat, fourth-grade penmanship:

Dear Mia,
I'm sorry that I made fun of your poem. I think I was jealous, because ~~your~~ you're super creative. I didn't know that, but Julie told me that's why I did it. She's really smart. She also made me write this letter and I said OK because I feel bad that you had to go to ~~the princi princep~~ Mr. S.'s office. I hope you're not in too much trouble. And I hope we can be friends, because I actually think you're pretty cool.

XOXO,
Sydney Sanders

When we finished reading, Sydney threw her arms around my shoulders. I hugged her back, but my attention was focused elsewhere. I scanned the room, finally finding Julie, who was watching us intently with a broad smile on her face. When I mouthed *thank you*, it only spread wider.

Once again, Julie Bailey had shown up for friends in need. In this case, one friend, and someone she'd turned into a friend. She truly was the best friend a girl could hope to have.

CHAPTER 8

now

"Mia?"

I startle awake at the sound of my name, and Julie jerks back.

"Hey. Sorry," she says. "I just wanted to check and see if you were planning on coming to church with us today."

Church? I probably should, all things considered. Thankfully there's no confessional at the Methodist church, so even if I do go, I wouldn't have to tell anyone but the Big Guy what I did.

"When are you leaving?" I stretch my arms overhead and point my toes, trying to recover from another night on this couch.

She checks her watch. "Twenty minutes, give or take."

"*Twenty minutes?*" I bolt upright, nearly crashing into her.

She rubs her stomach, already in protector mode for this little one, and rises to her feet. "How about this," she begins. "We go without you today and blame it on your entertaining Zoe with a late-night movie, but you're up and ready to go next week. You know Mom and Dad," she adds with a slight eye roll.

"Sure do. Thanks, Jules."

She pats my knee and heads upstairs, and once I hear the shuffling of feet and murmuring of voices subside a few minutes later I decide it's safe to take a shower.

I turn on my Belter Ballads playlist and brush my teeth while the water is heating up. And I snoop, just a little (but the Baileys have always said that I should make myself at home, so does it even count?), looking for the good face masks that I know Julie must have hidden around here somewhere. I figure I have a little over an hour until anyone's back home, so I'm going to pamper myself with the at-home spa day I've been craving for months.

My hair's sudsy and piled atop my head while I belt out *Driver's License* and rinse off the hardened mask, and I marvel at the acoustics in here. I may need to get the band on board with recording our next album in a little bathroom like this one, because my voice sounds *good*, even if I'm not the lead vocalist. After an *Illicit Affairs* encore, I shut off the water, dry off, and check my phone's clock. Assuming they come straight back to the house, I have about twenty minutes until anyone else is home. I wrap the towel around me and start my descent, only to bump into Elliott as he turns the corner out of the kitchen.

He lets out a gargled shriek and nearly chokes on his mouthful of Froot Loops. His eyes scan my body and he coughs, his mouth closed but partially smiling.

"What are you doing here?" I hiss, holding onto the towel for dear life.

Once he successfully swallows down his cereal, he responds. "I'm waiting for Zoe to get back from church. The whole family goes every week. It's a big thing."

"The whole family, huh?"

He nods.

"And you're still exempt from this?"

At this, Elliott shrugs, and he crams another spoonful of cereal into his mouth. "Looks like it."

There's a note of finality to the topic, especially when he looks down at his bowl and leans back against the kitchen island, shoveling in a few more bites. I can understand that he's had a hard time moving on from the past and the way he was treated, even though it was so many years ago. But even if I wanted to ask more I don't have the opportunity, because Elliott says—more to his cereal than to me—"We should talk about last night."

"We probably should," I agree. "When I'm dressed. And when we're not in your parents' kitchen."

"Well, it's not like we can be trusted on that couch again."

I wonder if we interpret the word *again* the same way. I wonder if he remembers. "And these seem to be our only meeting spaces." I force a smile and hope it looks somewhat convincing.

"So dinner, then?"

There's a part of me that softens a little inside when he suggests it, like a rose in bloom with soft, velvety petals. It's a part that's been hidden away forever, at one time all colorful and fragrant but now long overgrown with thorns. Inaccessible.

"We should talk about the baby shower, anyway. Hard to have that conversation here," he adds, and he has a point. "Besides. Zoe can be there to chaperone."

"I don't need your teenage daughter to chaperone our conversation about a kiss that never should've happened."

He nods, wiping a spot of milk from his bottom lip with the back of his hand, and it's not fair, drawing my attention to his perfect lips again. *Again*. "Glad we agree on that much," he says, with just enough hesitation that my inner teenager hopes he'll pull me into his arms and smother me in kisses. "But we have the shower to plan, regardless, and we can't do that with my nosy sister around."

"Okay, fine. You have a point. Where do you want to meet?"

He scoffs and shakes his head, then rinses his bowl and puts it in the top rack of the dishwasher. Word must not have gotten out about his kitchen cleanup skills, or there's no way he'd still be on the market.

"I'll just take you home with me tonight."

Sure. Let's just try to pretend I haven't waited half my life to hear him say those words.

"But Mia?"

"Hm?" I pull my mind out of the gutter and refocus it on the man in front of me, his dark eyes sparkling.

"You might want to get dressed. I just heard a car door, so they should be coming inside in five... four..."

I gasp, almost drop the towel, and dart to the basement door, latching it just as I hear voices emerge from the garage.

CHAPTER 9

now

JULIE AND JESS KNOW the baby shower's coming, and that the Baileys and I are planning it, but that's all they're getting from us. They know they can't coerce us into spilling any information. That doesn't mean they aren't going to try.

"Just one tiny detail," Julie begs, and even Jess is in on the action.

"Color scheme? Theme?"

I laugh, pulling on my coat. "No way. We're steel traps."

"Yeah. Our lips are sealed," Zoe adds, miming a zipping-her-lips action. She dangles the imaginary key at me and I take it from her and shove it into my coat pocket.

Elliott rests his hand on my shoulders and turns me around, looking back over his shoulder and telling his sister, "I'll have her back around ten. Unless she keeps talking. Then she'll either be back in half an hour or never."

"Hey!" I protest, swatting at his hand. Julie cackles behind us, and Zoe follows us out to the pickup in the driveway. She opens the back door and I throw myself into the seat before she's able to climb in.

She cocks her head. "I'll sit back here, Mia."

I turn into a defiant toddler, crossing my arms and shaking my head. "Nope. You sit up front. I'm not here to turn your life upside down."

"It's a seat in a truck, Mia." Elliott slides into the driver's seat and meets my eyes in the rearview. "I don't think she's going to be emotionally scarred if she has to sit in the back."

"Well, I'm already here, so." I shrug and buckle myself in. To my surprise, Zoe closes the truck door and jogs to the other side, hoisting herself onto the bench seat next to me.

Elliott massages the back of his neck and puts the key in the ignition, and we're all greeted with a familiar voice before he reaches over and smacks the dial, cutting off the music.

"Dad!" Zoe protests. "I wanted to listen to that!"

"She's literally *right next to you*, Zo." He gestures in my general direction, then gives in and turns the sound back on before pulling out of the driveway and onto the long lane that connects a handful of houses to the main street.

"I literally love The Fluorescent Flowers so much and so do all my friends. You're like, the coolest."

Her enthusiasm is so young and so pure, and for a moment I see no difference between the young girl I had last seen and the young woman she is now. Everyone says raising teenagers is so hard, and that they're so mean, but Elliott and Callie either got incredibly lucky or knocked it out of the park as parents.

Of course they did. Because Callie was perfect and Elliott's perfect and that's how they ended up together anyway.

"Can I tell you a secret?" I lean toward Zoe, catching Elliott's quick glance in the mirror. I drop my voice and half whisper, conspiratorially, "Word on the street is, their guitarist is a bit high-maintenance."

Zoe laughs, and there's a snort from the front seat, too. It might seem funny to them, but they don't know I'm totally branded this way by my bandmates. Mostly because they're all aligned about the clubs they want to go to and the old songs they want to sing, and I want to sit in my bus and write new music for us to perform. I feel like they're content to coast on all the things we did fifteen years ago to gain fame, but they don't want to do anything to grow and improve.

We sing along—more loudly than Elliott would probably like—to one of my favorite songs on the short drive back to his place. My job is to prep a box mix of brownies for dessert while they tackle dinner, which is spaghetti and homemade garlic bread, and I'm not mad about it. It's a ritual they've developed and perfected over time, and I'm equal parts casual observer and awestruck outsider.

Except they've never made me feel like an outsider. No one in this family—or, frankly, this town—has ever made me feel that way. Coming home is coming *home*, and I'm welcome and part of it, every single time. Even though I ran away, and even though I can only visit for a day or two every few years, it's why I will always come back.

♫♩

"That was delicious. Thank you."

Zoe's already cleaned up her seat at the table and gone up to get showered, so I take my plate and Elliott's to the sink as he closes the folder of baby shower ideas we discussed over dinner.

"It's probably nowhere near as good as what you're used to having."

"Are you kidding? They normally try to force-feed me tofu and mung beans, so this was like a Michelin Star meal."

He's dangerously close to smiling at my joke, and heaven help me if he does. I'm almost in a carb coma as it is, and his smile will knock me all the way out.

"You've got a good kid, El." Now I *have* to look away, because I know he's proud of Zoe and I know I won't be able to handle whatever his face does at the compliment.

"She's great," is all he says, and there's so much left unsaid that my heart swells and pulses with emotion. Things like, *She's great, even though she wasn't planned...* and *She's great, and I'm so proud...* and every possible thing in between. "Although," he adds, pulling me back from the verge of tears. "She does have one massive flaw."

"Oh yeah?"

He chuckles and stands, motioning for me to follow him upstairs. Zoe's in the shower, and he pushes open the door to her room. The startling difference between Zoe's room and my room as a teenage girl is that hers is immaculate. Everything is clean and tidy and in its place; there's not a "clothing chair" overflowing with reject outfits in sight. The one similarity is the nearly corner-to-corner display of band posters and shelf of memorabilia. On my walls it was creased posters from magazines, but Zoe's got stark white frames against her lavender walls, each one with posters of The Fluorescent Flowers throughout the years inside.

"Is that...?" I let myself into the room, hoping Zoe won't mind the intrusion.

"Yes. It's a Mia Montgomery bobble-head."

I tap the head of the plastic toy and watch it bob for a few seconds. "That's wild."

"What is? That someone's making bootleg bobbleheads of you and selling them on the internet?"

I nod, because *duh*. Of course that's wild. "And that anyone would care enough to actually have one."

Elliott props himself against the doorframe. "You're kind of a big deal, Mia. At least, that's what all the kids are saying these days."

Every fiber of my being longs to ask, *And you? What do you say?* But I know I can't handle the answer. Instead, I do my absolute best to look him square in the eye, unflinching, unwavering in my confidence, as I tell him, "I'm just me."

Suddenly it's suffocating, being here in Zoe's room, surrounded by pictures of myself and the rest of the band, like everything is perfect and we've got it all together. Elliott straightens as I push past him into the hallway, reaching out to grab my arm.

"You okay?"

"I'm fine," I lie. His hand lingers on my forearm a moment too long, and he begins the conversation I really don't want to have.

"About last night."

"A mistake."

"Yes. You've made that clear."

"So what is there to talk about?"

He licks his lips, and I try so hard not to notice, but there they are, saying the absolute worst thing he could say. "What if it wasn't?"

I feel like all the oxygen has been sucked out of the hallway. I'm dizzy. Disoriented. I gasp. "Sorry, what? You think that the two of us kissing is just totally normal? That it won't have some serious consequences if people find out?"

"That's not what I'm saying, Mia." I wish I could place whatever this is in his eyes. I wish I could figure out why he seems so sad and so hopeful, all at once, and why he's weaving his fingers into mine.

But there's no time, because the bathroom door down the hallway opens, and Elliott pulls his hand away like he's just touched the brownie pan without an oven mitt.

"Oh, hi guys." Zoe's in a pair of tie-dye pajamas, scrunching her hair into a towel. "You checking out the guest room, Mia? Dad said the couch down in Gigi and Pap's basement isn't great."

Does she know he was with me that first night? Does everyone already think we're spending nights together? There's no way, because Julie would have insisted on additional supervision tonight if she had any idea what had happened in her parents' basement.

"Mia wants to be close to Aunt Julie, so she's probably not interested in the guest room."

"Right," I add. I didn't know a guest room here was an option, which is probably for the better.

"Speaking of Aunt Julie, I promised I'd have Mia back soon, so we should head out."

Am I looking forward to sleeping on the couch again? Especially knowing that there is an alternative out there, with a real bed? No. But am I looking forward to putting some distance between me and Elliott Bailey? Also, but maybe less emphatically, no.

But the distance doesn't come immediately, because after a goodbye hug with Zoe, I'm in the front seat of Elliott's truck, the music off this time and an uncomfortable silence settling between us.

He sighs like it's imperative he releases every last molecule of air from his body, and looking out at the moonlit road he finally says, "I liked kissing you, Mia."

CHAPTER 10

twenty-two years ago

WHEN I WENT TO Julie's house on August thirteenth, I figured we'd watch a movie or make friendship bracelets or talk about boys. I never imagined I'd end up in a water balloon battle with Julie, Elliott, and some of the kids from their lane. Mostly it was a couple of boys in their early teens like us, but then the Hapshaw twins came over. Fifteen and gorgeous, with sandy hair and freckles that made them always look sun-kissed and fresh, Callie and Bentley were also super nice. I wanted to *be* Callie. It didn't hurt that she had boobs, and I was still trying to talk my parents into buying me a real bra, one with molded cups and an actual clasp instead of a simple cotton pullover.

We decided to split up by age: Elliott, Callie, and Bentley were older, so even though there were fewer of them, they felt confident taking on five of us "kids," as they called us.

The game was simple: Capture the Flag meets Freeze Tag meets Dodgeball, but with water balloons. Once you're hit, you're frozen until someone on your team tags you. We spent half an hour filling balloons, storing them in buckets across the lawn with most split between two large tubs near each team's base camp.

"If we run out," Elliott had declared, "then freeze tag rules are in effect."

Next, we hid our flags, which were really old rags from the Baileys' garage that Elliott tied to dowel rods from his dad's scrap wood supply. Ours was somewhat buried, tucked behind Mrs. Bailey's rose bushes that lined the front porch.

Finally, we lined up in the center of the side lawn, counted down, and took off.

And our team *struggled*. We had the numbers, but we lacked the strength and speed of the junior varsity athletes we were up against. It didn't help that their flag was well-guarded, atop the old playhouse that sat in their back yard, mostly unused except for the times Julie and I sat out on the attached swings to talk without her parents hovering nearby. We could see it, *barely*, but Elliott's arm was too accurate from years of playing baseball, and he'd take out anyone who got close. That is, of course, until we ran out of water balloons.

We planned it perfectly, banding together to use up his ammo so we could sneak in and steal the flag, cementing a victory for the little guys. Sure enough, Elliott eventually exhausted his supply of balloons, and Julie and Theo from a few doors down distracted him while I sprinted behind the shed to approach the playhouse from the rear.

I was at the base of the ladder when he realized what was happening, and by the time I grabbed the flag he was right behind me. I tried—valiantly, I might add—to get into the sliding board and liberate the flag. But Elliott's arm, strengthened by JV-mandated workouts, wrapped around my waist.

"Oh, no, you don't." He scooped me up, belly-laughing, reaching with his free arm to take the flag from my outstretched hand. Theo ran to the base of the playhouse, yelling for me to drop the flag, and then Elliott was gone, chasing Theo but just barely missing him before Theo mounted the flag in the traffic cone in the middle of the yard.

"We won!" Theo cried, and Dave and Adam came running, whooping and cheering our victory.

I took it all in from the playhouse, proud of our team, but feeling something new, too. Something warm and refreshing and wonderful.

Julie stood at the base of the playhouse, her eyes narrowed and her arms crossed. I met her at the bottom, wringing out my T-shirt as I rose from the slide. "You okay?" I asked, but she was unmoving, just staring at me.

"That was weird," she said.

I felt heat rush to my cheeks, unrelated to the August sun. "What was?" *Maybe if I play dumb*, I thought, *I won't have to talk about it.*

"Please tell me you don't have a crush on my brother."

She was so straightforward, to-the-point, so unlike herself that I knew this was an area where there was no room for compromise or negotiation. So I shook my head, and for the first time in our friendship, I lied to Julie Bailey. "Gross. No," I said, and she scanned my face.

"Good. You better not." She made her way to the center of the lawn with the rest of the kids, and I made a mental note that having a crush on Elliott Bailey was the one thing that seemed like it could actually threaten everything we'd built.

CHAPTER 11

now

I LIKE KISSING ELLIOTT Bailey.

I've liked the idea of it since I was thirteen. I liked it last night.

And I like it now, sitting in the front seat of his truck, his fingers woven into my hair and pressed into the back of my neck, greedy and possessive.

"We shouldn't be doing this." I manage to get the words out between hungry kisses.

"You're absolutely right," Elliott says, his mouth lingering just a breath away from mine.

I do everything I can to shove each hopeful physical and emotional response back down into hiding, behind the twisted thorns that have grown over my heart. We definitely shouldn't be doing this. But he likes it, and so do I.

Conversely, I present The Comprehensive List of Things I Do *Not* Like:

- The feeling that I'm betraying Julie.

- The hollow feeling in my chest when I'm alone, without Elliott, in the Baileys' basement after he drops me off.

CHAPTER 12

now

I SHOULDN'T BE CELEBRATING that it's a Monday and that everyone else has to go back to work, but I really need some time alone. I'm happy to be home for Julie and the shower and to see everyone again, but I've still got a job to do. And obviously the Baileys' house is not the ideal work location, with Mr. Bailey upstairs in Elliott's old room and intrusive thoughts of Elliott filling my brain when I'm at the kitchen table or down in the basement.

It's just over a mile walk into town, so I jam my iPad, notebook, and headphones into my backpack before bundling up and setting off on foot toward downtown Songbird Springs.

The café here is my favorite anywhere, and I park myself in a back corner booth with a maple chicken biscuit breakfast sandwich and an iced coffee, a thought tornado already spinning in my brain.

A few ideas from last night are scribbled across a page in my songbook. I add more now, fleshing out ideas for lyrics. It's been a while since The Fluorescent Flowers recorded anything new, and I feel like being back here is cracking my heart wide open, giving me all the inspiration for another album. The one benefit to a long-term unrequited love is that you always have heartache to lean on when you need a hit. And people eat it up.

I wonder if Zoe knows that her favorite song was written about her father. Actually, I'm sure she doesn't, because if she did I don't think it would be her favorite anymore.

Somewhere between writing garbage and rereading it for the thirtieth time, a tall blond at the table across from mine leans my way. "Excuse me," she says, her blue eyes sparkling. "I don't mean to interrupt your process, but are you a writer, too, by chance?"

Am I a writer? I was years ago, but recently—and now, specifically—it doesn't feel like it. But I shrug anyway. "Sort of," I answer. "How'd you guess?"

Her eyes travel to my hand, and I'm not sure how long I've been nervously tapping my pen against my notebook, but I'm pretty sure it's been a while.

"Ah, sorry."

"No need to apologize." She reaches out a hand with perfectly manicured hot pink nails. "Gwen," she says.

"Mia."

She shakes my hand. "Nice to meet another writer in town. Have you lived here long?"

"Off and on." I decide it's the safest way to answer. "You?"

"No. Just moved here not too long ago. Still learning the town, meeting new people."

"Gotcha. And you're a writer?"

"Yep!" She beams, and without an ounce of hesitation or shame, she adds, "I write romance novels." She reaches into the front pocket of her laptop sleeve and extracts a business card, passing it my way. "Here's my contact info, if you ever want to connect."

This town is magical. Here we are, two strangers, and already she's giving me her phone number and email so I can reach out about writing. I love her outgoing personality, and I'm totally going to take her up on her offer. "I'd love that. I'm actually in a band, back home during a break from our tour. I'm only here about two months before we have to record something new back in L.A. Hence—" I glance at the journal.

Her smile widens, authentic and excited. "That's awesome! What's the name of your band?"

I answer, and she bites the inside of her lip. "Sorry. I haven't heard of you before. My husband has me hooked on Taylor Swift's entire back catalog, but I should probably start to branch out soon. I'll definitely give you a listen."

We chat a while longer, about how she met her husband on a cruise ship and came to settle down in Songbird Springs, about the open mic nights here in the café and her upcoming reading in the bookstore two doors down the block, about tours and music and romance and writing.

"I feel like it's been so long since I've been able to get a good song on paper, and now I need a few that my bandmates will love. How do you churn out a new book every year?" I ask Gwen, long after we've secured our second cups of coffee.

She blushes and pulls her hair into a messy bun. "I draw from life, a little. My first romance novel was kind of a daydream—what I thought love could be. Then I met my husband, and the second book was what I knew love *was*."

"Ugh, you make even *that* sound romantic."

Gwen rests her elbows on the table and leans in, her head bobbing along as she shares her idea with me. "What if you stopped imagining your songs as songs, and started to imagine them as a story? Start to finish, write one story, not five, or whatever you're going for. Each song is its own chapter, with its own emotion. Make a few good, different songs, and you'll have something for everyone, right?"

I nod along slowly, wondering if I'll be able to retrain my brain to view the writing process in this way. It definitely can't be any worse than what I've been doing all day so far. Which is, of course, nothing productive.

Gwen's phone buzzes, and she apologizes that she has to take off to get ready for a call with her agent.

Alone again, I turn to a blank page in my notebook. *Chapters.* I can think and write in chapters.

Chapter One could be the excitement of realizing you have feelings for someone. Maybe Chapter Two is the tension when you think they might want you, too. Chapter Three: the sadness of being with other people when all you want is each other.

It's not long before ideas are pouring out of me, brain to hand to ink to paper, and the only thing that interrupts the flow of ideas is the nearby chatter that the café closes soon, and I should start the walk home.

I make it a block before I get the feeling that someone's watching me, and it's easy enough to check because the town is basically deserted. It's still cold out, which keeps most people home, cozied up by their fires and cooking hearty meals after a long day at work instead of out here wandering the streets in freezing temperatures.

But before I get a chance to turn to see who it is, a gray pickup rolls up from behind me. "Need a lift?" Elliott asks out the rolled-down window. The crisp air carries his words away in a tiny white cloud.

I should say no. Especially given the kissing that happened the last time I was in this truck. And *especially* considering the absurd amount of pleasure I felt while kissing my best friend's older brother.

I know. I *know* I'm an adult, and he's an adult, and Julie's an adult, and some comment from when we were teenagers shouldn't still be controlling my life. But the fact of the matter is, it doesn't really matter. Even if I thought there was a chance that Julie wouldn't freak out about us—not that Elliott and I are an *us*, of course—I'm leaving in two months to go back to L.A., and there's no way he's interested in a relationship. Especially a long-distance one.

So I really shouldn't get in the truck.

But that smile. That ridiculous smile gets me and I want nothing more than to devour it.

"It's cold as hell, Mia. Just get in the truck."

"Hell's not cold."

"It's an expression, Captain Obvious." He rolls his eyes—I don't bother to correct him that the expression is 'cold as hail'—and leans across the front seat to open the door for me.

I cross to the passenger side but hesitate before climbing up. He meets my eyes before rolling his again. "Don't worry. I'm not going to rip your clothes off or anything."

Even the idea of it does something to me and I let out one hearty laugh, which earns me a look like he thinks I've completely lost it. And maybe he's got a point, because all I can think of now is him actually ripping my clothes off. But I get in the truck anyway, because obviously that's ridiculous.

It's a short, quiet ride back to the Baileys' house, and I'm surprised when he gets out of the truck, too. "We always do family dinner on Monday nights," he says when I question him with a glance.

"And Saturdays?"

"A few nights, actually," he confesses with a maddening grin. Then he puts his hand on the side door's knob and leans in close just before twisting it. "Looks like we're going to be spending lots of time together."

CHaPTer 13

now

"You could just stay at my place, you know." Elliott engineers a patch for the air mattress he dragged out of a storage bin marked *Camping Gear*, and I'm so distracted by this awful feeling in my gut that I can't even muster a strong enough reaction to this new invitation.

"Yeah, no. That's a terrible idea," I say, trying to stop thinking about the tent I haven't seen in nearly twenty years that's now spilling out of a bin.

"Mia. You're a thirty-five-year-old woman sleeping on a forty-year-old couch or a busted air mattress in your best friend's parents' drafty basement. *This* is a terrible idea."

"It's fine."

"So help me, if you catch something down here and your manager even tries to sue my family for your untimely death..."

"I'm fine, El."

"You're stubborn, is what you are." He glances up then looks away quickly, scowling. "We have an empty guest room, and Zoe would love it, but fine, stay here and get pneumonia like a Victorian pauper."

Ooh, he almost has me. Tugging at my heartstrings by playing the make-a-kid-happy card. And an actual bed, and a room right next to a full bathroom that doesn't require me to ascend two flights of stairs carrying my underwear past my best friend's dad? Divine. But also, there's the whole bedroom-right-next-to-your-child-hood-crush-slash-muse thing, and that's where he loses me.

"Thank you for fixing the air mattress for me. Honestly, it's an upgrade from the tour bus." He shakes his head and rises, and I avoid his gaze as I tuck the fitted sheet around the corners of the mattress. "See? This will be great."

"Sure."

♫♩

It's not great.

Once everyone has gone to bed or gone home and I'm left alone in the basement, I pull out my journal and commit to writing a chapter. Gwen's advice earlier was really helpful, and I feel like I can get a first draft of a song on paper before my multiple afternoon coffees wear off.

The couch is comfortable for about three stanzas, so I give up and flop down on the air mattress to write like I did all those years ago: face down, propped over a pillow, scribbling down whatever comes into my head. The big difference between then and now? *Then* I had a real bed. *Now* I have a rapidly deflating air mattress. And it's as if Elliott can sense it, because a muffled *ding* chimes from the couch, where my phone is buried in blankets.

How's the air mattress?

Perfect. Couldn't be better.

Liar.

Did you rig this to self-destruct?

Wouldn't you like to know.

I wouldn't put it past him if he did. Elliott's a good guy, but he also likes to get his way. And there's no way on earth I'm going to give him that satisfaction.

I don't call, and I won't, because Elliott knows me perfectly well and hit the nail on the head: I *am* stubborn, and there's no way I'm going to call him to come and whisk me away back to his place.

But Elliott knows me so well he shows up anyway, uninvited, knocking on the basement's sliding glass door right around midnight. It scares the hell out of me, but I realize that robbers and axe murderers rarely knock before entering the home of their prey—right around the same time I recognize his flannel jacket on the other side of the glass.

I unlock the door and he's already talking before I can yell at him. "Figured you could use this, if you're so determined not to take me up on my very hospitable offer of room and board." He pushes past me, lugging a heavy-looking bag in his arms. "It's a bit newer than what you've got here, and it's extra thick so you're not going to end up on the floor."

He shuffles the old air mattress out of the way and starts inflating the new one, even unpacking special sheets that were designed to accommodate the extra height of this bed. Once everything's all set up—again—there's an awkward silence and I wonder if he wants me to ask him to stay.

"Alright. That should get you through." Elliott readjusts his backward baseball cap and starts a slow retreat toward the door. "Sleep well, Mia."

"Wait!" I reach for him, my fingers wrapping around his forearm as his other hand connects with the door handle.

He surveys the place where our skin meets, then slowly his eyes rise to meet mine.

"Did you want to watch a movie?" I ask, not yet ready to let go of his arm.

He swallows hard and shakes his head.

"Oh. Okay." I feel heat rush to my cheeks and I drop my hands, embarrassed for even asking. I drop my gaze to the floor, aware that his is hyper-focused on my head. I'm not sure how I read this so wrong. The kissing and the "I liked kissing you" and the flirty truck rides and his constant urging for me to stay at his place instead of here...what was it all for? What did it mean? It'll certainly give me something to unpack in song form, that's for sure.

"Thanks," I force out. I turn, desperate to keep him from seeing my face and whatever hurt or confusion burns there.

But he takes my hand in his and turns me toward him with one gentle pull. His hand is warm in mine. His breathing is slow, steady, measured, like he's calming himself, preparing himself for something big. And he's so close I feel each tiny puff of warmth as it collides with my head and begs me to look up. My body goes into ooey-gooey chocolate chip cookie mode, melting for him because this... this is not some normal taking of the hand. This is a loaded gesture, a moment filled with tension and heat and yearning, and I know it's not just my own.

"What are we doing, El?" I whisper. But I don't want him to answer. How do you even name what we're doing or this magnetic pull that seems to exist between us? How do you define it or describe it or control it? And is it wrong that I don't *want* to control it?

He hooks a finger under my chin and tilts my face up toward his, but I keep my eyes closed because I know beyond the shadow of a doubt that if I look into his dark amber eyes I will say or do something I should not say or do with my best friend's brother in my best friend's parents' basement, while said best friend and parents sleep upstairs.

"Mia." He rests his forehead against mine. "I really like spending time with you." And then his thumb traces the back of my hand, finding its way between fingers like he's dying to entwine his with mine. "It feels good, being with you." God, this man is ninety-six percent sexual urgency and ten percent restraint, and that percentage of overlap is the hottest thing ever. I feel like I'm reading a "choose your ending" story and I have no idea which way things are going to go. The only thing I know for certain is that I am totally going to write a song about this exact moment.

"I had an idea," he says, and the suddenness of it and its stark contrast to the rest of the moment makes me snap my eyes open, finally meeting his, though luckily he's pulled his face away from mine or we'd be so busy kissing right now I'd never hear his genius plan.

"Please, tell me."

"What if we pursued something here?"

If he wasn't holding onto me, I might fall over. *Pursue something?* Such a terrible idea. For so many reasons. Partially because, "I leave in two months. I don't think it's smart to start a relationship, knowing there'd be an expiration date. And I'm not interested in long distance."

"And I'm not interested in a relationship. Not really."

It reopens some old high school-era wounds for me, and I flinch at the fresh sting. "You're not remotely confusing, Elliott Bailey."

"I'm just trying to say—" he bites his lip, buying time to come up with the right words. "Being with you—physically near you—is nice. Like on the couch the other night, just watching movies. Hanging out."

"I don't think I'd call the past few days just 'hanging out,' El."

"Right. I mean, the kissing is great, too."

Oh, the kissing is *so* great. The words are like a bandage over the moments-old cut. I'm glad he enjoys kissing me, and I'll take all the joy I can in that.

"So, what are you saying?" I ask, because I truly am not following any of it, beyond *Relationship: Bad. Kissing: Good.*

"I'm saying, I think we should keep spending time together. But, like, *together*, together."

Crickets chirp. A pin drops and it echoes for days. Glass shatters and records scratch and I stare dumbfounded at Elliott. He's really going to make me say it.

"So... you want to be friends. With benefits." Be still my teenage heart.

His brow furrows and his lip quirks up. "I wouldn't put it quite that way," he says, but then he apparently considers it again and agrees that what he's asking for fits the definition pretty well. "Okay, I mean, we *are* friends. And it seems like kissing has felt mutually beneficial."

He's not wrong.

"Is this why you've been pushing for me to stay at your place?"

His expression shifts to something new. "No. I want you to stay at my place for you. Mostly." He sighs and rubs the back of his neck with his free hand. "Though I'd be lying if I said I wasn't being partially selfish."

"In light of this new development, I think it's best if I stay here. But also—"

He perks up at this. "Yeah?"

"You really are a great kisser."

When Elliott laughs, all is right in the world. He throws his head back and reels me in, all in one synchronous motion. Then his arms are wrapped around me and he rests his chin on top of my head.

"If we do this," I begin as he smooths a hand up and down my arm, "we need to set some ground rules."

"Of course. Whatever you want."

"Well, first—no relationship. I don't want to be attached when I go back to L.A."

"Done. I'm not looking for a relationship, either. Or feelings. I'm what my sister calls 'dead inside.'"

"Okay, check. Rule number two: no talking about your sister. It's weird."

Pressed against his chest, I feel his torso shake with laughter and hear it rumble through his ribs. It's one of my favorite sounds. "Fair point. No mention of her. Ever."

I nod. "And I guess the last one is, er—" It's good I'm at a loss here, that I can't bring myself to say what I need to say. Because if I can't say it, there's no way I'll ever *do* it. "Should we set some limits or boundaries or something?" There. I just asked my best friend's brother if we were going to take sex off the table without mentioning sex. Awkward crisis averted.

He pulls back and scans my eyes. "If you're talking about sex—" *awkward crisis initiated*— "I'm not asking you for anything like that. I just want to be around you, be close to you, you know?"

I do know. Because the last few nights have been incredible (kissing or no kissing). There's a connection here, and I don't feel so alone when Elliott's around. And not just because I'm not physically alone, either.

So as terrified as I am to say it, I agree to Elliott's idea: friends with benefits with rules and with*out* sex.

I'm excited to get to spend time with him.

I'm giddy, having this top-secret connection.

I'm looking forward to discovering what my membership benefits are.

And I'm so totally screwed.

CHAPTER 14

twenty years ago

ALL MY CLASSMATES WERE having massive parties for their birthdays. I don't mean that venues were rented out and parents were blowing money on balloons and cake for grid-worthy photos, because social media was non-existent and Pinterest wasn't around for inspiration, and no one in our then-rural town was in a position to spend that kind of money, anyway.

Instead, everyone had these big hang-out parties. It seemed like there was a requirement to have at least twenty kids show up, with very few presents actually changing hands, and do something pedestrian, like roast marshmallows around an evening campfire or have a table tennis tournament in someone's basement. There were some balloons, sure, and themed paper plates and napkins, but everything else was pretty chill.

I went to a dozen just like this. No frills, just pizza, or vats of spaghetti and homemade lemonade in Tupperware pitchers. Just kids being kids, loud and laughing and living.

And then there was my party. I don't know why I put so much weight into turning fifteen, but it felt monumental to me. Maybe it was because I'd been to Carla's quinceañera earlier that year, but fourteen-year-old me felt like I was knocking on the door of womanhood and everyone should care.

But the day of my fifteenth birthday party went something like this:

- Wake up to an empty house

- Anticipate Mom and Dad coming back soon with balloons and something special for me from their early-morning errand

- Witness Mom and Dad coming back with nothing more than leftover containers from their breakfast

- Help Mom bake a cake because she thought it would be more fun than ordering one

- Spend half my party hiding in my room because I'm worried everyone will see right through my smile

There were moments that were great, sure. Like Lyla Harper accidentally nailing Geoffrey Randolph in the nuts during a game of kickball in the back yard, or Julie squirting whipped cream directly into my mouth throughout the party, like she was a servant feeding me grapes in ancient Rome.

But having to cry to Julie that my parents didn't wake me up to join them for breakfast because they thought I'd want to sleep in (which, *fair*, I was a teenager), or detailing that they didn't even bring me back a to-go order of my favorite stuffed french toast, or the cake fiasco... hearing her jump in when she heard kids whispering about how there wasn't really *anything* that indicated this was an actual birthday... all of that sucked. And it made me really, really glad to have Julie as a best friend.

One by one, around dinner time, parents came to pick up their kids. Some of my friends walked or rode their bikes home. Elliott showed up in a beat-up truck for Julie and actually got out to talk to me when he parked.

"What's up, birthday girl? How was the party?" He mussed my hair, not for the first time, and it was a clear sign that I wasn't knocking on the door of womanhood in his eyes; I was trying to claw my way out of the kid sister basement he'd shoved me into.

"It was great!" Julie said, smiling in my direction but accidentally letting it fade before she was turned back to him. I could hear her, just under her breath, tell him, "I'll tell you about it on the way home."

He looked at her, looked at me, and nodded once as Julie pulled him back to the truck. "Well, happy birthday, Mia."

♫♩

We were in the living room, Mom and Dad in matching recliners and me sprawled on my stomach on the floor, watching Moulin Rouge at my request, when the doorbell rang. It was well after dark, so we all kind of looked at each other, silently asking, *Do you know who could be coming over this late?*

So Dad paused the movie and I, being closest to the door, sprang up to see who was there.

There were taillights already driving away, but left behind on the front porch was a gift bag and a card.

"Who's that from?" Dad asked, going into protector mode. He dropped the footrest on the recliner and almost looked like he was going to check the gift for prints. Almost.

"Um, I think Julie," I answer. She hadn't brought a gift earlier, so it would make sense that this was hers. But a quick glance at the envelope—*Mia* was scribbled without a heart-dot over the "i"—told me this definitely was not from my best friend.

"Ah." Dad rose anyway, turning to the kitchen instead of the front door, and went about refilling his and mom's cocktail glasses. Mom lifted a glossy magazine from her lap and resumed reading, which I realized then she'd been doing throughout the movie. So I snuck upstairs with the bag and accompanying card.

Buried beneath too much neon tissue paper was a black oversized T-shirt, a pack of neon iron-on flower decals, and a brightly-colored plush daisy. It was a seemingly random assortment of gifts from the craft store the next town over, and nothing at all like I would ever have added to my wish list.

But the card added additional insight:

Mia -
I heard someone say once that wildflowers are the
coolest because they thrive in the surroundings that
they're given. They aren't spoiled or tended to. They
just _are_. And they find a way to bloom and grow and
bring beauty into the world, even if no one weeds or
waters them. So I hope you like this stuff. And that
you keep blooming. Happy birthday.
                                        -El

Wow. Suddenly, this bag of random things felt like the most intentional, special gift I'd ever received. Like Elliott saw me as a wildflower, blooming and bringing beauty into the world. I didn't even bother going downstairs to finish the movie. I just picked up the phone (you know *exactly* to which clear plastic monstrosity I am referring) and dialed the number I knew by heart, hoping for once that Julie wasn't going to be the one to pick up.

Some people think birthday wishes are silly, but when Elliott picked up the phone I became a believer.

"Hi, El," I whisper-squeaked as soon as he answered.

"Hey. Mia?"

"Yeah. Hi. I, um... I just wanted to say thank you. For the present. That was really nice."

His voice rang through the cheap receiver and tunneled through my ear into a him-sized hole in my heart. "Yeah, of course. Julie said you had a rough day, so I just thought maybe a gift would cheer you up."

I mean, sure, the gift cheered me up. But it wasn't the gift so much as it was the *gift*. The thoughtful, hand-picked, *keep blooming* assortment and the encouraging words.

"It did. Yeah. Thank you."

"Sure." He got quiet, and I was quiet, not really sure what to say next. Not that it mattered, because Elliott added, "Hey, I gotta run, but I really hope your birthday was nice, all things considered."

"Thanks, El."

There was a moment of silent acknowledgement, and then there was nothing but the lightness in my chest and the knowledge that Elliott Bailey thought to buy me a birthday gift to cheer me up, swimming around in my brain.

I climbed into bed, holding onto the flower, circling its petals in a *he-loves-me, he-loves-me-not* pattern, around and around and around, and drifted off to sleep.

CHAPTER 15

now

TWO MORNINGS AFTER THE friends-with-benefits arrangement was made and we were both sworn in with a semi-platonic hour of video games followed by a not-remotely-platonic goodnight kiss, Julie descends the stairs and surveys the giant air mattress.

"Elliott brought it over."

"Oh." Her eyes snap to me and it takes me back to when we were thirteen.

"He is incredibly biased against the couch."

She scrunches her nose and I'm afraid I've inadvertently revealed too much, because why would he know anything about this couch's current state of comfort?

"He thinks an old couch must be wreaking havoc on my back."

This softens her up a little, and she slaps a palm against her forehead. "Yes. Mia, I'm so sorry. Maybe you should take the guest room and Jess and I should stay at the B and B."

"Absolutely not." Okay. Yes, it was the original plan for me to use the guest room. And yes, the bed there is memory foam and magical and it has the most incredible down comforter *and* west-facing windows which would let me sleep in a little bit more each day. But it also has a shared wall with Mr. and Mrs. Bailey's room that would make it challenging to have any sort of middle-of-the-night adventures with Elliott. It's exactly what I needed half a week ago and the opposite of what I want now. "Besides, I'm afraid it would damage your brother's fragile ego if I refused this generous gift."

She snorts, then wraps her hand under her belly. "I swear I'm going to dislodge this child with one over-enthusiastic laugh."

I shuffle some things out of the way and motion for her to sit on the couch, and she lowers herself down with a little less grace than she did a few days ago. She picks up my hoodie and folds it, then sets it next to her, moving my songbook out of the way, her fingers and eyes lingering on the pages longer than I'd like. So I clear my throat and rescue my things from her under the guise of tidying up.

"The real reason I came down here," she says, her interest in the book replaced by excitement, "is because we have girls' night tomorrow." She's positively beaming, and my heart is flooded with a kind of boundless youthful joy I haven't felt since the summer we went to Young Artists' camp and sang silly made-up songs at the top of our lungs in a kayak on Lake Misfit.

"I love girls' night."

Her eyes sparkle. "I know! It's been so long since we were all together. I mean—" she tries to correct herself but bites her lip instead, and I bridge the Sydney-sized hole between us and sit down next to her.

"It's okay, Jules."

"It just sucks. The whole town was at her funeral." She nestles her head onto my shoulder, and I'm glad she can't see my face. I've heard more than once how disappointing it was that I didn't come home for her service. Yes, I know everyone else was able to take off work for a day to be there, but not everyone else's work is in front of 9,500 paying customers. Not everyone else was across the country when it happened. Just because I wasn't there doesn't mean I didn't grieve. It just means I did it alone.

"She was great," I say, because acknowledging how much we all loved her seems like the right course of action.

Julie finds my hand and squeezes it, then rights herself and drags the back of her hand across her eyes. "Damn pregnancy hormones," she says, a sad little laugh escaping her lips. "Anyway. What are your plans today?"

I shrug. "More of the same, I guess. Too much coffee. Not enough progress on the new songs."

"Hm. Maybe that's a sign you should keep playing the hits, Mia. Everyone loves the classics."

It kills me that no one else seems excited for some new songs. Don't they get that the 'classics' were new at one point, too? And they learned them and loved them then, so they can do it again.

"Yes, I know. And they scream-sing them back to me. Out of tune. Every night."

"Well," she says, rising and picking an invisible piece of lint from her sweater. "If you want company, I took the day off. I have an appointment in an hour, then the rest of the day is wide open."

"Imagine the trouble we could get into."

"Imagine the snacks we could eat."

♫♪

In a perfect, seamless transition from high school to adulthood and back again, Julie and I are sprawled on the couch after her checkup, with containers of lo mein and fried rice scattered around us and a huge bowl of popcorn nestled in the space between us. She lifts a bag of chocolate chips and dumps a few more over the popcorn, then swirls the bowl to mix them before taking a heaping handful and tossing it back.

"Don't look at me like that," she says, narrowing her eyes at me as she finishes chewing.

"I'm just in awe of you. Truly. You're a shapeshifter. Somehow a thirty-five-year-old woman and a thirteen-year-old boy, all at once. Science will study you in perpetuity."

She throws a popcorn kernel at me and readjusts herself against the arm of the couch. "So tell me again why your manager has been calling you all afternoon and why you haven't picked up once."

I groan and wave my hand like *no big deal*, then give her the abbreviated version. "She wants updates on the new music, and there are no real updates to give. Plus, I'm spending a day with my best friend. Work can wait."

Julie nods slowly, thoughtfully. "Do you still like it? For real? Or is the whole celebrity thing starting to get old?"

"Most nights it's great. I love making music, playing music. I know, you're shocked." We share a laugh, and I'm sure her mind goes exactly where mine goes: making music videos—on VHS—in this very basement, playing guitar around campfires in high school, singing all the time (and most of the time not even realizing I was doing it).

"Yeah, but—" she dissects a piece of popcorn, tearing it apart limb by buttery limb. "Don't you think it would be nice to have a normal life? I mean, we *are* getting old and all."

It's become this inside joke between us, joking about getting old from the moment we turned thirty. Sometimes I forget that I'm not twenty-four anymore, but then nights like the first few I spent on this couch reintroduce me to reality. And I know that I look different—older, for sure—but generally I think it's been a bit of a glow up for me. Pregnancy aside, Julie just looks tired. Like her teaching job is draining all the life from her instead of giving her the purpose and zest it did when she first started. My stomach twists; it physically hurts to see my best friend's dream fall so short of her expectations for it.

"This life—this schedule and the traveling and the routine—all those things have become normal to me."

She looks down and smooths a hand over a spot on her leggings. It's not the answer she was looking for, but I think anything short of me sobbing into her shoulder that I've made a terrible mistake by chasing music and begging her to let me buy half her plot of land to build my own place where I can settle down with someone safe and our two-point-five kids and our dog is going to fall short of satisfying her.

"To answer your question, yes. I like it. I love it, actually. But I also like coming home."

Her eyes are wet when she raises them to meet mine again. "I really want you to be happy. But I also miss you like crazy."

I'm off the couch and on the floor, shuffling on my knees to her, throwing my arms around her neck. "I miss you too, Jules. Every day. But you know what?"

"What?" she asks and sniffles into my shirt.

"I'm here now. And I'm ready to kick your ass at Mario Kart."

It's the perfect thing to say because she throws her head back laughing and her tears evaporate.

But it's also the worst thing to say because when she turns the machine on, Elliott's game profile is pulled up, right there on the screen. A smoking gun.

"When did you say Elliott brought that air mattress over?" She tries so hard not to look suspicious, but I swear I can see her brain grow arms and write some calculus on the inside of her skull like it's a giant whiteboard.

I'm panicking inside, but I try to play it cool. First I shrug, then I say like it's no big deal, "A few nights ago. He brought this over after dinner. Stuck around for some games."

"Oh. How did I not know about this?"

"You were asleep already. And he came in this door so he didn't risk waking you or your parents."

She surveys the back door, the air mattress, the controller in her hand. Me. And I'm thirteen again, getting the third degree in a look from her. *You better not*, she'd said back then. And despite her passing me a controller and making it through an hour of faux driving without prying more, I have a feeling she's dying to say the same thing now, too.

CHAPTER 16

now

DINNER IS AT ELLIOTT'S house tonight, and Zoe's already hard at work when the rest of us show up.

By the time Elliott walks in, we've got a vat of turkey chili on the stove with fresh-baked cornbread and a tossed salad lined up on the table, which Jess and I set while Julie and the elder Baileys watched from their assigned chairs at the table.

He's a bit disheveled, tired-looking, with his fuzzy flannel jacket hanging open over pale blue scrubs that stretch across his broad shoulders and his lean waist. And yes, I have the authority to speak on his midsection because yes, I have had my arms wrapped around it a few times in the last week as we hugged goodbye.

What I'm not fully prepared for is how the scrubs also showcase a perfect ass that blue jeans don't do justice, and I have to remind myself to stop studying him as he hangs his jacket on a hook just inside the door before Julie—and everyone else, for that matter—catches me staring.

He waves an acknowledgement to everyone before bounding up the stairs, two at a time. Then he takes the world's fastest shower and is redressed, back down at the table, all within ten minutes of walking in the door.

"This looks great, Zo," he says, and he picks up the salad bowl to begin dishing.

But Mr. Bailey clears his throat and raises a brow at his son, and we all bow our heads and repeat the prayer they've said over dinner together for the past forty years, ever since the Baileys got married.

Then it's three conversations at once, and I'm not necessarily an active participant in any of them. Mrs. Bailey is continuing a slew of questions about Julie's appointment this morning, Mr. Bailey is grilling Jess on her thoughts about the local hockey team's recent string of losses, and Zoe and Elliott are quietly discussing their days at school and work, respectively. And honestly? It's nice just to take it all in. Not to have anyone need or want anything from me, not to have to entertain anyone for a few brief minutes. I'm high on this feeling of normalcy, of mundane, functional-family dinners.

And soon Julie is bringing me out of the fog with a laugh as she says my name. I straighten, wondering what I missed, but there's no question coming my way. Instead, Elliott and Zoe lean in conspiratorially and Zoe works her sweet teenager puppy-dog eyes on me with an invitation to help her with her homework. It's a hard sell, but she plays to my ego. I never really thought of myself as someone with a big ego, but let me tell you—it works.

"It's an essay about someone we admire. And I just think your story is so cool, I bet people would love it."

"Well, I appreciate that. But your dad is basically Dr. Frankenstein, taking stuff out of people to put in other people. Giving people life and all that jazz. Are you sure you don't want to use him?"

She rolls her eyes. "Only losers pick their parents."

I nearly choke on my water.

"Love you, too, Zo," Elliott deadpans from the end of the table.

As a normal teenage girl does, Zoe ignores him completely and turns her puppy-dog eyes to me again. "Please, Mia?"

You'd have to be a monster to resist these eyes. "Of course. Whatever you need."

She springs up from her seat with a squeal and runs around the table to hug me, and, half-choked by her surprising grip, I feel more at home than I have in years.

♫♩

"Dr. Frankenstein? Really?" Elliott chuckles as he passes me a freshly-rinsed plate for the dishwasher.

"I mean, sort of? Not in the whole cut-up-bodies-and-sew-them-together way. But more in the giving-people-a-chance-at-life way." I save a few crumbs of cornbread from a garbage disposal fate before passing the now empty platter to him. "What made you switch careers, anyway? Weren't you on track to basically run the firm in a few years?"

He shrugs, his smile evaporated. "Yeah. Maybe."

"Maybe? El..." I hoist myself onto the counter and cock my head toward him. "Your dad has talked for years about you taking the reins. I know I haven't been around much recently, but—"

"You're right. You haven't been."

It stings to hear the sharpness in his voice when he cuts me off, and his eyes snap to mine as I flinch at this sudden change in him.

"Wow. Okay."

"Mia." He closes the dishwasher and braces both hands against the counter, hanging his head. "I'm sorry. I just don't want to talk about it, okay?"

"Okay. Fine." There's an outburst of laughter from the living room, so I slide off the counter to join in on whatever fun thing is happening there.

"What'd I miss?" I ask, surveying the room. Mr. Bailey's in an armchair next to the loveseat where Mrs. Bailey and Zoe are currently laughing so hard they seem to be struggling to breathe. Across from them, Julie's stretched out on the couch with her feet propped up on Jess's lap at the opposite end, her head thrown back and her hands cradling her stomach. Or maybe she's holding on so she doesn't pee herself. It's honestly so hard to tell.

A chair from the dining room appears next to me as Elliott sneaks in. Then he sprawls out on the floor in the far corner. I thank him with a smile and sit, rejoining the family that included me at dinner.

"Grandpa was telling us a work story," Zoe says, and other than her dad she's the first person to acknowledge I'm in the room.

I want to know more—what kind of work story at an accounting firm is worthy of such a response?—but Elliott clears his throat and bellows from his corner. "Nope. No work stories once dinner ends. That's the rule."

It's a good rule, frankly, but the room goes quiet, like without work they have nothing to talk about.

"So, Zoe."

She turns her saucer eyes toward me. "Yeah?"

"Have you started thinking about prom yet? Do you know who you're going with?"

"Umm..." her eyes sweep toward Elliott and back again. "I haven't been asked yet. Not officially, anyway."

Julie shifts to lie on her side. "Prom-posals are *huge* these days, Mia. Nothing like when Theo Jeffries asked you senior year."

Elliott raises an eyebrow at the memory. "I forgot you went with him."

"Yeah. It was..." How to finish that sentence. "Not great," I decide. I'm over it now, but that night was a disaster. At least, most of it was.

Zoe's instantly bouncing on her knees on the couch. "Mia! You *have* to go prom dress shopping with us. I mean... if my mom's okay with it. And if you want to."

"That sounds really fun," I say, because I love fashion, but I love not being the one that has to squeeze into it more.

Conversation carries on for another half hour before Jess, Julie, and her parents are ready to head out. I'm slipping into my coat and shoes and Elliott's eyes are boring into me from across the room. If either of us knew Morse code I swear I would read S-T-A-Y in his blinks.

Regardless of what his blinks say, he *actually* says "See ya" as we climb into his parents' minivan. I'm relegated to the back seat because I am not old, pregnant, or wed to the pregnant person. Zoe, wrapped up in a plaid blanket, waves from the side door. Once we're all in and buckled, he gives a final look my way and closes the door.

CHAPTER 17

now

THEY SAY THAT WHEN one door closes another one opens.

Maybe that's why Elliott's sneaking through the basement door after a quick text to make sure I was okay with it.

"I'm sorry again, about snapping earlier." *How is this man single?* "It's really hard to talk about work stuff, especially with my parents around. They still don't quite get it. Or agree with it." A full apology, before he's shed his shoes and coat. Where do we stand on human cloning, again?

"It's totally fine. I mean, not that you snapped at me, but that you don't want to talk about it. Just say so. You didn't have to make it personal." I wrap my arms around his waist and breathe him in. He smells good, like brown sugar body wash and coffee and a little bit of vanilla. Like excitement and memories and hope. "If you ever *do* want to talk about it..."

"I have you on speed dial." He rests his chin on my head. "Thanks."

He pulls away first and grabs his backpack from the floor. "Mind if we do a little party planning?"

Am I in the mood to plan a baby shower right now? No. Not even a little. But am I in the mood to sit next to Elliott, our bodies touching as we both browse sites on his laptop to give Julie the kind of shower she's hoping for? Yes.

But this guy's always full of surprises, and once we're on adjacent cushions he pulls up a document filled with rose gold and balloons everywhere.

"This isn't what we'd talked about before." This is nothing like the sage and beige woodland theme we'd been working on for Jess and Julie, and I'm beginning to think he's gone rogue.

"Oh. Right. Different party. This is for Zoe's eighteenth."

I love that he's pulling me in, getting my input on her birthday. And I hate it. Because all those years of hurt and heartbreak come flooding back. But Zoe's special, and she and I are becoming friends, and I want her to get the party she deserves.

So we dive in. We look at vendors and decor ideas and the best cakes we can get within a thirty-mile radius and plan half the party over the course of two hours.

"Would it be okay if I did something special for her?"

Elliott closes his laptop and stows it in his backpack on the floor. "Special? Like what?" He sits back up, draping an arm over my shoulders, and I nestle into him, shrugging.

"I don't know. Maybe sang something? Gave her something auto-graphed by the band?"

"I love that idea," he says, resting his cheek against my head. "But will you still be around then?"

"*Shit.*" It's very possible that, with all the various event-planning tasks I have now taken on, I have forgotten that I have an actual job, and it's not being a party planner.

He laughs that warm, soft laugh that says yes, he's laughing at me, but also that he's a fan of my thoughtfulness. "Okay, rock star. Maybe just make her a friendship bracelet and give her a nice card. You were always good at that."

My heart melts. I am a *puddle*. I went through a phase—I guess Julie and I both did—where I made all my own greeting cards. If Mrs. Bailey got new scrapbooking supplies, Julie and I raided the storage bin drawers for new papers and stickers and die-cuts. And then the writer in me came out and I'd personalize every single one. A birthday card got a whole poem about celebrating life; a sympathy card got a stanza about finding comfort in memories. And cards for new babies... well, those got made and remade when dried teardrops warped the papers.

"You remember those?"

"Are you kidding?" He chuffs and pulls away, angling his face toward mine, and I dare to make eye contact. "Of course I remember them. They always said the right thing. Always made me feel special, you know?"

You are special. I want to scream it, here and now, and tomorrow and the day after and yesterday and twenty years ago and from the mountaintops and from lighthouses and in quiet cars on trains and to anyone who will listen when I tell them how special Elliott Bailey was and is, forever and ever.

But this is a 'no feelings' arrangement, and telling him how special he is to me definitely feels like feelings.

This chapter of our story, this one of mutual specialness, where I feel special from his remembering how special I made him feel... this will make a great song.

"You okay in there?" he asks, nudging my forehead with his.

"Very okay. I just didn't realize you cared about the cards." I consider, for the briefest moment, flinging open my suitcase and showing him how much I care, too. How much cards and notes and perfectly-timed gifts have always meant to me. But the desire to leave the couch vanishes when he smiles, just enough to give me a minor heart attack, and then he threads his fingers through my hair and presses his lips to mine.

Everything about Elliott is thoughtful: The time he's putting into Zoe's party. The gift when I was fifteen. The custody agreement he and Zoe's mom arranged when they were barely adults. Picking me up on my way home from the coffee shop. The way he cleans up after dinner every night, no matter who cooked or whose home he's in.

The way he kisses is no different. It's soft and gentle, permission-seeking, making sure I'm comfortable and happy and enjoying every second. And, have mercy, I am. Too much.

I'm so hungry for him, starved for the affection of this man I've wanted for more than half my life. And now I get a taste as my tongue skims his lips; on its next pass Elliott's tongue meets mine. It's better, but I still need more. And I don't think I'm rushing anything, because I've been waiting forever for this. And it's not like anything too serious will happen, because we both know the rules.

But this whole arrangement started because Elliott liked kissing me and because he liked spending time *together,* together. So let's be together, eh?

I shift up onto my knees, and his arm slides down until his hand is on the small of my back. Something possesses me—if we were in Salem circa 1692, I'd be burned at the stake, for sure—and with my arms wrapped around his neck, I swing my right leg over his legs so I'm straddling him.

He gasps and his eyes open and maybe I screwed it up. I pinch my eyelids shut, hoping he'll let me down gently. I know he's going to when he puts his hands on my hips. I'm waiting for him to lift me off of his lap and deposit me back on the cushion next to him before he takes off into the night sky, ne'er to return to me.

But *oh*, he grips my hips and holds me in place while he grinds up into me, and when my head lolls back in pure ecstasy he helps himself to my neck.

This. damn. couch.

Has there been a more magical moment than this? Not in my lifetime. Not when I won a songwriting Grammy (it wasn't televised) or when I met Taylor Swift (though that's a close second) or when I imagined this at any point in time in my existence.

But what does Elliott Bailey do? I swear he's from some hot-shot poker tournament somewhere, because now it's like he says *I'll see your magical hip-grinding moment and I'll raise you a little partial nudity* because his hands are under my shirt.

I applaud the seamless transition. Really. From his hands finding purchase on my hips, to his thumbs exploring my bare skin where my shirt shifts at my waist, to their leading the expedition for every single one of his fingertips to follow... well done, Elliott.

They hesitate there, not quite ready to venture farther north until the command center gives the all-clear.

We know the rules: No relationships. No feelings. No sex. And definitely not that other thing that I don't want to think about right now.

And I know the point of all of this is to feel good. To get a physical connection with someone we trust. And I've almost always trusted Elliott. I trust him fully right now. So I sit up and let our eyes lock as I raise my hands straight into the air.

It's a slow striptease that he does with my shirt. There's so much time to second guess this or come to my senses, so much time for him to change his mind, too. And bless him, because the only time we lose eye contact is when cotton passes in front of my face.

He was already hard under me but now he twitches, and his lips follow suit. "You're so beautiful, Mia." My shirt's still in his hand when he cradles my face and draws it to his, kissing me again, more deeply than before.

"Careful, El."

"What?" He pulls away and rubs my cheek with his thumb while he searches my eyes. "Are you okay? Is this too much?"

"I'm fine. But you're being too nice. That almost sounded feel-ings-adjacent."

He smiles. "I assure you, it wasn't."

"Sure. Maybe next time just *look* at my chest first before saying something like that? Just to make it super clear you're not being sweet?"

And now that smile reaches his eyes and I'm in trouble. "Next time, huh?" he asks.

I'm nodding, leaning in, ready for sparks to fly when our mouths meet again when someone makes it very clear they are out to destroy my happiness.

The basement door opens and footfalls land on the steps. "Mia?" It's Julie. There goes that rule.

"I'm naked!" I shout.

Elliott looks equal parts ready-to-puke horrified and ready to crack up at my admission.

"Don't come down. I need a minute."

"I just need to change some laundry around." There's another step.

"*Jules*! Upstairs. Please. I'll let you know when I'm decent." This is not remotely suspicious behavior between two best friends who had side-by-side lockers in the gym and who mastered the art of the quick-change backstage during all our musicals in high school.

There's a deep sigh, a huffy *"Fine,"* and retreating footsteps before the door closes and I am on my feet, frantically pulling my shirt back on while Elliott grabs his things.

"Hurry—before she gets curious and sees your truck out there." I whisper-yell and I chase him down to give him one more butterfly-inducing kiss as I push him out the door and lock it behind him.

Then I make my way up the steps and find Julie just on the other side of the basement door.

"What were you doing down there?" She narrows her eyes and takes me in, and I am far too flustered for this to resemble any sort of normal evening routine. "And why are you so out of breath?"

Because I just made out with your brother.

Because I just dry humped your brother.

Because your brother just snuck out of here like we're horny teenagers.

"No way. *Mia!*" And then she's losing it, cracking up as she saunters down the stairs. "I know exactly what you were doing!"

I gulp. One of those comically loud gulps that would have its own illustrated cell in a comic book. "You do?"

"Duh." She looks around like a detective searching for a piece of evidence that'll crack the case wide open. She finds my phone on the far arm of the couch and lunges toward it. "Let's see what kind of porn the famous Mia Montgomery watches in her friend's parents' basement."

"Let's not," I protest, swooping in and reclaiming my phone from a frowning Julie who couldn't get it unlocked with the passcode I know she attempted—the one we both started using years ago: the year we started kindergarten. "But, um, it's good stuff," I tell her, hoping that morsel will satiate her hunger for any additional juicy bits of gossip.

She snickers, then yawns, and I help her switch her laundry around, even carrying the full basket up the stairs to the living room for her. I don't know much about being pregnant, but I know from looking at Julie that bending to pick up the basket and then maneuvering it up the stairs doesn't seem exceptionally pleasant.

"Thanks, Mia." She sinks into a recliner and starts folding. "Can't sleep. Heartburn. Figured I might as well be productive."

I can imagine the loneliness she feels now, being the one awake in the middle of the night, going through this process of bringing life into the world with another person but being the one to do all the heavy lifting (literally).

"Did you want to watch something?" I ask, already lowering myself into the recliner's twin and reaching for the remote. I turn the TV to mute as soon as I hit the power button, and we're soon bathed in light from a home shopping network special.

"Watching something sounds lovely. As long as it's not porn." She throws a towel at me and I fold it, adding it to her stack, then stealing more from her basket and helping her with the laundry. She reclines when she's finished and we let the home shopping channel play with no volume, narrating the show ourselves until Julie starts snoring softly.

I finally turn my attention to the phone that's been vibrating in my pocket for the last hour.

> That was close.

> Also, very, VERY fun.

> …

> Mia. You're scaring me. Say something.

> Did she figure it out? Are you being interrogated?

> Oh no. You're chopped in a million pieces. She's broken your kneecaps. ARE YOU IN A REAL-LIFE MISERY?

> ISO: Signs of life.

> I'm alive.

FINALLY. And good. I'm glad.

Everything OK?

Yes. I'm fine. She's fine.

And you're right. That was too close. 0/10 recommend.

Hopefully you'd recommend SOME parts of tonight?

I mean, my shirt was off and his tongue was in my mouth and I know what he feels like through my pajama shorts, so this next text is flirty but not wildly inappropriate, right?

Nope. Not recommending. I want you all to my-self.

It takes him forever to respond, even though the timestamp shows it's only been two minutes.

No arguments here.

Okay, I know I'm overthinking this. But three words? Really, Elliott? You needed two minutes for three words? I wonder what he typed and deleted, then typed and considered and deleted. Lather, rinse, repeat. Or maybe he just went to the kitchen for a drink.

I have a long day at work tomorrow, but do you want to meet up after? Maybe grab a late dinner?

I would love to.

But I can't. Sorry.

It's girls' night.

CHAPTER 18

now

I REALIZE, AT GIRLS' night, that I am an absolute garbage human being.

"So, Jules, who is Elliott's new love interest?" Carla asks once our food is on the table, and it takes everything in me to keep my face neutral.

Julie lifts her steak knife and saws through her burger, rolling her eyes. "Elliott doesn't have a new love interest. Elliott is sulky and miserable and 'married to his work,'" she says, making air quotes around that last part, the knife still gripped in her palm.

"Well, that's interesting." Carla's eyes dance with delight as she purses her lips, and whatever she's about to say is clearly a juicy morsel of gossip. "I bumped into him at Johnston's earlier today."

Pregnant Julie is my favorite, because all this nonsense is keeping her from red meat and she is not having it. She shoots the most annoyed glare across the table at Carla, like *how dare you engage me in conversation about something as mundane as my brother being spotted at the pharmacy one town away—the town in which he happens to work—when there is meat to be had?* But somehow she edits all that down into the most bored, impatient "And?" I've ever heard. She arches an eyebrow, waiting—as we all are—for the significance of that particular sighting.

"And he was buying condoms."

Ho. ly. shit.

My heart stops and my eyes explode out of my face and I might actually be legally dead for a moment.

Julie falters ever so slightly before taking a defiant bite of her burger. There is *no way* she is going to show Carla that this rattles her, but I imagine she is rattled. "What's your point?"

By now, the whole table is turned toward the two of them, locked in a battle to see who knows more about Elliott's sex life. (I do, I think, but no way I'm telling *them* that.)

Thinking she has the upper hand, Carla smirks and raises her sangria to her lips. "Well, why would he buy condoms unless he recently exhausted his supply or he was planning to need them in the very near future?"

Kiko, always an excitable one, grabs Carla by the arm and leans in. "And why would he go out of town to buy them when the QuikShop sells them a mile from his house?" She gasps, which makes me jump. "Unless—he doesn't want to be seen!" I internally facepalm. Kiko's consumed the condom-conspiracy Kool-Aid.

"Wasn't he seeing someone a year or so ago, Julie? I thought it was super serious." Ali wrecks my whole world a little with this revelation, which was news to me. I do my best to read Julie's face, but she's a freaking statue, just blankly sipping her water. No help whatsoever.

"Maybe..." Kiko starts, but Julie slams her glass down and all heads turn toward her again.

"Enough, guys, okay? I really don't need to talk about my brother's sex life. I'm nauseous enough." There's a theatrical cradling of her belly to accompany her glare.

Kiko nods. "Right. What I'm thinking though, is maybe Elliott *isn't* seeing anyone. Maybe he bought them for someone else?"

"Well it wasn't me, that's for sure." Jules rolls her eyes and draws a laugh from everyone else at the table.

"Maybe... maybe they're for Zoe? She is at that age, after all?"

And this is where it becomes clear to me that I am a complete and total shit: I don't argue. I let them start a gossip train about a seventeen-year-old girl because I'm too scared to correct anyone and tell them that Elliott and I are sneaking around.

But also, what if they *are* for Zoe? Elliott and I said no sex, right? So they wouldn't be for us, unless he was planning to break a rule.

"You need a spy over there, Jules," Ali says. "Someone to report back and tell you who's coming and going. No pun intended."

"Gross. You volunteering?"

Ali scoffs at the offer. "Yeah, right. Like I could convince Scotty to babysit for a few days so I can play detective."

"It's not babysitting if *they're his kids,* Ali. It's called *parenting.*" At this, I give Carla a mental standing ovation.

Kiko interjects, giving Ali an opportunity to shrink back and question her choice of spouse and procreation partner. "What about Mia?"

Four pairs of eyes turn toward me, and I have never in my life wanted to be more invisible than I want to be right now.

"What *about* Mia?" Julie echoes.

I fold a fry in half, dip it in barbecue, and avoid everyone's gaze.

"It would totally make sense. Aren't you sleeping in a basement at the Baileys'? Why not infiltrate Elliott's place and report back next time with your findings?"

Every pair of eyes is urging me toward a yes. Except for Julie's, which are squinted like she is replaying that night in the basement over and over again in her head, when I tried (hopefully successfully) to convince her that Elliott randomly happened to drop off an air mattress and then played video games with me and there was definitely nothing else, wink wink.

Desperate to stop the telepathic attack of her internal voice, I remind everyone, "I think you're forgetting something just a tiny bit important. Which is, it's not up to any of us if I stay at Elliott's house. He would need to be on board, no?"

♫♩

"It wouldn't necessarily be the worst idea, I guess." Julie's pushed the passenger seat so far back that she's behind me as I drive her Corolla home from the restaurant.

It *might* be the worst idea. It might also be great and hot and wonderful, but also, 100%, the absolute worst idea. "You trying to get rid of me?"

"No." She winces, readjusting herself in her seat under the weight of what I can only imagine is some NFL linebacker's baby. She's huge. No thanks. "But you're so uncomfortable down there, and I think Dad's getting a little annoyed with you singing in the shower while he's trying to work."

Oh. Oops. *Note to self, shut up in the shower. Save the concerts for the stage.*

"Plus, Zoe adores you. And we would still do dinner together most nights. And, obviously, weekends."

"Obviously," I agree, navigating an S-curve on the narrow road. But I don't remember us actually making weekend plans.

"You should think about it. There's no way he'd say no if you asked."

I consider for the briefest moment what that could mean, until she adds, "He could never say no to Zoe."

CHAPTER 19

now

On Saturday morning I move into Elliott's spare room.

Not because I asked to move into Elliott's spare room, but because when I told Julie that there was no way on earth I wanted to move in and, additionally, no way on earth he'd agree to have his kid sister's bestie stay with him, she dragged me to his place to talk to him. With Zoe present.

Zoe shrieked, as expected. And El... well, Elliott looked at me with the most dangerously wicked smile I have ever seen.

Once both of my suitcases are unpacked, Julie whisks me away to New York City.

It's only about an hour and a half away, but it's definitely a full-day commitment.

We park in Hoboken and take the PATH into Manhattan, then hop onto another train to get up to the Theater District, which is buzzing with excitement and packed with people.

"I wanted to see *Chicago*," she says. "And once this baby comes, I feel like it'll be at least a year till I can get away."

She's still talking about how we needed to come this weekend before she grows too much more or her feet get more swollen or her body is affected in other ways by pregnancy.

Meanwhile, there I am, head hung low and fighting the wind, slightly bitter that *this* is the show we had to see, bitter because The Fluorescent Flowers' lead singer is playing Roxie Fucking Hart for six of the eight weeks of our break. It would be great to be here and see her—if we were on speaking terms.

We sit through the matinee and I clap extra loudly for Cell Block Tango (as one does) and then Julie insists on waiting at the stage door. We make it until Lily Asher (yes, the lead singer of The Fluorescent Flowers is named Lily) signs Julie's playbill with a little smirk and snide comment directed at me, and then Julie says she's hungry and asks if I know of any good places in the area where we can get dinner before heading home.

It's a tense ride back from Hoboken.

"I really thought you'd have more fun, Mia." She says it with such sweetness, but the underlying accusation seeps through. *I planned this day for you—well, really for me—and you were supposed to thank me and praise my awesome friendship.*

"I had fun. Promise." And I did! But not as much as she had. But I guess that was the point when she planned this day, wasn't it?

She slows at a red light just a few blocks from Elliott's house. "What do you want to do next weekend?"

"Honestly? Let's just hang out in your parents' basement. Like old times. Jess can hang out, too. And your parents and Zoe and El. Let everyone have popcorn and listen to Backstreet Boys and try to beat me at table tennis. I'll take on anyone, anytime."

I can hear the annoyance in her tone, like suggesting something so *normal* is offensive to her delicate sensibilities. "I can do that anytime."

All I want to say is *You can; I can't.* I want to remind her that the point of my coming home—of staying at her parents' place—was not simply to write or relax. I could have done that in L.A. or Bermuda or some remote lake town. The whole point is to see *her*. But I'm getting the feeling that *doing things* is more important to her than just being around me.

It's a delicate balance with Julie. Stand your ground but don't argue; tell her what you want unless she wants something different.

"We'll figure it out," she says, shifting the car into Park in front of Elliott's house. She couldn't even be bothered to pull into the driveway. She closes her eyes and rubs her stomach as I unbuckle my seatbelt, so I guess we're not going to even hug goodbye. We *always* hug goodbye.

"Sure. I guess so." There shouldn't be anything to figure out. I told her what I wanted to do, and after she focused today's plans on herself, I feel like I'm entitled to have the lazy day of hanging out I want to have.

Maybe that's why I don't say goodbye. Maybe it's why I slam the car door shut a little too loudly. And maybe that's why I don't feel remotely bad for wishing I had spent the day with Elliott, instead.

♫♪

"Fun day?" Elliott asks as I close the front door behind me.

"It was great."

He's lit only by a streak of streetlight shining through a crack in the curtains and the glow of the TV, paused on the evening news, and he leans forward in his chair. "I don't think I believe you."

"You caught me." I peel off my shoes and flop onto the couch across from him. "It was cold and busy and kind of lonely."

"Hm." He repeats the end of my sentence and scratches at the stubble on his chin. Then he turns on the lamp next to him and turns off the TV. Apparently, my feeling *kind of lonely* is something we're going to unpack right now.

I ask, "Remember how, growing up, you never took girls out to the movie theater on a date?"

The soft hum of laughter from his half of the room is a balm to the soul. "I remember. I didn't think you would."

I know I'm blushing, but thank goodness he can't see it. "Why didn't you? Take them to the movies, I mean."

"Because what's the point? You can't talk at all. So you drop ten bucks a ticket to sit next to each other but feel far away?"

"Right. So imagine that, times fifteen, for three hours. Watching your nemesis prance around onstage and everyone cheering for her as she gives the most mediocre performance Broadway's ever seen."

He leans back in his seat and crosses one leg over the other. "Nemesis, huh?"

"Oh, that." I wave a hand in front of me, like I'm shooing away the thought. "Never mind. She's just the worst. Anyway, the rest of it though... I just thought we'd do more old-times-sake stuff, you know? Kind of like what you and I have been doing. Sort of."

He laughs and I laugh, and he slaps his thighs before standing. "Alright. Let's go then."

"Go where?" It's nearly ten o'clock, and I can't imagine anything in Songbird Springs—other than O'Donnell's—is actually open past eight, even on a Saturday night.

He's pulling on his jacket over pajama pants and his old senior year basketball T-shirt, and I swear he winks as he says, "You'll see."

And that's how I end up in the front seat of Elliott's truck, going just above the speed limit through the town so deserted you'd think it was two a.m. on a Tuesday instead of bar o'clock on a Saturday night.

He spent a few minutes scrolling on his phone while I changed into warmer clothes at the house, and now I know why: there's a perfectly-curated playlist blaring from his speakers. All the old songs we'd listen to in the five-disc changer in the basement when we were kids; all the songs they played at school dances; the basketball team's hype song.

I'm absolutely crushing my rendition of an old Dierks Bentley song and he's smiling, singing softly in the driver's seat.

"Louder," I tell him, missing half a line but jumping right back into the song.

Elliott looks over at me, and his smile and his volume grow.

We drive like this for twenty more minutes, past the city limits and the onramp to the highway that is all too content to pretend Songbird Springs doesn't really exist. And we're content to let it act that way, because we love our sleepy town.

And then we're on a gravel road that juts off to the right, climbing up, up toward the brightest stars on the clearest night, and I remember—vaguely—hearing about places like this but never actually going there.

"Where are we?"

"It's Swallow's Ridge. It's a great lookout spot by day. Great for stargazing at night."

"Swallow's Ridge? Really?" The look I give him says *clearly, I don't believe this is just a lookout spot.*

"It's a songbird, Mia. Get your mind out of the gutter."

My mind *wasn't* in the gutter, but watching Elliott hop out of his seat with an armful of blankets and spreading them in the bed of his truck? Yep, my mind is firmly wedged in the gutter now. Like a bowling ball three sizes too big.

"Are there houses around here?" I might as well be asking, *is there any chance someone is going to catch us?*

But he just shrugs and looks around. "Probably about a mile or so in any direction. It's mostly woods. State land."

The music's still playing but this song's slower. Elliott shuts off the truck and the headlights, dropping his phone in the chest pocket of his flannel so we can hear it as he takes my hand and starts spinning me around in the gravel.

"What are we doing up here?"

He's humming softly, maybe singing the words just under his breath, and he doesn't stop leading me in a dance as he answers me. "Old times stuff." Then he pulls me in and I've got one hand curled up under his arm, gripping his shoulder, and the other held gently in his hand. I rest my face against the warm coziness of his shirt, and the humming resonates in my ear.

"I've never been here."

"Yeah, I think we killed it for you guys." He chuckles. "We would come up here junior or senior year after basketball games. A bunch of guys would bring beer or cigarettes or whatever, but I wasn't really into that. I just liked hanging out with my teammates. We came up here in the summer, too, which was nicer except for the mosquitos."

The song changes, and despite the faster tempo, Elliott still holds me close like it's the last slow dance of senior prom.

"Anyway. Trav Davies was an idiot, as you know. And he flicked a cigarette butt into the trees that used to be right over there—" he turns us and I feel his head gesture in the general direction of a clearing in the woods. "And then there was a fire. So the cops figured out what happened, but not exactly who was responsible, and they basically said that no one under twenty-one was allowed to park up here without more adult supervision."

"Wow. So Trav Davies screwed me out of the Swallow's Ridge experience, huh?"

"Yep. You have him to thank."

"Mmm. Noted. I'll write an angry song as my revenge."

Elliott stretches and I drop my arm from his shoulder, but he pulls me back toward the truck by our still-connected hands. Wordlessly, he climbs in and helps pull me up, and I follow his lead when he lies back on the pile of blankets. There's one off to the side that he pulls over us, and it's not the most comfortable or warmest arrangement, but it's beautiful under this canopy of stars.

There have to be thousands of them visible, all bright white and glowing, dotting the sky with the full moon. I'm looking at the cosmos; I feel Elliott's eyes on me.

"Why'd you come back, Mia? You could've gone anywhere for two months, but you're here."

"I missed everyone."

"Bull."

I backhand him gently on his arm. "I did! You guys are great!"

He catches my hand and weaves his fingers into mine, and I'm thirty degrees warmer with his touch. "What about Paris?" he asks, tucking his free arm behind his head.

"What *about* Paris?"

After a long moment where we're both stubbornly quiet, he sighs. "I'm surprised, I guess. That you didn't visit your parents."

I shrug off the statement. All the emotions tied to Paris are too big to talk about. So are all the reasons why I came back home. So I slide in closer to Elliott and rest my head on his chest, letting his slow, gentle breathing and the rhythmic thudding of his heart fill the silence around us. It's a steady beat and I can hear it already in a bass drum, the foundation beneath an airy vocal and an acoustic guitar.

And this. *This* is why I came back. Paris is gorgeous, but screw it. It doesn't have this moment or this man, and if Elliott was inspiration for three albums' worth of material before, I can imagine our new arrangement will be inspiration for at least one more.

"Paris is great, but it's not home," I finally admit to both of us.

He kisses the top of my head. "I'm glad you picked us."

"Me too." When I tip my head back to smile up at him he greets my mouth with his, and even though we've done this many times in the past few days, this kiss feels different. It's sweeter. Soft. His full lips pressed to mine, his arm wrapped around my back and pulling me closer. How dangerous is this, being curled up in his arms, under a blanket, in the bed of his truck?

He must feel it too, because a few minutes later he says, "We should probably get back." But his fingers are twisted in my hair, which says something else entirely.

In the vein of saying things we don't really mean, I reply, "Yeah. We should."

And somehow... somehow we manage to untangle ourselves from each other and the blankets and pack up and drive back in relative quiet. The grumble of his truck is the melody for the dance his hand does with mine on the armrest between us, and all I can think about the whole drive home is how different our lives might be if he'd taken me to Swallow's Ridge when we were teenagers.

CHAPTER 20
twenty years ago

I PICKED UP A guitar for the first time the summer after freshman year.

Some people might say I did it to spend extra time with Theo Jeffries, who was often found sitting on his parents' back deck, overlooking a cornfield, strumming an acoustic and tossing his pre-Bieber Bieber bangs out of his eyes.

Those people would be technically correct. In fact, but not in spirit.

Yes, I wanted to spend time with Theo, but not because I liked him like everyone assumed. I had hoped (it was misplaced) that by spending time with Theo, I'd forget all about Elliott Bailey and the weight my unrequited love for him placed on my soul.

(I should maybe take this opportunity to share that I was an incredibly dramatic adolescent.)

I stumbled into it, really. During a typical Saturday morning yard sale hunt, I found an old guitar that had seen better days. But I had twenty bucks from my shifts at Have a Ball, our mini-golf course's snack bar where I'd been working all summer with Julie, Theo, and Bentley, and I forked over my crumpled bills for the opportunity to own the instrument. I needed a hobby, per my parents and my guidance counselor who always felt I had too much energy.

"So wait, you're telling me you bought a guitar, and you don't know how to play it?" Theo asked, laughing like it was the best joke he'd ever heard, when he heard Julie and me talking about it at Have a Ball.

"How would I know how to play it before I had it?" I countered, but he just shook his head, like logic was lost on him.

"Come over sometime," he said, "and I'll teach you."

And that's how I spent half of July and most of August: working at Have a Ball, hanging out at Julie's house, and getting private guitar lessons from Theo.

I picked up the basics pretty quickly, like I was learning a second language during my formative years, and sure, Theo and I had a great time up there strumming away and looking for cool picks in the thrift shop or scouring the amphitheater at the park a few miles away where they hosted the free summer concert series, just in case anyone left any behind after their performance.

Playing guitar was fun. It was something to do in a place where—let's be honest—there wasn't much to do. Nothing was supposed to come of it, other than I'd play guitar instead of joining the marching band, because this was a little cooler than the French horn I'd picked up in fourth grade *and* it didn't require me to stand in the sun for eight hours a day, five days a week, during the hottest week of the year. And what the heck was "drill," anyway? And why was everyone so obsessed with rotating parallelograms?

Anyway... guitar. Supposed to be nothing. But the more Bentley randomly mentioned about Callie and Elliott hanging out, or the more I saw it with my own eyes at the Baileys' house, the more I channeled my inner Jewel, scribbling heartbroken poetry everywhere I could, whenever I could, trying to fit it into the chords I knew to turn it into music. Failing, every time.

"You guys are cute," Julie whispered as we were wiping down the counters at Have a Ball. It was our last shift before the school year, and I had never been so grateful for the little window AC unit that was keeping us from melting onto the floor.

"Who guys?"

She glanced around the room to make sure he was out of earshot. "You and Theo."

Theo had just asked if I wanted to walk around the first football game of the season with him, and I said sure, because of course I wasn't going to sit and watch the game. But it's not like that was a marriage proposal.

"Theo and I aren't a thing."

"I'm not sure he knows that."

"Jules." I rolled my eyes.

"Mia." She rolled hers right back, adding a smirk. "Think about it. You were at his house all summer long, you worked together, and you just planned to walk around the game with him."

"You and I did all those things too, except the game thing. Which we *would* do, but can't, since you're in the color guard."

"Well, we already know *we* have a thing." She wagged her finger between us. "He's cute, though, right?"

I stole a peek at him, from his black non-slip shoes and his white crew socks to his black shorts covered in dried drips of ice cream, from his navy blue Have a Ball T-shirt to the hair he kept tossing out of his eyes. And I just shrugged. "He's okay, I guess."

Objectively, Theo Jeffries was always better than okay, but when you have Elliott Bailey Blinders on, you don't see anyone that way but him.

My dad came and picked us up when the golf course closed, and we swung by our house so I could pack a bag for an impromptu sleepover night at Julie's.

"Have fun," he said through the open window as I trudged across Julie's driveway behind her, my backpack instantly plastering my shirt to my back and the guitar case heavy in my hand.

"Thanks Dad. Love you."

"You too, Kiddo." He smiled and gave a half salute, more like a tip of the hat he wasn't wearing, and took off down the lane.

Mr. Bailey had a stack of pancakes ready when we walked in. It was so nice, after an entire summer of making sure everyone else got fed, to have someone make you dinner at ten o'clock even though everyone else had eaten. Even more special was that Mr. Bailey had the most incredible from-scratch recipe and he took the time to make them for us that way that night, with maple syrup and vanilla added straight into the batter for the most insanely delicious breakfast I'd ever eaten for dinner.

He and Mrs. Bailey sat and talked to us throughout our meal, asking how we felt about starting tenth grade on Tuesday and if we thought we'd work at Have a Ball again next summer. It was easy, just sitting and talking to them like that, in a way that was not quite natural at home.

And maybe I was too focused on how good it felt, or still in a maple syrup stupor, because when we went downstairs to set up our sleepover I didn't even catch the start of the argument between Julie and Elliott. But Julie stood at the bottom of the steps, her arms crossed, hissing angry whispers at her brother.

Who looked pissed.

Who was seated next to Callie, who looked terrified.

"I should go," Callie finally said, checking her wrist even though her butter-yellow Swatch wasn't there. "Yeah, it's late. I'll see you tomorrow?" It was more a question than a statement of fact.

Elliott nodded. "Sure. Yeah."

Then Callie stood, straightened her tank top and skort, and brushed past Julie and me without making eye contact.

Elliott rose like he was going to follow her, but she was out of there faster than a Mariah Carey song shooting to the top of the charts.

"Thanks a lot," he grumbled, and if his ire was solely directed at his sister he didn't make that clear.

"*Me?*" Julie planted her fists on her hips and leaned in to scold him. "You're the one down here doing who-knows-what—"

And that's when I realized. Elliott's tight curls were disheveled, his T-shirt was stretched a bit and sloppy around his shoulder, and there was a pink sheen in random splotches on his neck and around his lips.

Elliott Bailey was making out on the couch where I was somehow supposed to sleep.

"Get over it, Jules. You're so freakin' immature."

He stormed off past her, his elbow bumping hers as he passed. I was still stuck on the stairs, a few steps behind Julie, but I made myself as small as possible when he started to ascend. Still, I was in his way, and I happened to catch his eye as he squeezed past me.

I don't know what he saw in my face, but clearly it was something he didn't like.

"What's your problem?" he huffed. But he never gave me a chance to answer. He just kept climbing, then closed the door hard. It was calculated: not quite a slam, because that would get his parents asking questions, but definitely harder than a normal close.

Julie cussed, which she didn't normally do within the confines of her parents' house, and we got to work setting up our sleepover site. We were so exhausted (and she was so angry and I was so devastated) that we didn't even talk and joke like normal. We just set things up and crashed. Or we tried to, anyway.

Julie did.

I tossed and turned and wished I could fall asleep, but every time I closed my eyes I imagined Elliott and Callie kissing. So I did what I'd done many times in my own bedroom all summer long: I grabbed my journal and pen from my backpack and started to write.

♫♪

"That sounds nice," Mrs. Bailey said, lowering herself into a rocker next to mine.

I'd been strumming quietly on the deck, scribbling and scratching in my journal for the last hour, finally feeling like maybe I was getting somewhere with a real song.

"Thanks." I smiled as she passed a mug half full of coffee my way. The Baileys were typically opposed to caffeinating the youth, but this mug appeared to be more milk than actual coffee. I set my pen down long enough to take a sip. It was bitter and sweet and made me feel a little like an adult, which was a change from the previous evening after Elliott called us immature.

"Would you play it for me, Mia?" Mrs. Bailey asked.

My heart raced. I hadn't really played for anyone but Theo before, and I definitely hadn't shared my poems or lyrics with anyone.

What I always loved about Mrs. Bailey is how she wanted to make sure everyone was comfortable, always. And that moment was no exception. "When you're ready, of course. If not now, maybe someday?" She patted my knee and smiled, then went back inside, leaving me outside with my guitar and my feelings.

And within the next twenty minutes, I put the finishing touches on what would go on to become The Fluorescent Flowers' first number one song.

and within the next twenty minutes I'm off the finishing touches on
what would go in the bedside. The fluorescent flowers are number one

CHaPTer 21

now

Sunlight streams through the window and my back doesn't ache
and I'm in a real bed. It takes a moment to register exactly where I am,
but it takes no time to register that I just had the best night's sleep I've
had in a week.

At first, I wasn't sure I'd sleep at all. The guest room is right next to
the bathroom, and after Zoe had gone to bed and I was reading in mine, I
heard water running in the bathroom. The faint creak of an old medicine
cabinet door. Footsteps in the hallway. And I lay there wondering if
(hoping?) he was outside my door, as tortured by this impermissible
proximity as I was, trying to decide whether to knock. So much of me
ached to meet him in the hall.

I slowed my breathing so I could hear better, listen for any signs that
he was standing just outside my room. I looked for movement in the
teasing gap between the door and the floor, but there was nothing. And
by the time I convinced myself to sit up, then stand, to go meet him, I
heard the soft but undeniable *click* of his bedroom door latching shut.

And then I spiraled with my thoughts for a long time but eventually
drifted off to sleep on an actual mattress and woke up okay.

Like, physically *great*, but mentally *meh*, which averages out to *I need
coffee*.

I'm half nervous to open the door, wondering if I'll collide with a
towel-clad Elliott (and if the universe could really keep us from accidentally dropping the towel in shock a second time), but I have to pee and
wouldn't mind ditching my morning breath.

I crack the door, then crane my neck to peer into the hallway, and Zoe breezes past me, already dressed and ready for school.

"Morning!" she says, and it's far too chipper, and also a little hurried. She pulls a maroon lip gloss from an acrylic cosmetics display on her dresser. "Dad's not here, and I'm running late. But I hope you slept well!" Then, with a smile and a wave, she's bounding down the stairs two at a time. There's a commotion on the first floor, a warm "Have a great day, Mia!", the rushed-not-angry slam of a door, and then I'm alone.

I duck into the bathroom for a shower, singing along to show tunes since there's no one here to judge me for it, and I emerge refreshed. Then I change into leggings and a too-big sweater, make my bed, and pack my bag for another trip to the café. After spending an hour at Swallow's Ridge with Elliott, I've got plenty to write about.

With my ear buds in for my walk into town, I'm ready to go. But "Come What May" comes on and all I can think about is Elliott, and his bedroom door is *right there,* just a few feet away. And I've always wondered what grown-up Elliott's room would look like. Would it be like his room so many years ago? Proof of his love of sports? Did he even still love sports?

I creep past the bathroom and gently press a palm to Elliott's bedroom door. It eases open, and inside is the most decidedly *Elliott* room there could be.

It's homey and warm and comfortable: The walls are a nondescript cream, save for the one behind the bed that's covered in wood slats, stained all shades of dark brown, stretching the width of the wall from floor to ceiling. In front is a beige tufted headboard and a queen-sized bed draped with a white and olive comforter. The bedside lamps have amber shades that, at night, probably make this place look even sexier than it does now, if it's even possible.

In the corner is a full-length mirror on a stand, framed in black, and it's there that I see movement, despite the fact that I haven't moved.

I spin, stumbling into the room—ohmygod I'm in Elliott Bailey's bedroom—and throw out a hand to catch myself on the doorjamb or doorknob or something before I topple over completely. Of course I miss everything I'm reaching for, but Elliott reaches for me and he doesn't miss.

"You scared the shit out of me."

A smirk plays at his lips. "What are you doing, Mia?" It's like he doesn't care that he scared the shit out of me. Or he's having fun knowing that he did.

"I was looking for you." I wasn't. But it sounds a lot better than *I wanted to see where you get naked every day because I've been obsessed with you since we were teenagers,* so I stick with it.

"You found me," he says. But he says it like he's not quite sure he buys my explanation for why I'm here. And then he challenges me on it. "So what's up?"

I right myself, steal my hand back from his, and massage my wrist. It buys exactly 2.3 seconds of time to think up an excuse. "I, uh— I was wondering if you were going into town at all later. I was going to go to the coffee shop. And I can walk, but I just thought..."

"Yeah," he answers with a shrug. "I can take you. No problem."

"Thanks!" It's too bright, too cheery, too awkward. Meh, no more awkward than being caught peeking in his room.

And he snickers. Rubs the scruff on his chin and the back of his neck. "Mia?" he finally says.

"Yeah?"

He takes a step backward and gestures to the hallway. "I need to get changed for work."

"Right." I'm reduced to one-word sentences now.

"Unless you planned to stay and watch." He raises an eyebrow, but his arms are still angled toward the hall.

I shake my head. "No. I'll wait downstairs, if that works for you."

"That works for me," he says.

I sneak past him and turn down the hall, pausing in front of my room for one last scan to make sure I've got everything (read: catch my breath and silently scold myself for being a dumbass). On my way down the stairs, I can't help but to look up one last time, through the rungs holding the railing along the hallway back to Elliott's room. He's left the door open, just enough, like he knew. Or maybe he thought I would be respectful enough not to look.

Either way.

I watch Elliott take off his shirt and I die a little inside.

♫♪

A little secret about me: I enjoy black coffee. But black coffee's cheaper, and it doesn't sell as well to women in the 16-25 demographic, so when the band was interviewed for an Indie Artist of the Year story, they encouraged us to pick something a little more appealing to the fanbase and a little more lucrative for their coffee chain advertisers.

And while I do enjoy a chocolate-covered strawberry mocha from time to time, today calls for no frills, no distractions. Just caffeine, and as much of it as possible.

I park with a gigantic mug of coffee at a booth in the corner and get to work right away. Writing, scribbling, counting beats, scribbling out my scribbles.

I've got a full song down in less than two hours. And honestly? It feels fantastic. And once I'm reunited with my laptop and guitar, I can put some chords and a melody to it, too.

Elliott, this town... they're good for me.

I'm about to get my second refill of the morning when my phone buzzes on the wooden table top. *Claudette* flashes across the screen, and I know I can't put off this conversation anymore. I channel my innermost happy person (not hard after just writing a barely-disguised song about making out with Elliott) and swipe to answer as I make my way to the counter.

"Claudette! Hi!" I say, and I feel her annoyance before I hear it.

"It's about time, Mia."

Okay. So we're skipping pleasantries today.

"You've been avoiding my calls."

"You've been calling at inconvenient times."

"Mia. Cut the shit."

"Fine. Sorry. I've just been busy out here."

"Lily Asher is literally the lead in a Broadway show right now, and she has time for me." She sighs, and the exasperation is palpable even across more than two thousand miles. "Whatever. Mia— tell me you've got something that'll be ready to record in L.A."

"Yes!" I'm so excited I'm screeching, and I lower my voice in decibels but not excitement. "I actually just finished something a few minutes ago. I just need to work on the music. But I should have a whole collection of lyrics to send you—"

"Wait." I can see Claudette pinching the bridge of her nose, just from the way she says that one syllable. "We talked about this. We just need the one song. It's an acoustic 'Best Of' album with a bonus track, not a whole new project."

It's not an unexpected response. I mean, I predicted the resistance to the idea of a brand new album, but it feels maybe a tad bit more pronounced in her tone than is entirely necessary.

"I just thought—" I start, but Claudette cuts me off.

"I know. I get that you want to do some new stuff, but I think we need to ease the fans into it. They keep singing the classics, and you may as well roll with that as long as you can. Fans don't always take to new stuff well. They like the nostalgia, and very specifically *your* kind of nostalgia."

Is every manager as diametrically opposed to progress? So content to rest on their laurels?

She sighs into the phone and I can hear her mindless pen-clicking in the background. "Maybe get me two or three, and we'll see what works with the girls. Sound good?"

No. "Yep."

"Great. And Mia?"

"Hm?"

"Next time, just answer when I call you."

CHAPTER 22

now

ZOE PLOPS DOWN ON the floor across the living room from where I sit with my guitar. "This is so cool," she says while I tune the B string. "It's like a VIP pass to the songwriting experience."

"Yep. Just like an old episode of 'Behind the Music.'"

"What's *that?*" she asks, pulling a face, and instantly I'm old.

Like, I-should-have-a-Life-Alert-necklace-just-to-sit-on-the-floor-like-this *old*.

Once everything is tuned and ready, I start strumming the opening chords to *Heartbreaker*, and she's giddy with delight.

"I love this song," she squeals.

I semi-gawk at her. "This one wasn't even a single."

But Zoe shakes her head. "Doesn't matter. I've heard them all."

"You really are a superfan, aren't you?"

She shrugs and gathers her long curls, sliding them over her shoulder. "I just think it's so cool that you're famous, and that my whole family knows you. And that I get to hang out with you." She pulls her knees up to her chest and crosses her arms over them, resting her chin on the backs of her hands. She's so much like her dad this way, with her intentional, full-body listening, like she's ready to absorb every little note and lyric.

"I think it's cool," I say, still strumming, "that I finally get to see *you* again. It's been a long time."

"It has. My mom said my obsession started the last time you were here."

"Mmm." It's like the air has been sucked out of the room at the mention of her mom. And obviously I know she has one, and that she's still around. But thinking about her mom makes me think of Elliott *with* her mom, and it's just perfect that I'm playing *Heartbreaker* right now. The strumming intensifies like every hurt the song touches on is fresh and I need to play harder to make something else feel the pain I don't want to feel myself.

"She listens to you, too. Says you were lucky to get out of this town," Zoe adds, and that right there is really something, isn't it? This woman procreated with the one man I've always wanted to be with, but *I'm* the lucky one? Sure.

"I don't know. This town isn't so bad these days." There's a warmth to Elliott's voice as he slips out of his flannel and scarf, draping them over a chair in the adjacent dining room.

I soak up the look in his eyes, the subtle shimmer that practically sighs *I just had a rough day at work but now I'm home with my girl.* "I didn't hear you come in," I say, relaxing my fingers around the neck of the guitar.

At the same time, Zoe says, "Hi, Dad," and he beams a smile right at her. His girl.

"Hi, Zo." He checks his watch and stretches his arms high overhead. "I'm going to grab a shower, and then we can head over for dinner."

There's a final smile, a gentle glance back as he climbs the stairs, and Zoe's excited *"Oh!"* that pulls my attention away from Elliott.

"I almost forgot to tell you, we're going shopping for my prom dress next Friday night. Do you think you can come?"

"Wouldn't miss it," I tell her. And I truly am thrilled to be invited, an emotion which is strengthened when her eyes light up.

"Cool! You always look so glam. Can't wait."

♫♪

Elliott's surprisingly dressed up for family dinner when he comes back downstairs in khakis instead of jeans, and a crewneck sweater instead of his signature flannel. I don't think much of it until we get to the Baileys' house and Zoe jumps out of the truck while it's still running.

"Have fun!" she shouts. "But not too much!"

Elliott rolls down his window and reminds her, "Be home by nine, no matter what Aunt Julie says."

She responds with an exaggerated thumbs up. "You got it. Love you, Dad. Bye, Mia!" And then she bounds across the driveway toward her grandparents' home.

My hand hovers over my seatbelt buckle. "We're not going in?"

"Nope," he answers with a shake of his head and the slyest grin I've seen from him yet. "We're going out."

"Out?"

"To dinner. We could use a night away from everyone else, don't you think?"

I'm brutally attacked by a swarm of stomach butterflies. Elliott wants to ditch his family to spend dinner—*a night away*—just the two of us? I curl my fingers and dig a stubby nail into my palm, a makeshift pinch. But I am, surprisingly, not dreaming.

"We have multiple parties to plan," he says, and the logic crushes the tiny part of my soul that thought this was an actual date.

"We sure do," I agree, dropping my hands into my lap.

It's like he senses this shift, because he reaches over and laces his fingers between mine. We ride in silence for a few minutes, his thumb grazing the back of my wrist as we head toward the town limits. And there, separating our town from the next, is Sunset Diner.

"Don't freak out," he says, killing the engine after giving my hand a gentle squeeze.

"About the roaches? Or the impending food poisoning?"

Laughter rumbles in his throat. And the way he hops out of the truck takes me back to high school, to the last time I was here.

CHAPTER 23

nineteen years ago

IT WAS A JUNE Wednesday, right after my sophomore year, when a streetful of teenagers piled into cars with Callie and Bentley and Elliott and drove to the parking lot of the Sunset Diner, which also doubled as a parking lot for people looking to boat, swim, or fish in Mud River. We parked and kayaked and fished all morning in the calm, narrow river, and once we were sun-sleepy we ordered a criminally large take-out order for a late lunch.

Then we sat around the Baileys' back yard, in a community of tents we'd erected the night before, gorging ourselves on greasy cheese tots and a whole smorgasbord of fried foods.

And then Theo started feeling sick. Then Callie, then Julie and Bentley, then Adam and Dave. Then Elliott and I were out there, alone, as the sun started to set.

"Your place is the best," I told him as we both stretched our legs in front of us like we wanted to take up as much space as possible, give the sun the largest surface area to warm before night settled in.

He scanned the large lot—an acre of clear lawn in the back yard alone, multiple wooded acres next to it—and leaned back on his elbows in the too-tall grass. "I love it here," he said. "But it's more the people, you know?"

I *did* know. Especially when he sat there just feet away, his curls hanging around his face, and looked at me with a sun-induced squint I mistook at first for a wink.

"Mia." His face went serious and I thought, *Okay, this is it. This is when he tells me he sees me, that he feels for me what he has to know I feel for him.*

"Yeah?"

"I feel..." He paused. Shifted.

I, embarrassed and excited and shy, closed my eyes in a long blink and inhaled. I opened my eyes just in time to see Elliott scramble to his feet, clutch his stomach, and stumble-sprint toward the house.

CHAPTER 24

now

"I promise—there's nothing to worry about anymore." He drops his hand to the small of my back and gently guides me to the door.

"I thought the health department—"

"Oh, they did," he says with a knowing smile, wrapping his fingers around the handle on the front door. "But someone bought it a few years back, fixed it up, brought in a new chef, and—"

He doesn't have to say anything else, because the second he opens the door his meaning is clear.

"Geez. It's gorgeous in here." And it is. Gone are the ripped pleather booth seats and the stench of grease, the sticky Formica tables and the old fluorescent lighting. In their place is a sophisticated blend of rustic wood and potted plants, wrought iron light fixtures and exposed brick, the aroma of something savory dancing toward our taste buds.

"Told you." He leans toward my ear, and his hand presses against me more firmly. "Shall we?"

I nod, taking it all in: The completely renovated, expanded, and chic interior. The excitement in Elliott's voice. His proximity to me. In public.

Once we're seated, he eyes me over the top of his cocktail menu. "You flashed back to that day, didn't you? Replayed every gory detail in your head?"

"Maybe. And now I need to schedule another appointment with my therapist."

"Well, hopefully the memory doesn't turn you off too much."

I choke on my own spit. Like I could ever be turned off where he's concerned. Hell, even all those years ago, I delivered Saltines and Gatorade to his room.

He arcs a brow at me as I take a sip of water. "You alright?"

"Yeah," I sputter. But the jury's still out, and I clear my throat. "I don't think you have to worry about... about me getting turned off."

"Good," he smiles, far too innocently. "Because I booked it for the shower."

"Oh. The shower. Right." The puzzle pieces shift into place in my brain, and *duh*.

Even with our arrangement, it's not like it matters if I'm turned off by Elliott. The stakes are pretty low for him—if I'm not into it, no big deal. He's back into Eligible Bachelor territory. Actually, he's already there, because our "thing" is nothing, all things considered.

We each order a cocktail, and then he leans in, his forearms resting on the table. "Is something bothering you? You seem... I dunno. Off."

"I'm fine," I answer with a shake of my head. "Anyway, we have some parties to plan, right?"

"We'll get there."

The server delivers our drinks—a smoky old fashioned for him and an elderflower cosmo for me—and Elliott raises his glass. "A toast?"

I raise mine in response. "To our party planning partnership?"

"Our partnership." He nods. Smiles. *Clinks* his glass to mine.

I guzzle half my drink in one gulp.

He relaxes in his seat, fingers tracing circles around his glass. "So, you and Zoe looked like you were bonding earlier."

"Over music and prom dresses, naturally."

"Naturally," he says and takes a sip.

"Which reminds me. I think her generation's broken."

When he looks at me so amused, I want to be inappropriately handsy. I want to earn that half smile and make his throaty laugh turn into a moan.

"They don't know about VH1? TRL? My god, El—am I..." I hush and glance around, partially for theatrics but partially due to shame at my realization. "Am I *classic rock?*"

He throws his head back and erupts with laughter. The few other patrons look only briefly, like they're conducting an obligatory wellness check at the sound, and go back to their dinners and drinks.

"It's not funny! Am I washed up? Irrelevant? Days away from being played exclusively on the oldies station?"

"Mia. Trust me. You are *very* relevant." His voice oozes reverence, or maybe I'm imagining it. Maybe I imagine the way he looks at me, my face, my eyes. The way his gaze dips a few small inches. The way my body responds to it.

"Anyway—" time to cut the sexual tension with the knife of mundane conversation. "How was work today? Short shift?"

It takes a beat for him to respond, and I wonder if we fill it with the same thought: *I wish we weren't in public right now.*

But he finally replies with a shrug. "Yeah, did a blood drive at the Lutheran church in Ferryton after their services today. They were doing a whole day of giving, and someone had the idea to invite us." His whole mood shifts, and when he takes a drink he's slow to lower his glass or lift his gaze.

"Hm. The Lutheran in Ferryton... isn't that where Syd went? I feel like I remember that from the funeral announcement."

"Yeah. Guess so."

I know Julie's mad that I wasn't there, but that doesn't explain Elliott's sudden frostiness.

In the nick of time, the server appears next to our table again with an indecent amount of food (some things don't change here, I guess) that I realize we never actually ordered.

"It's a tasting menu," he explains as he sets a trio of tiered platters on the table. "For your party, you'll choose two items from the hors d'oeuvre selections, two entrees, and three side dishes. Once you've enjoyed some of these options, I'll bring out dessert." He passes a small clipboard to each of us, each showing a list of the various options and including a pen for us to make selections, and leaves for the kitchen.

"Well, this is..." Elliott begins. "Fancy," he finishes, just as I say, "A lot of food."

Right away, from the thirty million options in front of us, I'm drawn to the sushi roll on the hors d'oeuvre platter.

"Guess we can rule that one out," Elliott says, just as I load two pieces onto my plate.

"Why?"

"Raw seafood. Julie won't be able to eat it."

I shove a bite into my mouth. "Jules loves sushi."

He looks at me like I've got three heads. "She does. But she can't eat it because she's pregnant."

"Okay..." I chew, thinking how wild it is that Elliott knows all his sister's new and temporary dietary restrictions. "But there are plenty of other options for her, if we think people would like the sushi."

He looks up from where he's scribbling notes on his clipboard. "Are you suggesting we serve a food Julie can't eat at a party *for* Julie? Have you met my sister? Do you think we'd ever hear the end of it?"

"Good point." I shovel the other piece into my mouth and wave my cocktail napkin like a white flag.

He snickers, and I watch as he crosses caprese skewers off the list, too.

"Do you hate good food?"

"It's the mozzarella. It's local. She probably can't have that, either."

I pick up a skewer and point it at him. "You must be the world's best big brother, if you've committed all this to memory."

He helps himself to a slice of roasted rosemary chicken and a side of green beans. "You think too highly of me. I've been burdened with this knowledge for more than eighteen years. I'm just glad to have a reason to use it again."

I know they split for the last time shortly after Zoe was born, and I know our arrangement isn't supposed to involve feelings, but of course I die a little inside every time he mentions Zoe's mom. Not for the me who's sitting here now, but for the me who wept herself to sleep for a week when we all heard what happened.

"Do you two ever think about getting back together?" It's official. I've lost my last ounce of sanity *and* my last shred of dignity. RIP to both. XOXO, This Question. "You don't have to answer that."

But he's already responding with the most respectfully violent head shaking I've ever seen. "No way. That ship has sailed. More like, it's sunk."

"Oh." A bite of the world's best scalloped potatoes can't even keep me from talking. "You guys just seem to get along really well."

Elliott nods thoughtfully. "We do. But we're just friends."

Just friends. Honestly, it would've maybe hurt less for him to say they were sleeping together. But I cram more potatoes into my mouth A) so I don't say that, and B) because I'm famished.

We make small talk through slightly suggestive food-induced moans, and we get refills on our cocktails, and finally dessert lands on our table. And while I'm thoroughly full from the other courses, I am absolutely going to devour my half of these treats, most of which are chocolate, and *yum.*

"Did you try the mini caramel apple pies?" Elliott asks, eating half of one in a single bite. "They're delicious."

I dissolve into a fit of giggles like I'm all of nine years old. We've now had refills on our refills. Elliott's already offered up his credit card and paid, and the restaurant is closing, and we've promised to send in final choices to the event manager tomorrow.

On her way out, an older woman rests a hand on Elliott's shoulder and coos at us about how adorable we are, and how happy we look, and how she hopes we have a long and wonderful life together.

"Thank you," Elliott says, while I'm across from him protesting perhaps too much.

"We're not... I mean. We're just friends."

"Oh. Apologies." She looks back and forth between the two of us and retracts her hand, like suddenly we're not to be trusted and admired.

Elliott meets my eyes, holds my gaze, tempers a smile. "We're friends," he almost repeats.

"Well, have a lovely evening, anyway," the woman says before finding her way to the door.

A quiet settles over us, like neither of us knows what to say now that we've been mistaken for—*gasp of gasps!*—a couple.

I'd been working my way through the chocolate-covered strawberries prior to the interruption, and I reach for my glass of water as a final palate cleanser before we leave.

"Good lord!" Elliott cries, catching my wrist, turning it to show me a streak of melted chocolate on my thumb and index finger. "You're a *monster*, Mia."

"Oh, yeah? Would a *monster* do *this?*" I ask, shoving my arm forward, leaning in with it, smearing the residue from my thumb on the tip of his nose. His grip tightens and/or I lose the will to move (either is equally likely at this point), and he examines my finger with his glassy eyes before the drinks really kick in—that's the only logical excuse for what happens next—and he brings it to his lips, licking off the chocolate.

Immediately, his eyes go wide and I feel my pulse in places I didn't know I could.

I pull my hand back as he starts to stand and avoids my gaze. "Sorry," he grumbles.

Are you? I wonder. "Don't be," I say.

This makes him pause, glance up at me, drop his gaze to my lips. Lick his own. "We should go."

CHAPTER 25

now

THERE'S NOWHERE TO GO.

I mean, there is, but not safely.

As soon as we're outside, we remember we're both too tipsy to drive.

"I could call Jules. Have her pick us up?"

"Nope. She would have too many questions about why we're here."

We stand side by side and stare at his truck, tucked into a dark corner of the nearly empty parking lot, overlooking the river.

"So." My fingers are still sticky from the chocolate when I pull my jacket tighter around me. "Now what?"

But we're staring at his truck. Tucked into a *dark corner* of the *nearly empty parking lot*. (Wink wink, nudge nudge.) This can go one of two ways: handprint on the steamy window (a la that scene in Titanic), or serial killer.

And Elliott's sworn life oath is to heal people. Or something like that.

"We wait a little, I guess, and then head home." And oh, when he says *home* like that to me. Not '*my place,*' but '*home.*' Like it's mine, too. Like I belong there with him.

He twists a keyring around his finger, slow and gentle, creating a timid *ting* of metal as keys jostle against each other, and takes a hesitant step toward the pickup. I follow his lead in the quietest minute we've shared since I got back into town.

Ever the good guy, he unlocks my door and holds it open while I climb into the cab. Once I'm in he shuts it and stands outside, his body square with the river, his gaze set in the direction of the dark water. His shoulders rise and fall. Once. Twice. Then he gets into his seat, starts the truck, and turns on the heat.

"You okay?" I ask, myself very much *not* okay now that his whole tone has changed. Plus, there's the whole sexy finger-licking thing we've just ignored.

"Fine."

"You're not acting like you're 'fine,' El."

He sits back and strokes his neck. "It's nothing."

Clearly it's *something*. But, just as clearly, Elliott doesn't want to be pushed. So I sit and wait and wait some more, and the patience pays off.

Elliott clears his throat and puts his hands at ten and two on the steering wheel, looking straight ahead, while we remain parked. "It's been a while."

My heart hammers in my chest. There are so many ways to interpret this, and I don't want to read into his words a story he's not trying to tell.

"A while?" is all I ask, because hopefully he expects that I'd be seeking to clarify what he means.

"Yeah." He drops both hands to six o'clock and glances my way from the corner of his eye. "A while. Since I've, uh, been out. With someone."

"Like, on a date?"

"Sure, I guess. I wasn't going to call it that, because I know it isn't, but—"

"But it's dinner at a relatively nice place, and you just licked chocolate off my finger."

He chews his bottom lip for a moment before breathing out "Yeah" on a sigh.

"For the record," I say, my fingers fidgeting in my lap. "This totally was not a date. Friends can also go out for dinner together."

Elliott nods, his shoulders a little looser now, his eyes not quite so tortured. It's possible he almost smiles when he asks, "And the finger-licking part?"

"I think that's related to the *benefits* part of our arrangement. But you can also plead temporary insanity or claim you thought you were at a KFC. Your choice."

He tips his head back and laughs. At first it's a little snort, a tiny burst of air from his nose. Then it grows into a chuckle, which snowballs into a full-on laugh attack. And it's honestly the best sound I've ever heard.

"It wasn't *that* funny, El."

He drags a hand down his face, stopping to muffle the remaining snickering. "It was *terrible*, Mia."

"But it worked." I jab a finger into his ribs. "You're laughing."

"I am," he says, almost like he's realizing it for the first time. He catches my hand in his and runs his thumb along mine. "I like laughing with you."

"I like laughing with you, too. It's, like, my second favorite thing we do together."

His eyes snap to mine, and a half smile creeps across his lips. Then he leans in, dangerous mischief lighting his eyes. "What's your first favorite?"

I answer with a kiss, mostly because I can't resist when his lips are this close to mine. It's sweet and hot, and the stubble on his jaw is soft on my palm as I hold his face in my hands.

When it ends, I exhale. Bite my lip. Meet his gaze. "Still not a date."

"Thank goodness. Wouldn't want to break the rules." Elliott's eyes move over my face, and then his hand moves over my arm, my side, my thigh. And my body reacts like a marionette, moving toward him like he's got some invisible string pulling me to him.

I'm up on my knees. "Technically..."

His mouth is on my neck. He reclines his seat and slides down, pulling me closer, like he's sinking and I'm going to drown with him.

"We didn't make a rule about dating." I ease my knee over him so I can straddle him, leaning into him, hot goosebumps rising on my arms at the feel of his breath on my skin.

"*We* didn't. But I don't want to break one of our rules to tell you about that one." His fingers glide up my back and twist into my hair. He gives a gentle tug and my head goes back, and his kiss is a whisper against my sternum.

Heat pools between my thighs and I groan, because *god*, that's good. And I feel the way he reacts through his khakis.

This is clearly not okay: not Elliott's lips and teeth moving lower on my chest, not the way his hands creep up into my shirt to feel my skin, not the way I want to get on my knees by the pedals and please him, not the way I want him to balance me between the hood of his truck and his thighs.

But it's fucking *amazing*, and I can tell he feels it too. We'd be so good together.

"Is this okay?" he asks, my sweater pushed up my ribcage, his hands ready and waiting to remove it altogether.

I swallow hard, because there are a million reasons why this isn't okay, but right now, none of them matter. "Yeah," I say. All of this so far is a repeat, of course, from his parents' house just a few nights ago. But once my shirt comes off, we're in new territory.

Like the way his eyes lock on my chest. This is *very* new. (Admittedly, this is the best bra I own, and I silently applaud myself for choosing to wear it tonight, even if the only reason I wore it is because my others were still drying after I did my laundry.)

"You remembered," I say, because of course I turn to humor when I feel like everything is turning too serious. And I seriously want to rip off the rest of our clothes right now.

His eyes flit to mine and then straight back to my chest. "Hmm?"

"To look. To avoid feelings."

"Oh. I'm feeling *something*." And then everything gets exponentially hotter, because he drops his face between my breasts and he presses a hot, breathy kiss into one.

A common misconception about rockstars is that we only do three things: Play the show. Make outrageous demands. Have lots of sex.

Maybe *some* rockstars do that, but I can guarantee that rockstars that have been hung up on their teenage crush for their entire lives absolutely do *not*. We may request that a hard-boiled egg never crosses our path, and we may have *some* sex, sure, because we're human. But it's not a super frequent occurrence.

So this whole moment here is not typical for me, is what I guess I'm trying to say.

And I've wanted this for so, so long. The way his hands roam over me and hold me. The way his breath warms me and creates goosebumps in its wake. The way he whispers moans into the confines of the cab of his truck; the way they're just loud enough for me to hear but not so loud others could hear them even if there was anyone else here. The way this feels like a secret (it is) but special (it *also* is) and good (it's fucking *great*).

He hooks a finger into my bra strap and slides it down my shoulder, and I reach for his belt buckle, and his eyes meet mine, and he takes a deep breath through parted, impatient lips, and he nods, and his face lights up.

And then there's a knock on the window.

CHAPTER 26

now

HE LOWERS THE WINDOW maybe two inches as I bury my face into his shoulder, pressing my chest against his, hiding as much as I possibly can. I didn't have a half-naked make-out session interruption on my bingo card.

"Uh—" says the interrupter, "sorry. I, uh… I saw the truck running, and we closed a while ago, and I was going to ask if you were okay. But. Um. I guess…" He chuckles, and I feel Elliott's chest deflate as he exhales the breath he's been holding.

"Yeah," he says, answering with a laugh of his own. "We're all good here."

"Got it. I should tell you, though. There're cameras in the lot, so maybe you want to take this somewhere else?"

"Absolutely. Thanks."

There's a mumble, and then the sound of the window sliding back into place.

"Is he gone?" I ask through the curtain of my hair that's fallen around my face.

"Yeah. He's gone." He rests his hands on my thighs as I peel myself away from the warmth of his sweater and start fumbling for my own. "I should've tipped him better."

I slide off his lap, back onto the seat next to him, and turn my sweater right-side-out. "So that he can pay for therapy now?"

"So he would've left us alone." Elliott's eyes drift downward again, and when he catches himself staring at my chest he bites his lip and meets my gaze.

I slowly slip into my sweater before turning and facing forward, and I pull the seatbelt across me and buckle it into place.

There's a delay before Elliott sighs, turns, and does the same.

And then there's a long, quiet ride back to his house, where the only questions are "Have you warmed up yet?" and "Any plans tomorrow?" and not "How far would we have gone had we not been interrupted?" or "Do you want to sneak into my room when we get home?"

It's just as well, because as I say the mundane ("Yep. Temperature's fine by me." and "Going to the café to write.") all I can focus on is the far more exciting and terrifying truth that swirls around inside my head: had we not been interrupted, I absolutely would have fucked my best friend's brother.

Zoe's already there when we get back to Elliott's house, and she's at the kitchen table eating what appears to be a slice of Mrs. Bailey's famous peach pie, eyes glued to the pages of a novel. "How was your night?" she asks without even looking up from her book. "You guys get into any trouble?"

I'm glad she's so engrossed in her book, because my face has to be giving "What did you hear" vibes.

Elliott brushes against my arm as he passes and drops his keys on the table. "It was good. Figured out some plans for Aunt Julie's party. How was dinner?"

"It was interesting."

"Oh, yeah?" Elliott asks. "How so?"

Zoe flips the book over to save her page and rests her elbows on the table. Her eyes dart between the two of us and then narrow as she focuses on her dad. "There was some conversation about who was missing. A few questions about why."

"Hm. That's strange. Grandma knew I had the reservation. Not sure what there was to talk about."

"I think maybe she thought that she would've been invited. Like all three of you would've gone or something. For planning purposes."

Zoe's eyes flit to me again, then back to her dad just as quickly, in a less-than-subtle hint that my involvement is a large part of the conversation at dinner.

Elliott must catch it, too, because he sighs. "I'll call her."

I take all of this as my cue to leave as nonchalantly as possible. I grab my water bottle off the drying mat next to the sink, fill it with ice and water from the refrigerator door, and say my goodnights to Zoe and Elliott.

Upstairs, I hear footsteps on the stairs as I brush my teeth and wash my face. When I open the bathroom door, Zoe's door is closed and Elliott's is cracked, and I hear him talking to—I'm assuming—his mother. The words that stand out most to my ears are "not" and "date" and "meant nothing," and that's all I really need to hear before I retreat back to my own room and close (okay, fine. *slam*) the door behind me.

I slip into my pajamas and plop down on my stomach on the bed, dragging my journal and pen across the nightstand to join me. And I write. I write about every single emotion I've felt throughout the night, every reaction to every time his lips were pressed against my skin, every laugh over dinner, every minute of silence on the ride back from the restaurant, every time I think about the words "meant nothing."

Zoe and Elliott go through the motions of getting ready for bed, too. Floorboards creak and water runs in the bathroom; doors open and close quietly in the hallway. The light that fills the crack under my door disappears, and I keep writing even after my phone vibrates on the floor. It's probably Julie, anyway, texting to remind me that her brother is off limits. Or to get details about her shower.

Bzzz.

Bzzz. Bzzz. Bzzz.

Bzzz.

I slam my pen down, my concentration fully wrecked at this point, and reach for my phone. But instead of Julie's name on the screen, I see a series of messages from Elliott.

> Hey

> Are you still awake?

> We should definitely talk about earlier. I know you don't want to, but I really think we should.

> I liked it.

> It terrified me.

> Mia please talk to me.

My fingers hover over the screen. The blinking cursor in the reply box taunts me, or begs me, or both.

I'm not going to pour my heart out to Elliott over a text. I can't do it. And I'm not going to fight with him over a text either. If he wants to talk, we can do it face to face. So I send back something stupid.

> U up?

There's a sound in the hallway, just outside my door. I jump up and open it, and there's Elliott, biting back a laugh.

"Hey," he whispers, composing himself.

"Hey."

"I'm up," he says. "Can we talk?"

I nod, pulling open the door and shifting my eyes toward Zoe's room next door, concerned she'll hear whatever conversation we're about to have. But he jerks his head toward the opposite end of the hallway. I follow him to his room.

In theory, this is the smarter room to meet in. It's further from Zoe and affords us more privacy. But now that I'm here, I don't know what to do. Sitting on his bed seems dangerous, but it's not like he has other furniture choices in here. So I stand awkwardly in front of his dresser as he pulls the door closed with a near-silent *thud*.

Elliott maintains his position just inside the door, and he turns my way with his head hung. He exhales and raises his gaze.

"I'm sorry," we say simultaneously. His eyes light up, so I yield to him.

"What a night, huh?" he asks on another exhale, but this time his mouth curls upward at the corners and I think he thinks he's being cute.

Damn it. He *is* cute. But I'm still kind of annoyed with him.

He must be able to read on my face just how unamused I am.

"I can't stop thinking about—"

"Our *not date*?" I interrupt, and his face falls. I shrug and double down. "Funny how something that's *nothing* can stick with you like that."

At this he drops his head and massages the back of his neck. "You were listening to my conversation with Mom."

"Not intentionally, no. But certain key words stood out to me as I was getting ready for bed."

He nods, rolling his neck, and stares at the ceiling. He licks his lips. Draws his bottom lip between his teeth. Sighs. "I don't know what to say."

I don't need to be as mean as I'm being. I don't need to be accusatory and hurt-sounding and angry, because what we have is really, truly, *nothing*. That's the point, right? Friends with benefits. No strings. No relationship.

"Mia—" he begins, and I can see the torment in his eyes, like he can't decide if he wants to remind me of the rules or kiss me again or kick me out of his room. "I had fun tonight," he finally decides to say.

I wait for the 'but' that is inevitably coming, but there isn't one. We search each other's eyes for any sort of follow up until Elliott finally lets out a puff of air and drops onto the bed. He rests his elbows on his knees and stares at the floor like his life depends on never breaking eye contact with a particular tuft of carpet.

"I had fun, too. Obviously," I admit. "And I don't just mean the ending. Or... right before the ending, I guess."

This earns a chuckle from him, and then there's a sniffle, and then I'm next to him on the bed, my knee nudging his and my fingers curling around his forearm.

"I know the rules, El. I know this is informal and we're not actually dating. I think it threw me, just hearing you say I meant nothing—"

"Whoa, Mia." He straightens his back and turns toward me, and his misty eyes scan my face. "I never said you meant nothing."

"Oh." The dangers of trying to interpret one side of a conversation, I guess. I reclaim my body parts and fold my hands in my lap.

He slides his palms backward and forward on his thighs, and I assume he's going to clarify. But instead he says, "I fell in love. Years ago. Head-over-heels, madly, fully in love."

Oh. It might honestly hurt less if he rewound the tape and told me I meant nothing. Because knowing Elliott was capable of loving so deeply—and that he *had* loved that deeply, but never felt so strongly about me—that might be the worst feeling in the world.

"It was this all-consuming thing for me," he adds, unprompted, and I think I might die. "I was all in, and for the first time in my life I actually saw a future for myself with someone." He takes a deep breath and further examines the carpet.

"So what happened?" It sneaks out of me, this betraying, too-interested, bringing-up-bad-memories question.

And he looks at me, finally, his eyes glossy and lips parted. But he doesn't answer.

"How did it end?"

"Abruptly," he eventually says. He seems so tormented, like he can't decide on the balance of what he wants to tell me and what he should, and his eyes fix on mine before sweeping to his dresser. "She left me." He rises and rummages through his top drawer.

No, not rummages. His hands move with precision, repositioning piles within the drawer until he finds what must have been buried underneath: a small black velvet ring box. Then he turns and holds it between us, his eyes glued to it, his words meant for me.

"I thought I'd found forever. I made plans. I put all my hope for happiness into her, and when she—" His voice breaks. He clears his throat, regains composure. "When she was gone, I fell apart."

He raises his eyes slowly and meaningfully to meet mine. "You're not *nothing* to me, Mia. You were never nothing to me, and you never could be."

"But I'm not *that,* either. I get it."

Elliott's heart breaks a little. I can see it in his face, the moment he catches my shaky exhale, the poorly-disguised hurt in my voice. To his credit, he demonstrates a great deal of concern, plopping the box on top of his dresser without even looking as he finds his way back to the spot next to me. He wraps an arm around my shoulder and rests his cheek on my head, tucking me into his side, wrapping me in his warmth.

We sit like this for what feels like minutes, and my head finally gets my heart under control.

"It's okay that I'm not... *that.* What you had before. Rule number one, and all that." I plaster on half of a smile, and since he can't see it I guess it's mostly for myself.

"Rule number one," he repeats.

"But we're still friends," I remind him. "That's half of our arrangement, right?"

He sniffles again and lifts his head, putting distance between us. "Yes. Friends."

The brush of his fingers on my shoulder softens, a ghost of the comforting touch he'd given when he first sat down. A letting go. A prologue to a goodbye. A reminder that Elliott and I are not destined to be some great love story, and that our less-than-ideal arrangement has an expiration date.

It's all too much and exactly what I need to force myself to rise and excuse myself to my room.

CHAPTER 27

now

ELLIOTT BAILEY IS A gorgeous distraction. Or he has been, or was, but can't be for the next few weeks.

Have I enjoyed having his hands on me and my mouth on him?

Yes. And that's the problem.

I've gotten a little swept up by this whole Elliott thing, which is going nowhere. After the other night, that's crystal clear. So the past few days I've been putting music to some of my lyrics, completely annihilating a Hi-polymer eraser in the process, and shopping for eighteenth birthday and baby shower gifts that will hopefully convey how much I care about the recipients.

With all my free time now that I'm avoiding her father, Zoe and I are really connecting and spending time together in the evenings. We go out for pedicures on Wednesday, Chinese on Thursday, and on Friday we make our way to Ferryton to stuff our faces with popcorn and footlong hotdogs during a Ferryton Falcons game. I never thought I'd be into ice hockey, but Zoe is obsessed with one of their wingers, so we treat ourselves to sweatshirts and beanies from their merch shop and yell at the refs and cheer when the right red light goes off and generally have a magnificent time.

Zoe's driving us home in her blue RAV4, both of us laughing, our ears ringing after the crowd erupted for the big win by the Falcons. She flicks on her signal and slows, then turns off the main road and quiets, her smile fading.

"This is where it happened, you know," she says. It takes a moment, and then it finally registers. "Have you been here, since?"

I shake my head and croak out "No."

"Do you want to stop?"

"No, that's okay." I do. Eventually. I swear, I want to sit and weep and remember and apologize and say goodbye, but I don't want to do it with Zoe or anyone else there with me.

Thankfully, Zoe seems to understand, and she accelerates as we drive past.

"I get not wanting to visit," she says a moment later. "Dad was the same way at first. He'd go out of his way to avoid this road and that intersection."

Elliott? I didn't think he was one to change his travel route just because his sister's friend died. "Really?"

She nods. "Yeah. He was there, when it happened. I mean, not *right* when it happened, but right after. It really messed with him."

"I can imagine it would." Julie hadn't told me any of this—not that Elliott had been there, not that he was so affected by Sydney's death. But then, we didn't really talk about Sydney, not since I didn't come home for the funeral and Julie still hasn't forgiven me for it, and we didn't really talk about Elliott, because she didn't know I wanted to know everything that was happening in his life.

"Anyway. Sorry to bring the mood down." Zoe adjusts the angle of the air vent and skips a track on her playlist. "Did you have fun tonight? At the game?"

"I really did. Thanks so much for inviting me."

"You bet." She smiles, and though she never takes her eyes off the road I can see the mischievous glint in them. "What'd you think about the center? Number thirty-two."

I try to remember the player in question, but my mind draws a blank.

"He's the one who started the big fight?"

Ah, yes, now I remember. Blond curls matted to his forehead as he tossed his helmet to the ice and swung at a player from the Cedars. Full set of teeth. Devilish grin. "Right. He was fine."

"Fine? Or, like, *fine*?"

"The first one?" I shrug, and Zoe laughs. "I mean, I like that he was defending his teammate. Clearly the guys look up to him because he's the captain. But I think maybe he's a little... old for you."

Zoe's laugh fills the car, and it's such a gift to be in the presence of her joy. Even though I'm pretty sure she's laughing at me. "No. Ew. Not for me, Mia. He's like, thirty-four years old."

I roll my eyes and use my most dramatic voice. "Oh *no*. He's absolutely ancient."

"In hockey years, yes. But mid-thirties is the new mid-twenties of the dating world. Wink wink," she says, not actually winking, because she's a remarkably careful driver.

"Ha!" I snort. "No way. I'm barely here another month anyway."

"So? I'm not saying you should marry the guy! But you could totally arrange a meeting. Go on a date. Have some fun. That is, unless you've got a secret guy out there somewhere."

I drop my gaze to my lap and exhale. "No. I definitely don't have one of those."

"Great! Then you should go for it."

They say the apple doesn't fall far from the tree. I know Zoe is only Julie's niece, but the similarities between the two are, at times, jaw dropping. Like the way they both take care of everyone around them. The way they both light up a room when they walk in. And the way they end a conversation by turning up the stereo and singing along at the top of their lungs.

CHAPTER 28

now

I GAVE MYSELF PERMISSION to sleep in since it's Saturday, but my REM cycle had other ideas. Specifically, the idea to continuously blast Polaroids of that intersection clearing, with its little cross and array of flowers, into my brain.

So when I emerge from my bedroom, I'm not surprised to hear Elliott say, "Damn, Mia, you look like hell."

"Thanks." I rub the sleep from my eyes and yawn, then try to focus—or not focus, as the case may be—on him, shirtless, brushing his teeth. Worry dances with amusement in his expression. My vision and my resolve steady simultaneously, and I barge in to brush my teeth next to him like it's no big deal. We're silent for a few moments, the only audible sound the hurried scrubbing of bristles on enamel, but I feel his eyes on me. I meet his gaze in the mirror and quickly look away. He bends, spits, and takes a drink of water from his cupped hand before holstering his toothbrush in its holder and turning toward me.

"Are you okay?" he finally asks.

"Fine," I answer around my toothbrush.

"Because we haven't really seen each other since our conversation, and—"

"I said I'm fine." I spit out the toothpaste and rinse the foam down the drain.

Elliott adjusts the towel that's wrapped around his hips before crossing his arms over his bare chest. "I just feel like you've been avoiding me. I miss talking to you."

He's not wrong with the first half of his statement. "I don't know what we'd even have to talk about," I say in response to the second.

His lips part and he knits his brows, and I know the comment has landed like a hot ash on the skin.

I'm not a monster. I don't want to hurt the man who's already been hurt so much; who was ostracized in the community nearly two decades ago and who was left by the woman he loved… loves?… and who held the hand of his sister's friend as she lay dying on the side of the road.

"We're good, El," I lie. He straightens and breathes before settling back against the wall, his shoulders more relaxed this time. I put the travel cap back on my toothbrush and return it to its spot on the counter before mustering up the most normal smile I can. "Besides. I have to go get ready for brunch with your sister. She's probably already waiting outside."

Back in my room, I have a half-dozen text messages from Julie waiting for me. I scroll through each bubble, past each emoji and exclamation point, and reply that I'll be ready in fifteen minutes. Once I'm sure that Elliott is finished in the bathroom I sneak in, take a quick shower, spray dry shampoo into my hair, and throw on a sweater dress and chunky boots.

Julie's pulling into the driveway when I walk out the side door. It's chilly but not cold, like the winter is giving us a respite from the frosty days we had earlier this week.

"You look cute," she says, scanning my outfit as I climb into the passenger seat. She's in a pair of black jeans with a black T-shirt and a long, open cardigan. I open my mouth but she holds up a hand. "Don't even lie to me. Winter maternity clothes suck."

"Well, I think it's nice."

"I have to wear these because I can't even reach to tie my shoes anymore." She rolls her eyes and gestures toward the slip-on shoes on her feet. "Being pregnant sucks."

"I'll take your word for it."

She puts the car in drive and navigates toward Ferryton, to the restaurant that she says serves a "better-than-sex" brunch. This car ride is everything our day in New York wasn't: It's early-aughts music and laughter. It's catching up, sure, but reconnecting on a deeper level, too. Like years of memories have happened without the other but like no time at all has passed.

And brunch... Brunch is good. Great, even. Brunch is easily the best non-Mr.-Bailey's-pancakes meal I've eaten in the last year.

"You weren't kidding, Jules. This is delicious."

She leans in close, wiggling her eyebrows and dropping her voice. "Better than sex?"

I pretend to think about it and tap a finger to my temple. "Depends who it's with, I guess."

Julie cackles, which draws a few amused gazes. She leans back in her chair and cradles her stomach from below with one hand while she strokes gentle lines up and down with the other. "I bet it's good, right? I mean, as good as it can be with men." She smiles when she says it; it's the smile that says *I'm going to pry and prod and learn everything I want to know, so you might as well tell me everything.*

"It's..." I set down my glass of water, trying to think of the best way to answer. "It's rare."

"Rare?" she parrots.

"Rare." I repeat.

"Rare in which way? Underdone? Hard to find?"

"The second."

Her mindless belly-rubbing ceases and her eyes go wide. "You're seriously telling me that you, Mia Montgomery, rock star extraordinaire, are not regularly getting laid?"

Our server picks that exact moment to stop by our table with the check, and her cheeks flush. "So sorry to interrupt," she says. "I'll take this whenever you're ready." She hustles off, glancing back only briefly once she's halfway across the dining room.

"Are you happy with yourself? You scared a teenager."

Julie shifts in her seat, leaning in now with a joyful intensity. "I'll scare whoever I have to scare to get my answers. Now. Tell me. What is happening? Why are you in a drought? Is it self-imposed?"

"Why do you care so much?" I match her playfulness with my own; if she wants to play detective, I'll make her work for her information.

"Because! You're my best friend, and I need to make sure you're well taken care of!"

I nearly spit out a sip of orange juice, just thinking about the way Elliott was taking care of me in his truck, on their parents' couch...

"Is there someone special, at least? Some hot-shot actor or something you're hiding, even from me?"

"If I were hiding him, I wouldn't tell you about him now, would I?"

When she laughs, the sound is airy. It's like a mild rustling of delicate sea glass chimes. "You *should*, Mia. We don't keep secrets, remember?"

CHAPTER 29

nineteen years ago

MAYBE IT WAS HAVING grown up watching the news reports of regular school shootings, wars, terrorism, and a steady diet of emo music, but our teen years were a bit dark. Sydney's seemed a shade darker than most.

Granted, we'd all gone through it together, but Sydney felt things in a way that very few other teenagers did. She was an empath, able to put herself in others' shoes. During our seventh-grade field trip to the zoo, she cried because she imagined what it would be like to be in a cage, separated from her home and family. On our ninth-grade trip to the art museum, she stared for an hour at a painting of a little girl chasing her hat toward the edge of a canvas, imagining all the emotions the girl might be feeling, examining all the possibilities for what was just beyond the frame.

And then, early in eleventh grade, she wrote poetry.

Truth be told, we all did it. The dark, teen-angsty poems layered with poorly written metaphors and symbolism, all about abysses and voids and longing. We posted them to now-defunct websites for our friends to see, embedded them line by line in instant messages, scribbled them across journal covers.

Though we pretended they held our deepest secrets, we put them out there for the world to see and, hopefully, to praise.

One Saturday night, at the Baileys' house, we gathered for our usual movie night. It was Sydney's turn to choose, and she wanted to watch The Philadelphia Story. We'd seen it so many times, but there was something about knowing a black-and-white film by heart that made us all feel elegant or mature.

"Is anyone going to help me with snacks?" Julie asked, dropping a stack of old blankets on the couch cushions.

"Sure," Sydney said, less enthusiastically than she normally did.

"I'll get the movie ready," I volunteered. I clicked on the TV, then rummaged through Syd's backpack to find the DVD case. But when I pulled it out, a folded piece of paper tumbled to the floor. Its center crease opened as it fell, and I could see Sydney's frantic handwriting on the lines of the page torn from her college-ruled notebook.

I had no intention of reading whatever she had written. We all shared what we felt comfortable with others seeing—which was a lot—and we didn't share what we didn't. No way was I going to snoop. But as I picked it up to slide it back into her bag, three letters stood out to me, and I found myself reading every word, not having to work too hard to determine the meaning of her poem.

Tears stung the corners of my eyes when she and Julie descended the stairs, popcorn and candies and Frescas in hand, and when I met her eyes she froze, knowing.

"Seriously, Mia, you had one job," Julie said, sighing at the commercial on the TV screen. When she turned to deposit the snacks on the couch, she caught me with the paper in my hand and my eyes on Sydney. Her gaze bounced between us. "Weird vibe. What's going on?"

Sydney swallowed, her face full of fear and fury, but her feet full of lead. "Why do you have that?"

"Why do *you*?" I spat back.

She didn't even bother to answer the question. She didn't deny anything. "Put it back," she hissed, taking a step in my direction.

"No. Not until we talk about it."

Julie, still between us, still watching us like she'd watch a tennis match, interjected again. "Can someone *please* tell me what is happening?"

Sydney lunged for me then, diving over the couch on her way to get to me. "Give it to me!" she shouted. "You have no right!"

I flopped backward on the couch, pinning the poem between my back and the cushion, just as she fell beside me, capsizing the bowl of popcorn—at least two bags' worth—on her way down. Over her shrieking and the sound of her smacking me with a nearby pillow, Julie's voice rang out.

"Knock it off! Both of you!" She reached for Sydney and pulled her, panting, off of me. "Someone tell me what the hell is happening. Now."

Sydney and I had a wordless stand-off, and finally she dropped onto the floor, hugging the pillow to her chest. "That was never meant for anyone to see." A quiet sob bubbled from her chest, escaping her lips, and I handed the paper to Julie as I slid to the floor next to my friend.

"Well, I'm glad I *did* see it, Syd. You shouldn't go through those feelings alone."

A glance toward Julie showed each moment of realization that dawned on her, couplet after couplet, until the very end.

"Sydney." Julie lowered herself down so she was on the other side of our friend, resting her head on Syd's shoulder. "You could've told us. You *should've* told us."

Sydney shook her head, burying her face in the pillow, her shoulders shaking with each fresh round of sobs.

"I'm sorry," I finally said as the crying slowed, "if we don't make you feel like you're good enough."

"No." Sydney straightened and wiped her eyes and cheeks with the back of her sweatshirt. "Don't say that. You guys are the best."

Julie looked across our friend at me, then back at Sydney, shrugging. "Then why? Why did you say you want to... you know."

"To die?"

"Yeah," Julie said.

Sydney tugged the cuffs of her sleeves over her hands, her fingertips barely visible, and fiddled with a loose thread. After a few regulating, shuddering breaths, she answered. "I don't. Not really. But it's... it's a lot. My parents are splitting up, and they're trying to figure out who's going to take me, and then they're putting me in the middle, asking what I want. What I *want* is for them to stay together. To choose our family. And then there's college, and you guys basically have it all figured out, and I have no idea what I'm going to do forever, and all of it makes me feel so lost." She sniffled into her sleeves, and Julie and I instantly wrapped our arms around her.

"Are you kidding, Syd?" Julie buried her face in Sydney's shoulder. With a smile in her voice, she said, "I have no idea where the hell I want to go after high school."

I chimed in, "And I'm a freaking mess. And I totally get the thing about parents. They suck sometimes."

"Sometimes?" Sydney chuckled, rolled her eyes, and lolled her head to the side, resting it on Julie's. "I'm sorry. I'm fine, I promise. Just—" She sighed. "I don't know what I'd do without you guys."

"Same," I answered. "And never apologize for feeling the way you feel."

"And promise you'll ask for help, anytime you think you might need it," Julie said.

"And no more secrets," I added.

Sydney agreed. "No. No more secrets."

CHAPTER 30

now

THE WEEK IS A dance—carefully choreographed moments and movements.

It's staying in my room an extra five minutes in the morning until I'm sure Elliott is downstairs.

It's pretending to be asleep when he knocks on my door at midnight.

It's calling Gwen for a writing session at the café—which turns into a writing session at her place—because I feel more creative around other creators.

It's trying to plan more dinners with just Julie and me and then making excuses for why I can't attend the family dinners when she says she can't hang out one-on-one.

And then it's Friday, and Elliott and I cross paths as he returns home from work and Zoe and I head out for prom dress shopping.

Zoe ducks past him just inside the garage with a quick "Bye, Dad," but Elliott isn't going to let me go so easily.

"Mia."

I avoid his eyes as I slip my arms into my coat. "We're going to be late."

"Mia, come on. You've been avoiding me all week."

"Not avoiding. Just busy."

"Seriously?"

"Yes." No. Sort of. I mean, I *have* been busy avoiding him, so it's not a total lie.

Elliott sighs and shakes his head, and my heart softens in response. God, I've missed him. And it sucks knowing that he's all mopey and it's all my fault. I meet his gaze, and he raises a hand to fix the collar of my jacket. "Can we talk later? Please?"

Instinctively I nuzzle into his palm. His thumb strokes my cheek; his eyes scan my face. How nice it must be—no, more than nice. Lovely. Perfect. Blissful. Dreamy. How dreamy it would be to have him come home to me like this every day, to have him look at me with this much longing every morning before he left for work, to touch me this tenderly whenever he wanted. But all of this... it's *only* a dream. I clear my throat and straighten, coming back to reality. "Sure. When I get home."

"Great," he says.

From the garage door behind me Zoe's voice emerges, a new tinge to it. "You ready to go, Mia?"

I spin to face her, Elliott's hand falling away as I do. "Yes. Ready." Without a glance behind me, I follow Zoe out to her car.

♫♩

You hear a lot of stories about how communities change, but one thing I love about small towns is the way certain businesses persist. In Songbird Springs it's the café, the book store, the bed and breakfast, the hardware store, and the bridal boutique. They're all staples from my own childhood, like our weekly Saturday morning trips to the hardware store for whatever Mom and Dad needed for their newest project, or when we paid by the hour for internet service at the café so our parents could use the landline at home.

It's surreal to pull into the bridal shop's parking lot again, especially with Zoe in the driver's seat. The last time I was here was to look for a dress for senior prom, which I nearly asked Elliott to be my date to until Julie decreed we should just go as a group of friends and everyone else agreed.

"Do you have an idea of what you're looking for?" I ask, unbuckling my seatbelt.

She kills the engine and stares out the windshield at the white brick building.

"Zoe? You okay?"

She shrugs a shoulder and worries at her bottom lip. "This might be crazy," she says, frowning. "But is there something going on with you and my dad?"

I never claimed to be an actress, and my reaction is a great example of why I never got into the art. Dumbfounded, I pick my jaw up from my lap and try to find a smile on my face. "What makes you think that?"

Zoe taps the steering wheel with a long blue fingernail. "I don't know. I felt like maybe there was a thing, right before we left. And if there is, cool, I just—"

"No," I answer. Sure, I consider telling the truth, but A) it's overrated and B) it might be over anyway. No reason to freak out the teenager. "Nothing's going on."

"Okay," she says, pressing her seatbelt button and opening her door. "Let's go find a dress."

♫♩

"Crazy, isn't it? How fast the time goes?"

Callie hasn't changed a bit since high school, other than somehow becoming even more beautiful. I haven't seen her in years, but back then she was a relatively new mom, disheveled but still dewy, carrying the weight of other people's judgment with the lightness of someone whose father controlled the narrative around her pregnancy.

The narrative that villainized Elliott.

It's why they never stood a chance—not really, anyway—once Mr. Hapshaw went into damage control mode and destroyed Elliott's reputation.

But I guess that's the consequence of sleeping with the pastor's daughter.

"She was just a kid the last time I saw her," I reply.

"You guys know I can hear you, right?" Zoe meets our eyes in the mirror with a raised brow.

"Yes, sorry, just a little sappy over here," Callie says. "It's not every day you see your little girl looking so grown up and glamorous. I'm going for a little walk down memory lane. Sue me."

The saleswoman, oblivious to or not caring about the conversation happening around her, asks Zoe, "What do you think?"

Zoe's drowning in a glittery baby pink gown, a full tulle skirt ballooning around her lower half.

"It's, um..." She's trying so hard to be polite, tilting her head and turning her hips to examine the dress from a different angle, but there aren't many redeeming qualities to find.

"You're allowed to say you hate it, Z," Callie tells her daughter. "You hate it, right?"

Zoe nods, looking both relieved and scared, like she's going to personally offend Carol, who is not getting enough commission off this sale to warrant the client staying in a dress a second longer than is necessary. They disappear back into the fitting room.

Callie shakes her head and lowers her voice. "I keep trying to teach her to speak up for herself, you know? But it's hard when the world is teaching them something else altogether." She sighs, and I sigh, because I completely understand what she means. "She looks up to you, you know."

There's a tug at my heartstrings, gentle and tight, and I don't know how to respond, so I just wait.

"Every night she's at my place, you're all she talks about. She's always thought it was cool that Elliott and Julie know you, but now that she's gotten to know you, too? Everything is 'Mia said this' and 'Mia did that.'"

"Sorry," I reply, and I don't know why because I don't actually think I've done anything wrong, except maybe been the topic of too many conversations between Zoe and her mom.

Callie laughs and re-crosses her legs. "Mia, there's nothing to apologize for. I love that Zoe has another strong role model in her life. Especially one who uses her voice."

Sometimes compliments feel like indictments, much the way that Callie's does right now. I've got bandmates and a manager I don't stand up to, a best friend I can't come clean to, and Elliott...

Lock me up, I guess, because I can't tell Elliott how I feel.

I'm about to protest when Zoe reemerges in an old-Hollywood style gown with off-the-shoulder sleeves. The bias-cut fabric drapes beautifully on her, and beside me, Callie gasps.

Zoe's repeating "I love it, I love it," before she's even on the podium, now complete with giggles after getting Callie's initial reaction.

"It's literally perfect, honey," Callie says, and though she's smiling, she wipes a tear from her eye.

Zoe turns toward me. "What do you think, Mia?"

I think it's perfect. Gorgeous and elegant and simple enough to let her radiance be the focus. "I have thoughts, but the most important thing is how you feel in it."

Callie smiles in my periphery, and Zoe admires herself in the mirror.

"This is it," she tells Carol. "This is the one I want."

Details are discussed and shoes are selected and Zoe disappears one more time to FaceTime her friends before changing back into her street clothes.

Callie and I are waiting by the door after she pays when she looks at me and says, "Thank you."

I'm not sure what she's thanking me for, exactly. "I didn't really do anything," I reply.

"You've done more than you know. And not just for Zoe, either." She smiles and adjusts her purse strap on her shoulder. "Oh, come on, Mia," she says, rolling her eyes as her grin widens. "You think I don't hear stories about Elliott, too?"

The tiny pluck on my heartstrings is gone, and there's a crashing feeling now, like a toddler gripped the neck of a violin and swung it like a baseball bat right into a wall. My mouth goes dry and my hands are clammy and I marvel at this family's fascination with my situationship with Elliott.

"I think it's really great for him to have a friend around. Ever since... well, you know. He's just been down. He isolates and dives into work, and honestly? I'm worried about him when Zoe goes to school next year. It's nice to know he's got an extra person in his corner, and one that makes him light up a little bit again. Lord knows he's had his share of heartache."

A shadow of pain flits across her face, disappearing just as quickly as it came as Zoe bounds toward us.

She squeals and hugs her mom, thanking her over and over again as we exit, and then Callie pulls me in for a parting hug.

"It's so great to have you back, Mia. We're truly all so happy that you're here." She gives me a final, knowing look before kissing Zoe's forehead and waving goodbye as she walks to her car.

Zoe and I climb into her car at the opposite end of the parking lot, and if she remembers our earlier conversation she doesn't let on. She cranks up the music and talks over it, breaking at times to sing along, giddy and full of excitement.

When we pull into the garage, the inside door opens and Elliott's waiting expectantly. He beams when he sees Zoe, then softens his smile for me, but it's warm and hopeful and I want to throw my arms around his neck and thank him for making space for me in his life.

I don't, of course, because Zoe is here, and I've promised her there's nothing happening between us.

"I was thinking," Elliott calls out, closing the door as he follows us into the house. He raises his voice so Zoe, who has disappeared inside, can hear him. "What if we did a movie night? After you show me this perfect dress."

Being able to put off the conversation we're supposed to have for an extra two hours? Count me in.

"Can't, Dad. Sorry," Zoe replies, leaning over the railing on the steps that lead to the bedrooms upstairs. "Katelyn just asked if I could spend the night. Would that be okay?"

Elliott agrees with minimal hesitation, and within moments, Zoe is packed and bounding back toward the garage. "Love you," she says, giving him a sideways hug. "See ya, Mia." She gives me a wave and takes off.

And then I'm—dangerously—all alone with Elliott Bailey.

CHAPTER 31

now

"So." Elliott shoves one hand into the pocket of his pajama pants, massages the back of his neck with the other.

"So. You mentioned a movie?"

It's interesting, the way we come to find ourselves in certain situations. Like the time I signed up for a 10K run and promised myself that training would start tomorrow, and too many tomorrows came and went before I found myself hobbling across the finish line near the end of my age group after walking a good portion of the event. Or the time when I took my guitar to New York City for a day to play on the street, found shelter in a coffee shop when a storm rolled in, and ended up filling in for a no-show at their Caffeinated and Amped night. That's where Lily's friend found me, and the rest is history.

But tonight there's no café, and there's no guitar and there's no music or overthinking or running away. There's just diving right in: to hope, to tomorrow, to Elliott.

Unlike his sister, Elliott is not a popcorn guy. He tasks me with finding a movie while he preheats the oven and readies a tray of pizza rolls. He finds me in the living room, rummaging through a drawer of DVDs in his entertainment console.

"You know I have, like, three streaming services, right?" he asks, passing me a beer bottle.

"Yes, but they're only streaming their own movies these days. I want a classic."

He shakes his head, smiling, as he returns to the kitchen.

I riffle through a few more titles in the first drawer; though I've had to read some synopses, most titles are comfortingly familiar to me. There are a few holiday classics we watched together every year as kids, a handful of romantic comedies that Mrs. Bailey must have passed down, a few Best Picture winners from three decades ago, and a few of Elliott's favorite horror and action movies. And then, right on top when I open the second drawer, the familiar faces of Cary Grant, Katharine Hepburn, and Jimmy Stewart greet me. I haven't seen *The Philadelphia Story* in more years than I care to count, but I'm taken back to that night with Sydney in a heartbeat.

I set the case next to the TV and push myself off the floor. "On second thought," I call to Elliott, "maybe we should do something else. Like... a puzzle or something."

"It's a Friday night, and you want to do a puzzle?"

"You're right. It's a terrible party game. We should play Twister."

He rolls his eyes, and I feel the heat rush to my cheeks at the thought of being tangled up with Elliott and at the thought of him thinking about us being tangled up together.

"Yeah, see how dumb that sounds? We're practically forty, dude. That's primo puzzle age."

"Fine," he says. "Let's do a puzzle."

What I forget—and immediately regret—is that puzzles don't make noise. And when an activity doesn't make noise, the people partaking in said activity tend to fill the void. And that's how I find myself, my mouth full of pizza roll so hot it's like Satan wrapped himself inside, answering Elliott's question about the weirdest fan encounter I've ever had.

"No," he laughs. "I refuse to believe that someone said that to you."

"What part of someone offering to pay for my completely unnecessary oral surgery so they could keep an extracted tooth seems odd to you?" I deadpan, cocking my head to the side.

He flips the last few puzzle pieces right-side-up as I slide a section of the border into place.

"Do you feel safe out there? With tooth-seekers and fangirls and the general population?"

I shrug. "I guess I don't feel any less safe doing what I do, traveling around the country with a small group of people I know, than I think I'd feel if I were just here living on my own, you know?"

We puzzle a while longer, and Elliott laments that he didn't have anything smaller than a one-thousand-piece option.

"Sure we can't do a movie?" he asks. "I think my brain hurts too much for this. It's been a week."

I totally understand. It's absolutely been a week, and I could use a break from thinking. I nod in agreement.

"What sounds good?" he asks as he heads into the living room. I find us a carton of chocolate chip cookie dough ice cream in the freezer.

"Maybe something light? Like an old rom-com I already know?"

I plop onto the couch, setting the ice cream lid upside-down on the coffee table and digging in with the singular spoon I brought with me.

He's standing at the TV, his back to me. His voice is shaky when he turns, holding the case I'd set aside earlier. My heart plummets into my stomach. "Did you—" he starts, then clears his throat. "Uh, did you want to keep working through the Jimmy Stewart filmography?"

Shaking my head, I answer, "That's Syd's favorite." Three words. That's all it takes to make the tears well in my eyes. *The Philadelphia Story.* Or, *that's Syd's favorite.* I should have said that *was* Syd's favorite, but I still struggle to talk about her in the past tense. She's a part of me. Always.

"*Shit.* I'm sorry," he says, returning to the couch empty-handed, the TV still turned off. He lowers himself into the cushion next to mine and angles his body toward me. "What if we just talk instead?"

Talking would sound so much better if I could get my emotions under control.

"You're allowed to miss her, Mia."

This simple declaration—this statement of fact—tears my heart wide open. There is no controlling the emotion that accompanies this, and Elliott envelops me in his arms as soon as the first tears hit my cheek. He carefully extracts the ice cream from my hand and sets it onto the table, never once breaking contact with me. Years of sorrow pour out of me and I feel myself sinking into his hug, his arms and shoulders supporting my weight.

I don't know how long we sit like this. I don't feel the passage of time; I feel Elliott's fingers stroking my spine, his warm breath whispering "it's okay" and "let it out" against my temple. I feel the weightlessness of being seen, held, cared for. Loved.

After a long, wordless cry, my eyes dry and my cheeks are salty. I pull out of the hug and wipe my face with the back of my hands. Though we separate, Elliott stays close.

"Did you ever get the chance to grieve? Like, *really* grieve?" he asks me, brushing a hair from my face before reaching for the ice cream again and holding it between us. The top layer is peak meltiness, and I skim a bit onto the spoon.

Shaking my head, I swallow the ice cream. "There wasn't really much opportunity. I got the call right before I went on stage at Red Rocks. And the next morning I had a radio show interview, then another show that night, and a photo shoot the day after. I just kept going and going because if I didn't, I'd fall apart."

He's quiet, thoughtful. Laser-focused on the ice cream.

"You okay?" I nudge his knee with mine, trying to draw him back to earth.

He nods, eyes still on the cookie dough. He opens and closes his mouth like he wants to say something but can't decide what, then does it again. Finally his voice comes out, cracked and broken like my heart. "She was really special. I mean, I know how special she was to you."

It's the tenderness in his tone that gets me, and the words. Sydney *was* special, and I didn't tell her enough when I had the chance. Tears fall again, but Elliott reaches over and smooths a hand over my cheek, drying them with his calloused thumb.

"Sorry to be all mopey." I sit up and wipe my eyelids, pulling just out of Elliott's reach. "It's not like I'm the only person to ever have lost someone, you know? Ugh." I shake my head, sniffle, and swallow back the faint taste of bile. "I'm fine. I know you've been through a lot, too. You just keep it together so much better than I do."

"I wouldn't say that," he replies, shifting in his seat. "I think I've just had more opportunity to figure out how to move through it."

Move through it. Not *get past it* or *get over it* but *move through it*. This terrible "it" of suffering and sorrow and shame and the greatest heartache I've ever known.

Elliott always seemed to me wise beyond his years. Even as a teenage boy, I felt he was so much more mature than other guys his age. He just seemed so thoughtful, always ready to listen, actually hearing and thinking before responding. It's one of the things that drew me to him then, and not a damn thing has changed.

"What did you want to talk about?" I blurt, and it catches him off guard.

"What do you mean?"

"Earlier. Before I left with Zoe, you asked if we could talk when I got back."

He inhales and shakes his head. "We can forget it. It's not a big deal."

"Well, that hardly seems true." When he arches a brow at me, I add, "You were so serious, all dark and moody and sexy when you said it."

"Mia—"

If I've learned anything from thinking about Sydney at any point in the last two years, it's that life is short, and we're not always guaranteed a second chance. Is it the smartest idea I've ever had to just lay it out there for Elliott? No. But I'm known for great music, not great ideas.

"It's one of the things I've always loved about you, actually. Your intensity. Your intention. So I don't believe for one second that it was not a big deal."

He says nothing. He licks his lips and scans my face and says nothing. He swallows hard and reaches for the ice cream and shakes his head and says "It's really not important right now" but really says *nothing*.

"Wow," I mutter, running my hands along my thighs. "Wow. Okay then."

He protests, of course, rising when I do, trying to reason with me to just let it go for tonight, that we've already talked through something big and this conversation doesn't need to happen right now. But I'm so tired of holding back with everyone in my life—with Julie and my parents and Lily and Claudette and with him—and now, now he gets it all.

"I don't need to be babied, Elliott. I'm not a little girl anymore and I haven't been for a long time. I can talk through my feelings and deal with my emotions, but what I can't... no, what I *won't* deal with is being used to fill some sort of void. I get that you lost someone you cared very much about, and I'm sorry that she blindsided you when she left. I thought I could handle this arrangement between us, but I can't give you what you need if you can't give me what *I* need."

"And what do you need, Mia?" His voice is steady, but barely, like he's concentrating hard on not faltering.

It's been such a long time since someone's asked me that, that I don't even know how to answer. And looking at Elliott now, a lifetime flashes before my eyes. One full of longing and loneliness and joy and jealousy, all rolled into one big, messy history.

I have loved this man since I was sixteen years old. I'm sure of it. There's no way anything other than love can explain the pain of losing him when he was still right in front of me; feeling his hurt; not being enough. Not then, not now. And suddenly the answer is crystal clear: "I need something *real*."

We both know it's not something he's capable of giving right now, or something that he wants to give. He recoils, and the confusion or hurt or incredulousness shapes every feature of his handsome face. He says my name, timidly and tenderly, and I refuse to let him see how real my hurt is.

"I'm going to bed," I say before he can convince me otherwise. I spin on my heels and march upstairs.

I brush my teeth quickly, skip my skincare routine, and shut myself into my room. With the blankets pulled tight around my shoulder I calm my breathing, waiting for a knock that never comes.

CHAPTER 32

now

AN OUT-OF-TUNE GUITAR.

A sniffling singer.

A fresh layer of frost on the ground.

A cross on the side of the road.

It's a sad scene for a Saturday morning.

"I've missed you, Syd."

I let her speak in the silence; she responds with the gentle sway of pine branches. Sydney always did have a presence about her. You knew when she was there.

I pluck at the strings on my guitar, just enjoying the stillness, the quiet, the frigid air of home.

"It's funny... You accused me once of having a thing for Elliott. Turns out, you were right. Obviously Julie can never know. When we were growing up, there was no way I could do anything about it because I was so sure she'd find out, and there was no way he'd be interested in me, anyway. But now..." I bite my lip, just like I would if Syd was here in person, the last protective barrier to a secret I'm bursting at the seams to share.

"I may have kissed Elliott. Actually, full disclosure, he kissed me first. And then this whole thing started, and we did this 'friends with benefits' thing for like, two weeks. And holy shit, Sydney, he's incredible. Everything I ever hoped for and expected and even more. He's so smart and thoughtful and funny and hot, but, turns out, I was right about the whole 'he could never be interested in me' thing."

I play a chord, and a phrase I've been playing on repeat in my mind comes out as a song: "Every love song I sing is about the same thing."

"I know it sounds silly, but literally every song I've written has been about Elliott. Except for maybe two. One of which was, incidentally, about you," I tell her. I stop strumming and rest my palm on the strings, feeling the vibrations die under my skin.

"I'm sorry I wasn't here. I'm sorry I missed the funeral. I'm sorry I missed girls' nights and coffee dates and just spending time with you." I thought I'd be a blubbering mess, confessing all my regrets to one of my best and oldest friends. Instead, I'm resolute in my decision to have left in the first place, to seize the day, to chase my joy and purpose. I just wish I would have called more, texted more, skipped the interview with KLQT Radio and been here right after, at least.

I inhale, letting the icy air fill my chest, and exhale, letting my lungs expel the burden of regret. I can see it, carried on the fog of my breath, evaporating into the morning.

Few cars have passed by this morning, and I've drowned out the sound of their tires and the hum of their acceleration from my spot down the embankment next to the road. But a car door slams and footsteps crunch the frozen grass behind me, and a quick turn of my head reveals Elliott standing there, a small bouquet of eucalyptus and dark plum hellebore in his hand.

He looks equally as surprised to see me as I feel to see him here, but he rearranges his expression into a neutral look. "Sorry to interrupt," he says, keeping his distance a few steps back.

"You're fine."

"I'm surprised to see you here. Most people visit her grave, not the spot where... well."

I shrug and pluck at the strings again. "I thought about it, but I didn't have a car to get to Ferryton. Plus, I wasn't sure if the cemetery would be crowded, and I kind of wanted alone time, just to talk."

"Right." Elliott swallows and shifts his weight from one foot to the other, looking anywhere but at me.

"There's room, if you want to sit." I scoot to one side of my blanket, freeing up a space for him.

Instead, he passes me and sets the flowers carefully at the base of the cross, pausing for a moment with his knee in the grass. He rises, returns, and hesitates before lowering himself next to me. Even though the blanket isn't spacious, he's careful to avoid contact.

What a change from two weeks ago.

His eyes stay locked on the little cross and the grass that separates him from it, even as he speaks again. "Sure it's okay if I sit here a bit?"

"Of course."

He doesn't seem to mind my guitar playing, and it fills what would otherwise be an awkward silence between us, so I play the first few chords from *Hollywood Love Story*.

"I knew this one was about her," he says, and for the first time since our puzzle time last night he smiles. It's gentle, understanding, and he taps the toes of his heavy boots together. "Julie told me I was reading too much into it, with the 'Hollywood' piece. But I knew."

"Most people just think it's a love song."

"Most people don't know you, Mia. And I know how much you loved Sydney, and how much she loved you."

There are a few types of strategies when it comes to putting together a puzzle. Some people want to see everything from the very beginning and start by turning every piece right side up. Some people begin by separating the edge pieces from the inner pieces and making the border first. And then there's me, and I am typically a border-maker, but I will absolutely stray from my tidy little outer pieces if I see something that looks like it fits together, even if I don't really know where it's going. And that's how I feel right now with Elliott and his showing up here with his flowers and his knowingness of how much Sydney loved me and his copy of *The Philadelphia Story* at his house.

"How do you know how much she loved me?"

Now he looks at me. "What?"

"How do you know? How do you know so much about her?"

"Mia, we've all known each other for thirty years. Julie has held girls' night once a month since she moved back after college. I see people. I hear stuff." He pinches a piece of grass and plucks it from the ground, twirling the blade between his fingers.

"But that doesn't explain why you have her favorite movie at your house, or why you bring flowers here."

He sighs and closes his eyes. "I bring flowers here every week, because someone should."

"Okay, but it doesn't have to be you, just because you were the first one here."

"I don't bring flowers because I was the one who found her after the accident. I bring flowers because—" Elliott exhales, shakes his head, and sucks his bottom lip between his teeth. Finally, shakily, he says, "I bring flowers every week because it's my fault that she's dead."

CHAPTER 33

now

IT WAS A QUIET ride back to Elliott's house.

Inside, he's busied himself with making a fresh pot of coffee and changing into dry jeans, and I've been sitting shell-shocked by the admission that has yet to get an explanation.

"Let's go warm up. Then I'll tell you everything," he said. I followed him back to the truck and the only sound on the way home was the heavy *woosh* of heat filling the air around us.

Everything turns out to be quite a story, I learn, as he sets a mug in front of me and takes the seat across from mine at his modest dining room table.

"Promise you'll hear me out, all the way through," he says before adding "please."

"I guess it depends what you have to tell me."

He wraps both hands around his mug and hunches his shoulders. "Fair enough. First and foremost, I can imagine where your mind has been going for the past half hour, but Sydney and I were friends. That's it."

It provides little comfort, just a tiny relief, to hear him assuage my initial fears. But there's still the matter of *he thinks he's responsible for her death*, and I remain uneasy.

"We started hanging out a year or so before... before she died." There's a heaviness in his voice, like no matter how many years pass, this will always be raw for him.

"We bumped into each other at O'Donnell's. I'd been on a terrible date, and she'd been there with Kiko—did you know they worked together?"

I nod. It had come up exactly three times in text messages: once when Kiko got hired at the pediatric hospital where Sydney worked, once when they accidentally showed up to work in matching sloth-print scrubs, and once when Kiko left that job for a marketing role at a healthcare company. (Sydney was not pleased with that choice, and she let me know it in a string of all caps messages.)

"Anyway, we ended up just sitting at the bar for a while, and then we bumped into each other again at the state championship game for Songbird High—did you know we won?—and then we ended up watching Sunday Night Football together the rest of the season."

"I thought Sydney hated football."

"Oh, she used to." Elliott's cautious veneer cracks and a smile breaks through. "But her nephew played second string on the varsity team, so she got really into it. And you know she liked to yell at people in charge. You should have heard her yelling at the refs each week."

I can absolutely imagine that. Sydney was a spitfire, through and through, and she wasn't afraid to make her voice heard (even if the people she was yelling at couldn't hear her).

"And then, when football season ended, she decided she needed to educate me on the classics, and we watched pretty much every black and white movie ever created. Filtering in some *I Love Lucy* reruns, just for levity."

"And she left her DVD here?"

"It must have gotten mixed up with some others."

"Okay..." I readjust the mug in my hands and my butt on the wooden chair. "I get that you were friends, but why do you think it was your fault she died?"

He shakes his head, like he's trying to scatter the more vivid parts of the memory. "We talked a lot, too. Not just movies and football, but she'd confide in me. Things she couldn't tell Julie or anyone else. I don't really know when it started, or how, other than I think we were both feeling like we had secrets, and sharing them with each other ensured mutual destruction if one person blabbed."

"What secrets could she possibly have that she wouldn't share with Julie?"

"Trust me, she had her reasons, and they were good."

"Fine. What about you?"

Elliott coughs a laugh. "Not a chance. Anyway." He clears his throat and takes another drink of coffee, then stares into his mug. "The night of the accident, we'd met for dinner at O'Donnell's. Sydney was telling me about some personal stuff and we got into an argument about it. She was emotional and left quickly, and by the time I paid and got out to my car, she was long gone. I tried calling her, but she sent my call to voicemail. I texted her, but nothing. I started driving home, but I had this feeling like something was wrong, you know? Anyway. I couldn't have been more than five minutes behind her, but it was raining hard, and I was trying to take it easy. And then I got to Seventh and Elm, and I saw the headlights near the tree line, and I just knew. I knew it was her, and I pulled over and ran to her—" He swallows, hard, his Adam's apple bobbing and his jaw clenching, and my heart races and breaks all at once, all over again.

"You have to know, Mia, there was nothing I could have done."

Unlike the smorgasbord of awkward silence moments we've shared since I came back to town, this silence is a blanket. It's the comfort of closure that has the power to suffocate you, if you let it.

"I know." An olive branch, to stave off the suffocation. "I'm sorry that you've been living with that for two years."

Another olive branch: I reach across the table, my palm up. He looks at it, then my face, then accepts the invitation and slides his hand into mine.

"Is this what you didn't want to tell me last night?"

He watches the place where our hands are joined and weaves our fingers together. "Yes. I figured you'd had enough for one night."

"It was…. a lot. This was a lot. But Elliott— it was a lot for you, too, and you shouldn't have to shoulder that burden alone just to try to protect me. That's what friends are for— to help each other through those times. And I know I wasn't here two years ago, but I'm here now."

His brows pinch, and his thumb traces the lines on my palm, and he's not at peace with this. Not yet.

"Last night—when you went upstairs, it felt just like that night. I hate that we argued, and then you took off—and I can't lose you, too, Mia. Not again."

"Why didn't you come talk to me?" There's more desperation in my voice than I'd prefer, and I swallow to try to clear it before I add, more quietly, "I waited for you."

Elliott leans back in his chair, pulling his hand from mine. "I never liked those games. I figure if you lock yourself in your room, you want to be alone, and I'm not going to harass you. It's why I didn't try to follow Sydney when she drove off, either. I figured she just wanted some time alone and we'd talk about it later."

"Can I ask you something? About her accident?"

He nods.

Putting these fears that I've carried for two years into words makes my mouth go instantly dry. "Did it seem..." All the emotions from decades ago flood back, from finding that poem in Sydney's bag. "Do you think it was intentional?"

"Not for a second," he answers, with no hesitation. "And she hadn't been drinking, either. It was dark, the roads were wet, and she was driving fast. The area's known for deer. I think she swerved to miss one and lost control."

"Earlier, why did you say it was your fault? It just seems like an accident based on what you told me."

After a sigh, he says, "I was supposed to pick her up at her place after work, but I was running late. If I would've driven her, she'd still be here."

Quiet envelops us again. A wall clock ticks as I stare at my coffee, willing myself not to think of the details of the accident, shaming myself for not wanting to think about it when Sydney had to experience it in her final, horrible moments.

Elliott's chair slides back and he emerges from the kitchen with the coffee pot, warming up our mugs. "If you want me to chase after you, I will. Just say the words." He shuffles back to replace the pot, and it strikes me how much older he seems, like the weight of Sydney's secrets and his own, and the weight of feeling like this was all his fault, have aged him in his shoulders and how he carries himself.

"I appreciate that you gave me space." I sit back, warming my hands around the mug, smelling the coffee more than drinking it. "But I felt like you didn't care. And I know that's really unfair to say, but anyway, I thought you'd appreciate the honesty."

"I do appreciate it, thank you. God, it feels good to be honest with someone again." He rests his mug on the table and extracts mine from my hands to do the same, then he sinks into the chair next to me and wraps his hands around mine. "But let me make one thing abundantly clear—I absolutely care. I always have, always will. I care so much I slept on the couch because I was afraid you were going to leave and I wanted to stop you if you tried."

I throw my arms around his neck—a move that surprises both of us, if his delayed return of the hug is any indication. But he rises from his chair, bringing me with him, and I'm wrapped so firmly in his arms I can't breathe deeply.

Elliott is safety personified. He's warmth and comfort, goodness and strength. He's steady, and wonderful, and I hate that I can't be as honest with him as he is with me. He and Sydney had their secrets, and I have mine: I am—deeply, hopelessly, and forever—in love with Elliott Bailey.

CHAPTER 34

now

THE ENTIRE FAMILY IS bundled in beanies and coats when Elliott, Zoe, and I walk into the Baileys' house. Everyone, of course, except for Julie and me. A delicious scent wafts in from the kitchen, and Julie beams in the entryway, rubbing her belly.

"Are you ready for the best girls' night of all time?" she asks, ushering us in.

She's peeling my coat back off my shoulders before I can answer. "Absolutely. Also, mostly I'm excited to stay warm."

Jess, the mastermind behind tonight's plan, *tsks* me as she wraps a scarf around her neck. "You don't know what you're missing. The Outdoor Adventure is the best event in hockey. The Falcons host it each year and they always pull out a W."

Mrs. Bailey looks less enthused about the prospect of sitting outside for three hours to watch local hockey.

Zoe counters Jess's argument. "Yeah, but our goalie kinda sucks this year—I hear they're looking to trade up next season. At least the center is good. Right, Mia?" She waggles her eyebrows at me.

"Oh my gosh, you should totally go out with him," Julie agrees. "One of the kids at school just did a presentation on the team for his public speaking assignment and I remember thinking how cute some of them were. If you're into that sort of thing."

Elliott's eyes dart to mine.

"Nice save." Jess gives Julie a quick kiss on the forehead and a hug goodbye. "Have fun tonight."

"You too. But stick to spectating—all the fighting should happen on the ice."

"It happened *one time*," Jess laughs, playfully punching Elliott in the arm.

"Yeah, and you started it," he retorts. "No fisticuffs between family." He holds up his hands in mock surrender, and the family loudly and excitedly exits.

Julie rolls her eyes and grabs my arm, pulling me along with her as she rattles off the menu, highlighting everything from the batch of mocktails she made to the desserts she picked up in Philly and the main course currently in the oven. "If cheesesteaks are considered a main course, then I don't know why people think cheesesteak egg rolls are just for appetizers."

"These are the issues that keep me up at night."

Julie laughs and claps her hands. "Right. So, egg rolls for dinner, but I have a cheese, fruit and cracker platter to start."

"A charcuterie board?"

"Yes. But why is that word so hard to say?" She passes a glass of wine to me and fills her own cup with water before propping herself against the pantry door. "So. A Falcons player, huh?"

♫♪

Carla brought red wine, and Ali brought white wine, and Kiko brought Jell-O shots. We collectively agree to donate our mocktails to Julie (after sampling half a glass each with appreciative accolades) and are sufficiently tipsy within thirty minutes.

Ali's animatedly retelling a story about a mishap at home caused by a rogue LEGO piece and a full coffee mug while the rest of us lounge on the basement couch and the floor, munching on crackers and grapes, laughing at her husband's misfortune but having the courtesy to feel a little bad about it.

Carla nudges me when Ali's finished. "Any updates on your top-secret mission? What have you found out about Elliott?"

I shrug, because even though I've learned a lot about him, there's very little I want to share with this group instead of keeping all to myself. "He's definitely not seeing anyone, unless he's very good at hiding it."

"Interesting. Maybe it's a casual thing, like he's sneaking out with someone, coming home in the middle of the night smelling like her perfume."

"It's possible, I guess, but I doubt it. We hang out almost every night."

Kiko raises an eyebrow while Ali and Carla exchange a look, and there's a faint glare shaping Julie's expression. I feel heat flood my cheeks, knowing how that must sound. "I don't know if you know this, but the Baileys eat dinner together like, five times a week. There's really no opportunity to escape."

There's a collective chuckle at that, at least, and Julie tries to stand as an alarm goes off on her phone.

"Time to grab the egg rolls," she says.

But Kiko rises and tells her to sit. "Mia and I can get them. Come on, Mia. We have catching up to do, anyway."

It seems odd to be singled out, because of everyone here Kiko and I were always the least connected, but the interrogation that begins as soon as we're on the other side of the basement door helps to clarify everything.

"What did he say about Syd?" There's no easing into it, just a shove into the deep end, and Kiko has no interest in throwing me a life ring.

"He said very little, actually, other than they were friends."

"Uh huh." She puts on a pair of oven mitts to pull out the tray, then drops it on the stovetop and turns the oven off. "You and I are friends. Syd and I were friends. But Syd and Elliott? You really think that's all there was to it?"

I've wondered this since last night, putting the puzzle pieces together in my mind, seeing if they all match up or if there's something that doesn't quite fit. But when it comes down to it, "I trust him."

"We talked the day she died, you know. She told me she was going out for dinner with him, which, fine, they did that sometimes. But she was so nervous about something, some 'big leap,' she called it... and I've always wondered what it was." She presses the heel of her hands to her eyes. "Sometimes I feel like I didn't know her at all."

Mrs. Bailey's old platter, the one she served treats on when we were kids, is right where it's always been: the narrow cabinet between the stove and the fridge. I start stacking the egg rolls on top and find the special sauce Julie bought to dip them in. "I'm sure you knew her very well, but we all have our secrets, and that's okay. I bet there are things you've shared with Carla that I don't know about, and I get that."

"On the topic of secrets." She moves to the basement door, but instead of opening it, she blocks it. "Is something going on with you and Elliott? Be real with me."

"Nothing." Not anymore. "I promise."

She seems to think about it, scanning my face for any sort of tell she can identify, before opening the door.

We—rather, the delicious-smelling food we're carrying—receive a welcome reception back in the basement.

"I see we've opened more wine," I say, sinking down next to Ali.

"Don't tell Julie—" She pulls me in close, but her voice is well above a whisper and I'm grateful everyone else is gushing over Julie's cooking because I know she's hyper focused on the praise. "My water bottle is filled with frozen margarita."

Leave it to Ali, the soccer mom with three kids under age seven, to smuggle tequila into the party.

I don't mean to laugh as hard as I do, but there's something so refreshing and downright fun about being here with most of my oldest friends, learning who they really are these days, and not just who they pretend to be on Christmas cards and social media.

"You okay over there, Montgomery?" Carla asks, her mouth full of egg roll, her eyes full of humor.

"I'm so good," I answer, raising a glass of wine in a distant *cheers*. "I just really love it when we can all get together and hang out like this."

"Oh brother, she's going sappy on us!" Julie rolls her eyes and softly smacks my shoulder with a throw pillow.

Kiko throws her arms to the side, nearly smacking Ali in the face, with a loud "*Guys*" that gets everyone's attention. "You know what was so fun when we were teenagers?"

"So help me if you say braiding each other's hair..." Julie says, to an answering chorus of laughter.

"Did we ever even do that?" Kiko asks, then shakes her head. "Anyway. I was thinking... we should play *truth or dare.*"

The mix of groans and agreements is truly mind blowing, considering the small number of people in the room. We vote on it, and we don't even care that some people have two hands raised in favor of the motion to play.

"To make it more fun," Carla announces, "instead of choosing for yourself, you should have to flip a coin. Heads, truth. Tails, dare."

A quiet "ooh" falls over the room, and that idea, too, is met with swift agreement.

First up, Ali, who flips a tails and is dared by Kiko to do a lap around the back yard in her underwear. We huddle around the sliding glass door to watch and throw a blanket around her as soon as she makes it back in, red-faced and frozen.

Julie gets heads. Ali gets to ask her anything but lands on "What's your biggest fear about becoming a mom," which brings the overall vibe of the party down a bit in its raw intensity.

But Julie comes up with a response that leaves half the room howling with laughter: "Our sperm donor is six-five, which looks good on paper. This kid is going to be supermodel gorgeous. Statuesque. But we never considered the practicality of birthing a giant."

Kiko and Carla both get tails and their dares have to do with prank calling a guy Kiko had a crush on in high school (turns out his parents still use the landline number found in the phone book that's been collecting dust in the Baileys' coat closet since 2002) and doing a one-minute handstand while consuming three Jell-O shots.

When I flip the coin, Carla's quick to cheer when it lands heads up.

"Okay, Mia. Secretive, mysterious Mia. I want to know..." she taps her chin and frowns, trying to think of something juicy, no doubt. "Ah, got it. Tell us about your first kiss."

CHAPTER 35

eighteen years ago

THE INVITATION WAS CASUAL enough—we were opening up the snack hut at the start of spring, when the weather was warming and mini golf was apparently at the top of everyone's to-do list. Theo was wiping down the booths while I restocked straws at the soda fountain.

Julie's critique of Bentley's tux (shown in a grainy Polaroid his girlfriend, who was in our grade, took at the store) wafted from the kitchen into the dining room. Theo looked up, amused, as Julie continued her commentary.

"Do you have a date to prom yet?" he asked with a flick of his head, sending his bangs fluttering away from his forehead.

"No. Julie wanted to go as a group with some girls from band." (It sounded much more pathetic than it promised to be. The band girls knew how to have fun.)

"Oh. Well... do you want to go with me?"

It took me a moment to respond, partially because I was shocked he asked me and partially because I was actually looking forward to going with my friends. But Julie must have overheard the question because when I instinctively turned toward the kitchen she was making a *shoo*-ing gesture with her hands and silently squealing.

"Sure, yeah. That sounds fun," I answered.

"Cool." He smiled, and his cheeks flushed, and it made it seem like the invitation wasn't just a spur-of-the-moment impulse. We went about our business for the afternoon, scooping ice cream, delivering trays loaded with french fries and chili dogs to various tables, not really bringing it up again until Theo was getting ready to leave at the end of his shift.

"So, um, I guess we'll talk about details, and I can buy our tickets Monday at school. Do you have a favorite flower? For the... the wrist flower thingy?"

"The corsage?" Julie butted in.

"Yes. The corsage. Right."

I wasn't really a flower aficionado, so I don't know where the answer came from, but I very confidently replied, "I like daisies."

♫♩

Julie and I somehow managed to survive a joint prom dress shopping venture with our mothers in tow. There was a lot of head shaking and cringing from everyone involved, but eventually Julie ended up with a canary yellow dress with a neckline that plunged into a bejeweled brooch, and I walked out of our mall's budget-friendly department store with a shimmery aquamarine mermaid gown that shed its glitter on every surface with which it came into contact.

The day of prom, Mom took me to her salon to get my hair curled, pinned up, and shellacked so thoroughly that I could remove all the bobby pins and the style wouldn't budge. Then Sydney did my makeup at Julie's house since I had no idea how to do it myself. We took photos on the porch and in front of Mrs. Bailey's blooming forsythia bushes while we waited for Theo to pick me up.

He showed up in a silver Mustang—borrowed from a family friend's dealership, I learned—and looked nice in a black tux with a tie and cummerbund just a shade off from matching my dress. He told me I looked nice and put a corsage made of a pink gerbera daisy and baby's breath around my wrist. Mrs. Bailey helped me pin a boutonniere to his lapel while mom snapped pictures on a disposable Kodak camera, the winding of the wheel after each shot grating.

After the photo shoot, Theo and I took off with Sydney and Julie close behind.

♫♩

The event itself was great. We had dinner (stuffed chicken breast with mashed potatoes and green beans), dessert (tiny apple pies), and spent the night dancing under a disco ball in the conference center of the Ferryton/Songbird Springs Inn & Suites while the DJ played a mix of boy bands and pop stars and rap filled with innuendo we were too young and sheltered to understand. (It was very different, growing up back then.)

Theo and I slow danced, keeping our distance in the beginning but gravitating closer and closer, it seemed, as the night wore on. I could feel Julie's *hubba-hubba* eyebrows trained on me with each passing dance, and I liked the nearness with Theo. It was nice to feel wanted, and when he held me closer during a Mandy Moore song I dared to rest my head against his shoulder instead of awkwardly avoiding eye contact while we slowly turned in circles, like I'd spent the rest of the night doing.

"I like you, Mia," he whispered as the song came to a close. Something upbeat and reeking of an incoming group dance flooded our ears, but he held on, pulling back just enough to look at me.

"I like you, too," I confessed, because I *did* like him. We were friends, and guitar buddies, and I didn't want to hurt his feelings. He smiled, so I smiled, and I realized years later how much of my affection was reciprocal in nature and how I very seldom took the lead on sharing my love first.

Sydney bounded toward me and took me by the arm, dragging me into a line between her and Julie as we followed the instructions from the music. Theo disappeared a few measures into the song, which was understandable since I'd been the one to ditch him, even if it was not by my choosing.

When the song (and the one after that) was over and I went looking for him—the last dance of the night was coming up soon, the DJ promised—I wasn't surprised to find him in the hotel's much cooler, much less noisy lobby. I was, however, shocked to see him there with his tongue in Stacy Goldblum's throat and his hands, well... they were all over her.

I didn't even think I cared, honestly.

Was I confused? Hell yes. This guy told me barely ten minutes ago that he liked me and then he pulled this?

But still, I didn't care. Theo was a work buddy, a guy from down the street, a classmate.

Julie, however, was *livid*.

"What do you think you're doing?" she cried, her voice filling the lobby and more than a few heads snapping our direction. Theo stepped away from Stacy and dropped his hands, but even if we hadn't caught them kissing the pink gloss smeared around his lips would've given him away.

Stacy slid to the side, as if she could make sure she avoided Julie's wrath if she was far enough from ground zero.

"Where do you think you get off, inviting someone to prom and making out with someone else instead?"

He was clearly uncomfortable, and I was, too. Actually, everyone within earshot seemed to be.

"You said you liked me," was all I could muster, and Theo's face fell. He moved closer, trying to reduce the size of our audience.

"I was going to say more, but you responded so quickly, and then you disappeared."

I looked between Stacy and Theo for any kind of help understanding. "What do you mean?"

The DJ called for last dance, and most of the other students took off for the end of the party, leaving Julie scowling and standing with her arms crossed just watching the soap opera playing out in front of her.

"What I was trying to say was, I like you, Mia, but just as a friend." He took a breath and swung his bangs out of his face and sent a sappy look over to Stacy. "I thought you knew I had a thing for Stacy."

I mean, I'd totally heard he had a thing for her, but no way was she going for him when quarterback and all-around cute-but-shallow Bryan Tucker was flirting with her from the seat next to her in English.

Turned out, we all discovered in a dingy hotel lobby with peeling beige wallpaper and musty burgundy carpet, Bryan Tucker was only interested in Stacy for her note-taking skills and his girlfriend/prom date was just as gorgeous and vapid as he was.

So when Theo came across a teary-eyed Stacy during the Macarena he decided to make his move.

And I couldn't even be mad at him, or sad for me that he didn't actually like me.

But I absolutely was sad for me that *no one* seemed to like me the way they were clearly capable of liking other people, and that's how I came to leave my prom in tears, flanked by my two best friends as we walked out during a Vitamin C song.

♫♩

Sydney couldn't spend the night, but it was always the plan for me to stay over after prom. I had just hoped I'd be less snotty and gross.

The glitter trail stretched the whole way from the front door up the stairs to Julie's room where we changed and put our dresses back in their garment bags.

I decided to sleep with my hair still intact, just to see how it would look in the morning and to avoid the Medusa style I feared awaited me if I took the pins out, and I brushed my teeth and washed my face and headed downstairs in short shorts and an oversized hoodie that I borrowed from a hamper of folded clothing in Julie's room. For it being late spring, it was a little chilly in their house, and after the night I'd had I needed some kind of warmth.

Julie needed more time to shower and get ready for bed, so she sent me down to the basement to set up whatever I wanted—video game, movie... whatever. I'd turned on a music video channel before turning to my journal, and maybe it's because I was so focused that I didn't hear the footsteps on the stairs, but I jumped when I saw movement in the form of Elliott walking across the room.

"Don't freak out—I'm just here for the laundry," he said with the kind of teasing smile that I'd come to adore. "I like your hair. How was prom?" He passed the couch en route to the dryer, where he shoveled clothing out into a laundry basket before re-stuffing the machine with wet clothes from the washer. "Will it bother you if this is running for a little bit?"

"No," I sniffled and wiped my nose. "It's fine."

"Whoa," he said, pressing the start button on the dryer. "You okay?"

I bit my lip to keep myself from crying and nodded, but it was all in vain. My lip quivered, and tears fell hot and steady down my cheeks before I could hide my face with my hands.

"Hey, it's okay." Elliott rushed to my side and dropped onto the far end of the couch. "Tell me what's wrong."

I recounted everything I could, from the clumsy invitation to actually being excited for the dance, to Theo telling me he liked me, to Theo showing me that actually, he didn't.

"And I'm just so tired of not being wanted, you know?" I cried, wiping my lower lids with the edge of my sweatshirt sleeve cuff.

"I know how that feels," he said, and I felt bad complaining to him of all people, who got dumped in January when Callie went back to campus after winter break even though rumor has it they'd thrown around the *L*-word over the holidays. "But of course you're wanted," he said. "I don't know if you noticed this, but my sister is kind of obsessed with having you around."

"That's only because it's too late for her to train someone else to be her friend."

He chuckled. "That's fair." He grew only a fraction more serious when he said, "You're really funny, Mia. And smart, and talented. And also a really good person. Theo's just a dumbass if he doesn't see that."

Then he reached up to the strings of my hood and playfully tugged the ends. His fingers lingered there, his gaze moving from the cord in his hand to my lips, and I'd watched enough romantic comedies to know what that meant. My heart skipped a beat.

"Do you really think so?"

Elliott's eyes dashed to mine, then back to my lips and up again. "I really do. He's such an idiot if he thinks Stacy Goldblum is half as special as you."

I did a final swipe of my eyes and nose. "You're just saying that because I'm crying and you feel bad for me."

"No," he whispered, his voice hoarse. I could hear him swallow, feel his breath on my lips as we drew together.

"Are you sure?"

He understood every interpretation of the question and nodded. "I've never been more sure of anything." He gave a final pull on each of the hoodie strings, until our mouths were an inch apart. "What about you?"

"Positive."

He tilted his head a few degrees and closed the distance between us, pressing his lips softly to mine.

Elliott Bailey was always intense but gentle. Like when he played soccer, he was aggressive, but he'd also extend a hand to anyone who went down on the field. At Bailey family game nights, he played to win, but was gracious no matter the outcome.

The way he kissed was no exception. His lips were pillow-soft, and the hand that cradled my neck held me like I was porcelain, but the fact that it cradled my neck at all conveyed a wanting that I never expected from him.

I had been kissed exactly once before, behind an oak tree where the mulchy part of our elementary school's playground met a grassy field. I was eight, and he was nine, and he was sent to detention immediately. With a black eye, courtesy of Julie.

Elliott's kiss was nothing like that playground kiss. This one was, though impromptu, somehow still intentional and careful and perfect. So perfect I moaned, just a little, but then it was over.

Elliott pulled away, his eyes wide, his fingers still on my skin. "Oh my god."

"I'm sorry," I said, because obviously he regretted it and it was all my fault.

"Don't— don't apologize. I, um... I liked that."

I liked it too. So, so very much. I felt like I was floating, or at least my heart was, like an astronaut untethered in space, just drifting.

"Julie's probably coming down soon." His words were an unwelcome gravity.

My mind was dizzy from the free-fall, the plummet back to Earth, trying to make sense of things, find which way was up. "Right."

He rose and reclaimed his laundry basket from the end of the couch, but he paused before heading to the stairs. "I didn't get a chance to tell you earlier, but you looked really beautiful in your prom dress."

A parachute, opened just before the point of impact.

"And," he said, leaning in to peck me quickly on the lips and tug again at the hoodie's strings, "you look hot in my old sweatshirt."

Then he winked and took off up the stairs, leaving me, soaring, on the couch.

CHAPTER 36

now

"I don't believe for one minute you and Theo Jeffries didn't kiss at *least* once." Ali is scolding me from the floor, chucking a kernel of popcorn at my head.

Julie jumps to my defense, as she often does. "Ew! After the way he treated her at prom?"

"You had that whole summer of playing guitar together, and guitar players are hot." Kiko tosses her hair behind her shoulder as if there were a guitar player (other than yours truly) in the room right now and she's trying to put her best assets on display. "You're telling me he never... plucked your G-string?"

"That is so gross, you horndog!" Ali elbows her before refilling both their glasses of wine.

"For sure nothing happened before prom. And *definitely* not right after it. But I seem to recall someone being a little too excited about the mistletoe at the B&B's Yule Have a Ball party when she was twenty-two, and Theo definitely had a glow-up, once he got his hair situation resolved, and he looked good that night, before he went missing for an hour."

Leave it to Ali to bring *that* up. I definitely will not be divulging the details of that awful evening when I learned the hard way that our mayor's definition of "a little bourbon" did not align with my own when it came to his eggnog recipe.

But yes, twenty-two-year-old Theo's hair was *much* better than high school Theo's hair.

"If you're thinking I made out with Theo in some random closet at an event that was basically the adult equivalent of prom—remember prom, when he ditched me to play tonsil hockey with someone else?—you're going to be very disappointed."

"Okay, fine. I'm convinced." Julie holds her hands up in mock surrender. "But I still don't believe your first kiss was some rando at a bar in New York."

Kiko leans in, resting her elbow on her knee, narrowing her eyes at me. "Yeah, Mia. Are you sure there wasn't someone else before that? Other than the weird elementary school thing Jules already told us about?"

I shrug in response, avoiding her gaze. "Sorry my story wasn't what you were hoping for. Now, who's next?"

♫♪

Kiko and Ali have committed to an old-fashioned sleepover, even though Carla can't stay the night. The air mattress Elliott had leant me had been deflated and set off in the corner, meant to be returned but forgotten. We find a pump and inflate it, and Kiko quickly claims it for herself.

"I've heard all about this couch," she says.

We have no business eating more snacks, but we're rummaging through the pantry and cabinets when Julie's family returns home, and like raccoons in headlights, we're caught red-handed.

But all anyone can do is laugh.

Mr. and Mrs. Bailey shrug out of their jackets to greet our friends, and Jess asks Julie if she's sure she wants to sleep downstairs on the couch that was so uncomfortable it forced me to turn to Elliott's house for a good night's sleep.

"How's it going? You guys having fun tonight?" Elliott props himself against the same wall where I stand, but he leans in and crosses his arms, and he really does ooze casual sex appeal.

Kiko watches from the kitchen table, sending a conspiratorial look toward Ali who has the common decency to act like everything is normal here; her neutral expression seems to say 'there's nothing to see here; move along,' and I realize I never gave her enough credit for not wanting to start the next thread of gossip.

There's that moment, where one person yawns and another looks at their watch and says 'oh look at the time' and everyone acts like they're shocked at how late it is and parts ways. The Baileys and Jess climb the stairs and Julie finishes a final raid of the refrigerator before leading a convoy back to the basement.

"Did you want me to pick you up tomorrow? Maybe around ten?" Elliott asks, adjusting his coat on his shoulders before he leaves.

"I don't want to interrupt your morning. I'll just get a ride home from Ali or something."

He pauses, his hands on the zipper of his coat, and arches an eyebrow at me.

I don't know if he's more interested in why I don't want him to drive me or why I used the word *home*, but it doesn't matter. Julie's head emerges from the doorframe and she gives an exaggerated *pssst* that makes it seem like she's been drinking, even though obviously she hasn't been.

"Elliott! Quit yapping. I have a MarioKart tournament to win down here, and I need Mia to witness my dominance firsthand."

He answers her laughter with his own. "Okay, sis. I'm so sorry that I wanted to make sure she had a ride home tomorrow." Then he turns to me, and it's not lost on me that he said *home* too, and I know it's just the easiest term to use and it shouldn't mean anything, despite the fact that Elliott's house has felt the most like home to me in a long time. "I'll see you for lunch, probably?"

"Sure," I answer. I try to sound nonchalant but probably seem cha-lant as hell, all bothered in the best possible way by his gravelly voice and his warm smile and his general heat, in both the fuzzy feelings and *hubba-hubba* categories.

With Julie still watching, the goodbye feels awkward. Hell, it feels awkward because I'm in love with him and he's not with me, and all 've been thinking about for the last hour is our first kiss on the couch downstairs, and for two weeks we'd at least hug or *something* before bed but now we're in our hands-off era, and all those factors add up to a weird half-wave and a heartless "See ya" before Elliott leaves and Julie locks the front door behind him.

Then she drags me, willingly, laughing, down the stairs and I let her beat me in half of our MarioKart races before we decide one a.m. is late enough for us old ladies to be awake and we curl up in our respective beds.

I have a missed text from Elliott, who I'd been regularly texting with between races. This last message came in during my final victory over Julie when I couldn't afford the distraction of reading it. So far he invited me to lunch. Told me to text him when I was ready to go and he'd pick me up if Ali couldn't or didn't want to drive me back. Wished me luck in the Grand Prix. Was, of course, his perfect, charming, unobtainable self.

So, the hockey player, huh?

Why bring this up now? Unless, of course, he's been thinking this very question since Julie and Zoe mentioned him earlier. I pull my blanket over my head to dim the light of the phone and avoid disturbing anyone else as they're trying to sleep.

It has been suggested that I pursue him, but 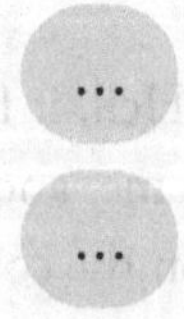

I've had a fair amount of wine, and it's late, which automatically makes me goofy, and I'm coming off a pretty good victory high from this video game, and also? Fuck it. Nearly eighteen years ago he kissed me and told me I looked beautiful—then hot—and if he could flirt with me when I was eighteen I can flirt with him now.

You jealous? 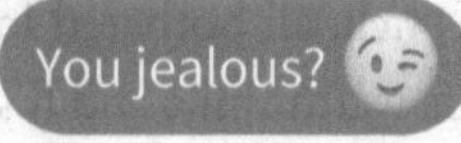

...

...

Let's talk tomorrow.

My heart skips a beat, and I *love* his text, then I hatch from my little cocoon and set my phone face down on the cushion next to me.

Ali's already snoring and Julie flops to her side on the recliner, but Kiko's face is bathed in light from her own phone, probably checking work emails and pulling up her sleep playlist, if the earbuds she's wearing are any indication.

My phone vibrates one more time, but when I check it I'm surprised that it's not Elliott's name on my notifications screen.

Instead, Kiko's message is there waiting for me, and I blush with the knowledge that she is absolutely, without a doubt watching for this very reaction.

How's Elliott?

CHAPTER 37

now

At our last group sleepover, we stayed up till three, told each other our thoughts and dreams and fears, ate far too much sugar, and slept till noon.

Maybe some of us can still do that, but by the time eight a.m. rolls around I'm wide awake. Begrudgingly, but still. There's movement upstairs as the Baileys shuffle about getting ready for church, which I'm assuming Julie is exempt from this week considering she's still snoring.

I venture upstairs to the bathroom, and as I pass through the kitchen Mrs. Bailey extends a mug of coffee to me. We make small talk for a few minutes until Mr. Bailey is ready to go, and then I rummage through their fridge for the tube of cinnamon rolls I know they've got hiding in a corner.

"Predictable, aren't they?" I don't even hear the door open behind me, but there's Kiko, fresh from the basement. "You know what I did *not* predict?"

"Hmm?"

"You actually going for Elliott. Good for you, Mia. It's about damn time." She squats and opens a cabinet door, looking for the glass pie dish we always used for Saturday morning breakfasts when we all slept over during tax season and Mr. Bailey wasn't around to make us his special pancakes. I know that it's a Sunday morning, and that we're not all here, but when I close my eyes I imagine the table surrounded by teens, planning out which movie they wanted to see as they perused the Friday night paper for showtimes at the Movie Palace.

"Nothing's happening."

"You can keep telling yourself that, but I see how you look at him. It's the same way you looked at him when you were fifteen. And he's no better, honestly, making puppy dog eyes at you and sending you flirty texts in the middle of the night."

"Why do you think they're flirty texts?"

Kiko grins and sets the pie dish on the counter. "Because I saw your face last night."

She finds the dish and lightly coats it with cooking spray before I drop in eight rolls, flakes of cinnamon smooshed into each perfect, doughy one. She puts the dish in the oven and leans back against its door, crossing her arms and smirking at me.

"Fine," I answer quietly. "Maybe a text or two got flirty. And yes, I've liked him for a really long time. But like I said, nothing's happening."

"Except that you like him, and you're living with him, and he's flirting with you because he wants you, too."

Normally I wouldn't let myself get excited about the thought, but the last thing he texted me was that we should talk today, and why would he need to tell me again that he wasn't interested? So I'm hopeful about our conversation, if cautiously so.

"Please don't make a big deal about it. And definitely don't say anything to Julie. She'd freak out if she knew I ever even had a crush on him."

"Yeah, of course. On one condition, though."

I pause, nervous, holding a small stack of plates just above the countertop. "What's that?"

Kiko once described herself as spicy, and when we were teenagers—heck, when we were in our twenties—I didn't fully understand it. Now it's on full display in the way mischief dances in her eyes, the way energy emanates from every limb and pore, like wisps of smoke giving away a fire on the other side of a door.

"Meet me for coffee tomorrow to tell me everything."

♫♪

"I would've picked you up."

Coming home to Elliott like this feels like *coming home* to Elliott, and I have no right thinking about how glorious it would be to come home from a day in a recording studio, or an interview with the local news station, or anywhere I am, just to have him meet me at the door like he's done this morning, taking my coat and smoothing my beanie-staticked hair. Every family sitcom I've ever watched has taught me that he should lean down to kiss me, quickly and gently, even if only on my forehead.

Of course he doesn't; instead his eyes rake over me and he steps aside so I can set my boots next to the door.

"I know, but Kiko was heading this way, anyway, and I wanted to get washed up before lunch."

"Sure." He shifts his weight from one foot to the other and shoves his hands into his back pockets.

Twenty-four hours ago I was tucked against him in the next room over; now he's coping with nerves in the ways he always has and that he doesn't realize I'm aware of. Not in a stalker way but more of an observant fan kind of way, I know all his mannerisms, all his habits; I can see he's nervous but I have no idea about what.

His idea of lunch is quite different from mine. I imagined we'd find ourselves at the café or Sunset Diner, but instead Elliott drives us to Green Fable Gardens. Just inside the gate is an incredible vegan restaurant—so amazing that even meat eaters like the two of us sex-moan at our first bites—and we split a dessert before we're finished. Dangerous, considering that last time we did so I ended up straddling him in his truck, topless.

The *talk* of 'let's talk tomorrow' fame has yet to come, unless I missed it while I was analyzing my burger, searching for traces of meat to prove that this experience is a hoax and beef does, in fact, reign supreme.

Elliott insists on paying, but I get him to agree to my terms of my paying for gas on the way home since he covered the gardens admission and lunch.

We stroll toward the conservatory, past ponds of waterlilies and illuminated fountains, bubbling against the day's chill. Elliott tugs his jacket closed around him and I cross my arms as we walk along the paved path.

"So tell me more about this game of truth or dare."

I'd started to tell him about the sleepover as we waited for our food, but once we had deliciousness in front of us the conversation morphed into a series of raves about all of our favorite meals. Regardless, this is not the exact topic I'd hoped to discuss coming out of last night.

But I channel my inner Boromir and answer, "One does not simply reveal the secrets of truth or dare."

He chuckles, his shoe scuffing the ground as he steps. "Okay, I don't need all the details. Can you at least tell me what you chose?"

If I were a braver woman, I would stop in my tracks and refuse to move until he tells me what he wants to talk about, why he cares about the stupid hockey player. Julie would do it, if she and I were here together and I had information she wanted. She'd probably sit down right in the middle of the path and wait until I gave in and told her everything. I, however, am a bit of a coward, so I answer his question.

"I got *truth*."

"Ah. What did they ask you?"

Maybe I should say I'm *mostly* a coward, because I'm not afraid to make him sweat a little. "They asked about my first kiss."

It's like I can see the calculations swirling in his head; the question marks and the flashing alarm lights; the way he recovers after the smallest stumble in his step.

"What did you tell them?"

"The truth, obviously."

"Mia—"

"Elementary school playground. Adam Bradley. Third grade."

He cocks his head. "The one Jules punched?"

"That's the one."

We've reached the doors to the conservatory and he grips a handle, opens one, and motions me inside. "No way they accepted that answer."

"That's an astute assumption." It feels nearly tropical in here, and I peel off my coat, also regretting wearing the sweater underneath.

Elliott knows he was my first kiss, and since I know he's holding back on whatever it is he wanted to talk about, it's fun to watch him squirm a little.

"You're killing me. You know that, right?"

"Relax. There were two possible outcomes to me telling them about us. First, Julie's totally okay with it and no one felt the need to comment on it when you all got back from the game last night. Second, Julie murders both of us. Yet here we are, alive, and with no accolades upon your return from hockey."

I pause in front of a statue with ivy creeping up from its base. It's a dancer, posed with a careful arch to her back and her arms delicate but powerful overhead, and I understand it all. She's reaching up, strong and stone, looking skyward to something great, while vines twist around her feet, grounding her, holding her back, away from what she wants.

I have no interest in being held back.

"Why'd you ask about the hockey player?"

He snorts, and when he doesn't answer I turn to him. His eyes are glued on the statue, either avoiding me or just taking it in, trying to understand it, and I want to scream at him, *she is me and you are the ceiling and our past and your sister and our lives are the ivy, and how I long to cut them all away.*

But stone is stone, and even without the ivy strangling it, it's not reaching the ceiling.

"We're doing a blood drive, and the Falcons are all participating, trying to get more people involved. We always have shortages, and their P.R. team is always looking for community involvement opportunities. So." His eyes flick to mine, then back to the statue, then to the ground as he brushes a foot over the walkway. "If you wanted to meet him, I could help arrange that, is what I guess I'm trying to say."

CHAPTER 38

eighteen years ago

I WOKE UP IN Elliott's sweatshirt, my lips still tingling at the thought of the previous night's kiss, my whole body in want.

Sunlight streamed through the sliding glass door and there were voices upstairs. Not the usual, jovial voices of Sunday mornings and pre-church breakfasts. This was different, quietly intense with the shuffling of pacing feet and pushed-back chairs and muffled scolding.

Julie was missing, so I changed and turned to my journal, not wanting to interrupt whatever was happening upstairs, assuming Julie was in trouble for some unfair reason she'd tell me all about later.

Then there was stomping toward the garage, the slamming of doors, and, finally, quiet.

I dared to emerge upstairs.

Elliott was alone at the kitchen table, his back to me, his head hung with his fingers locked behind his neck. My heart leapt at the thought of being alone in the house with him, and it was seeming increasingly likely that that was the case, considering I heard no sounds elsewhere.

"Hi! Where'd everyone go?" I asked, my voice cautiously bright.

"Church."

I checked the clock on the microwave as I rummaged for a snack in the pantry; it was already eleven, which is when they typically got home on Sunday mornings. "You didn't go with them?"

"No. And I probably won't go back for a while."

"Oh." It was weird, sure, for everyone to go and to leave him behind, and weirder still for him to predict he wouldn't go back for a while, but maybe he found a job that required him to work on weekends, or maybe he was having some sort of existential crisis and needed to find meaning elsewhere. We could talk about it, if he wanted to. But, first things first. "So, I was thinking about last night."

I kept my voice cheery, mostly because I couldn't control it. He'd told me I looked beautiful *and* hot, and he'd kissed me, and sue me if I was maybe a little bit happy about that. I sat across from him, setting a bowl on the table and pouring in cereal. "I was thinking maybe, since we're alone, we could talk about it." I added a few ounces of milk and stirred the oats and marshmallows in so everything was thoroughly coated, so focused on my cereal and nervous about mentioning the kiss out loud that I didn't even look at Elliott's face until after he spoke.

"I can't, Mia."

I should've known from his posture that something was wrong: Elliott Bailey was never a head hanger, was never a one-word-answer kind of guy. But there he was, body bent, sniffling tiny sentences at me.

"Oh my gosh, what's wrong?" I dropped my spoon next to my newly abandoned cereal.

He looked up, met my eyes, and came undone. "I really screwed up. And I am so, so sorry."

I'd never seen him cry at all before, and definitely did not anticipate seeing him cry like this, ever. Shoulder-shaking sobs, gasping for air, and later, I found, for mercy.

I didn't know then what had happened, what he felt was so terrible. All I knew is that Elliott, *the* Elliott, *my* Elliott, was falling apart in front of me and all I wanted was to hold him together, to glue all the pieces back into place, to make him whole.

I circled the table, fell to my knees, and wrapped my arms around his waist. It wasn't the kind of hug you return, not from that angle. It was the kind you just accept, that you use as a shield or strength, as a sign.

Elliott rested one hand on my head, wiped his face with the other, and broke my heart with just five words.

"I think you should go."

Julie seldomly came to my house. We had freedom at hers, with a whole basement to ourselves most days, but my place was cluttered with Mom's craft projects and simultaneously sterile from Dad's need for cleanliness, and with an open floor plan it was hard to find privacy.

But that Sunday Julie arrived in the middle of the afternoon, her regular school backpack and a duffle bag over her shoulders. "I need to stay here tonight," she announced, and I followed her up to my room.

Five minutes later I was on the floor, leaned back against the bed and hiding my face from Julie, who had sprawled on her back on my bed, torturing the stress ball I'd gotten at the winter carnival the school held in January.

"I thought they broke up," I said. "Like, months ago."

"Yeah. She dumped him four months ago, but I guess, I mean, she's six months pregnant, so."

"And no one knew?"

"She was too afraid to tell anyone, and with it being winter she was just wearing sweatshirts and stuff, and now she can't really hide it anymore. And her dad is like, freaking out, saying Elliott should've known better, and Mom and Dad are losing it because obviously now they're on damage control, trying to protect everyone and keep up their reputation, and home is just a lot right now. So thanks for letting me stay here. And for keeping it secret, as much as you can, I guess."

I inhaled, feeling the air rattling in my chest like it was rearranging my organs, and I knew I was changed. Gone was the naive girl who believed in the happy endings of children's stories and romcoms; gone was the hopeful young woman who believed in the possibility of a relationship with Elliott. She had to be gone—because she wasn't a child, and stories and romcoms were fiction, and Elliott was months away from becoming a father. Of someone else's child.

"Sure," I confirmed to Julie. "Whatever you need."

I promised to look out for Julie, but I also needed to look out for myself. And that was the night that I decided that as soon as I graduated, I was leaving Songbird Springs.

CHAPTER 39

now

IT WOULD TAKE APPROXIMATELY 20,895 balloons to carry this statue thirty feet to the ceiling.

And there's not a drop of helium in sight.

CHAPTER 40

now

I'M SCHEDULED TO DONATE blood on Friday. Not because I'm trying to meet a hockey player, but because people need it every day, and it's an easy way to be a superhero. (Also, I *am* going to meet the hockey player, but I'm not, like, into it.)

For now, though, I'm pouring metaphorical blood, sweat, and tears into this last song, polishing up the rough edges before I send five new songs off to Claudette. Today is drastically warmer than yesterday, and the café has opened its brightly-painted wooden door so only the thin storm door separates us from the outside world.

Gwen, the writer, breezes in around eleven o'clock with her blond hair billowing behind her as she approaches from next door with a paper bag in hand. She spots me at my usual booth and rushes over for a hug. "I just wanted to say hi, but I won't keep you," she says.

"Are you kidding? You're always welcome to stay." I gesture toward the table, but there's not a free spot to be found in my strewn papers. I shuffle them into a haphazard pile while she's ordering her drink, then she lowers herself into the bench opposite mine.

"So, you've been busy." Gwen always has this gleam about her, something fun and colorful and bright, like she's a glittery rainbow bomb just waiting to explode.

"Just a little," I tell her. "I should have gotten more done, but life actually *has* been busy, which means I have inspiration, but not necessarily time."

"I get that."

She asks what's going on, and I tell her about Elliott and our history, complicated by the controlling best friend character, complicated by the unplanned pregnancy, complicated by distance and time and masking the truth.

"I would never do this to you, because I respect you and your privacy," she says, "but you know that your whole thing would make a pretty good romance novel, right?"

I roll my eyes at that, laughing a bit at the ridiculousness of it all. "It sure doesn't feel like it."

Gwen reaches a hand across the table and rests it on mine. "Mia. No matter what, you're going to be fine. I have faith that you'll do the thing you need to do, whether it's telling him everything, coming clean to your friend, or getting out of here with a few new, incredible songs and zero love-interest drama."

She squeezes my hand and it's like a hug my whole body deflates into. The weight is lifted, and I realize every option she named is a viable possibility... it just depends on *what I want* to do.

The only thing that could make this better is if I knew what, exactly, that was.

♫♩

Gwen is nice enough to give me a ride to Swallow's Ridge. Yes, she laughs at the name when I tell her about it, and yes, she tells me she plans to bring Sawyer by later for some stargazing. (And yes, she winks when she says the word *stargazing*.)

My guitar and I settle in on a large rock overlooking the hills and trees below, the first colors of spring barely visible in hesitant buds.

It's here that I allow myself to think, to breathe, to feel. I close my eyes and just finger the strings, letting the familiar notes and chords drown out the noise of the world around me and the warring voices in my head.

On a deep inhale I ask myself, *What makes you happy?*

On the exhale, I see Elliott's face, projected on the inside of my eyelids like a feature film at a drive-in for one.

I breathe in again. *What actually brings you joy?*

I see Elliott again, this time with context. It's not just him anymore, but he's standing there smiling, a blurry crowd around him.

Ugh. Okay, self. This can't be it. Yes, I love Elliott. Yes, I have for a really long time. (Like, my love for him could legally drink, long time.) But no, I can't put all my eggs in the Elliott basket. There has to be happiness for me outside of a world where I am—impossibly, I should remind you—all wrapped up in him.

I try one more time. Deep breath. And now the picture is clearer.

Elliott's there, but so is Julie, so is Zoe, and Kiko, and Ali and Carla and Mr. and Mrs. Bailey, *and* my parents, all there in the crowd, and I see them all staring at me, just beyond the top of a microphone. I'm making music, and people, Elliott included, love it.

I feel myself smiling and I know this is it—this is the future I want. I want to sing, to write songs, to have people appreciate my words and connect with them, *and* I want to be near the people who raised me, who love me, whom I love.

Ideas course through me, lyrics and melodies jumping between synapses until they make their way out of my mouth and this—*this* is the song I need to send to Claudette.

I scribble a few things in my journal, then play it again and again until it's committed to both paper and memory. Then I wait forty-seven minutes for an Uber to take me home.

♫♪

Elliott walks in two minutes after I hit *send* on my email to Claudette, one minute after I click the refresh button in my inbox for the third time. He's wearing his scrubs, and he looks really sexy in them.

Okay, listen. I know that when we talk about loving a man in uniform, most women are getting all hot and bothered about firemen and Marines and, I don't know, astronauts? Maybe? But I will happily take these sea-foam, green-blue, paper-thin, ass-hugging scrubs that remind me that Elliott has dedicated his life to saving people in response to his own personal tragedy; that he saw a need and a job with a name a lot of people don't know how to spell and no real glamor or celebration, and he decided, yeah, I'm going to do that. And he went to school and got trained and is now organizing blood drives with local athletes who will get all the recognition and glory and he'll get the satisfaction of knowing every pint collected can save a life.

So yeah, I'm totally, 100% lusting over Elliott Bailey in his uniform.

Which is maybe a little problematic considering how we ended things yesterday at the gardens, when I told him sure, I'll meet the hockey player, because why the hell not?

Well, the *hell not* is standing across the kitchen and dining room of the modest home he's been generous enough to let me stay in for the past month, and he's avoiding me. I can feel it.

"I sent in a song," I blurt out, and he startles and spins to face me.

"Shit. Mia. I didn't realize you were there."

"Sorry."

"It's fine." He grabs the nearly-empty jug of chocolate milk he pulled from the fridge and brings it closer to the dining room, keeping his distance as he leans back against the doorway. "So, you sent it in, huh? What's this one about?"

I watch as he twists the cap off and gulps down what's left, except for the frothy bubbles, and I'm fourteen again, watching Elliott chug chocolate milk after soccer practice, careful not to let his mother see him drinking straight from the carton.

But now no one's here to yell at him for drinking straight out of the jug. Now no one's here at all, except me and Elliott, and I consider that I could come clean to him right now.

"You."

His body changes; shoulders stiffen and brows furrow and jaw clenches. "Me?"

"Sort of. More like the collective 'you': the whole Bailey family and my friends."

"Oh." I wish I could tell if that was relief or regret in his expression and that single, unhelpful syllable.

"It's called *Home*. And I know I haven't said it enough, but thank you, for letting me stay in yours."

He shrugs and retreats to the kitchen to rinse out the milk jug. "Anytime. You're practically family."

Ugh. Dagger to the heart, El. And after everything that's happened the past few weeks. "That's, uh... never mind."

"Yeah, I heard it." He chuckles, his head shaking as he drops the milk container into the recycling bin and closes the drawer. "Please forget I used that particular f-word. I promise I wasn't trying to imply that I viewed you as another sister—"

"Please stop talking," I groan, internally grateful that we seem to be back on more playful terms.

"Fair enough." He meets my gaze through the cutout in the wall between the kitchen and dining room, and he smiles, if only fleetingly.

"I'm going to grab a shower," he says, just as I ask, "Did you want to watch a movie tonight?" Zoe's at her mom's for the week, and I figured a quiet night in together would be nice.

His expression clouds as he draws his bottom lip between his teeth. "I can't," he finally says. "I'm meeting up with some work friends for dinner."

"Oh. Got it."

He pauses a moment, like he wants to say something else but won't let himself, and then passes me on his way up the stairs.

CHAPTER 41

now

KIKO AND JULIE BOTH answered my 'anyone up for a trip to O'Donnell's?' text with an affirmative within mere minutes; Carla and Ali are unable to make it, unfortunately.

But it's perfect, because I never called Kiko for coffee this morning, so when she picks me up an hour later, thirty minutes after Elliott left in dark jeans and a black button-down shirt, I'm able to finally fill her in, as promised.

She intuits so much about other people, and I'm sure she senses that something is off. It might be because I never send out texts like the one I sent earlier, kind of desperate-sounding and pitiful, but let's pretend it's just Kiko's excellent people skills.

"I'm sorry I didn't call you about coffee earlier. I was a little distracted."

Kiko maneuvers a turn past a stretch of fields on our left, past my dream house when I was growing up: a huge stone farmhouse with a wrap-around porch and candles in the windows that always made me feel like I was in a cheesy made-for-TV Christmas movie, no matter what time of year it was.

"No worries. I figure you're more likely to spill the details if I give you wine instead of coffee, anyway." I can practically hear the wink in her voice.

"I told you yesterday morning, nothing's really happening. Just some long-term crushing."

"Long-term *reciprocated* crushing."

"It's really nothing as exciting as that."

The drive to O'Donnell's is short, and Julie and Jess are going to meet us there after their own dinner with Mr. and Mrs. Bailey since it was already in progress when I texted, so Kiko and I have time to catch up in the car and at the bar until they arrive.

"Mia, can you honestly tell me that there is *nothing* going on? No cuddling on the couch or midnight make-out sessions?"

Okay, there have actually been both of those things. I try to come up with an answer that's neither an admission nor a lie, because I'm not comfortable with either, but I hesitate just long enough that Kiko turns her head momentarily, her jaw dropped. "Holy shit. You *did!* Which was it? Cuddling? Kissing? Both?"

"It's not like we're sleeping together or anything," I say, which is totally the *wrong* thing to say, because Kiko gasps and giggles and latches onto the extreme scenario.

"So not sleeping together, just... second base? Oh my god, Mia... *third* base?!?"

"Not exactly," I answer as she puts the car in park at O'Donnell's.

Kiko gawks at me. "This is simultaneously worse than I thought and the absolute best thing I've heard so far this year." She interrogates me more as we walk inside, her whole body bouncing with excitement as she asks questions without giving me time to answer them. "How long have you liked him? Were you hooking up before you moved in with him? Is that *why* you moved in with him? Did you write your first album about him? I don't know if I should listen to 'One Night' ever again." She shudders like she's thinking through the lyrics and picturing Elliott as the main subject in the song.

"Breathe, Kiko. And chill—Jules and Jess could be here any minute, and you have to keep this between us."

"Fine," she sighs as we weave our way through tables and bodies to a corner half-booth/half-table near the bar. "I don't know why you don't just tell Julie. We're all adults."

I shake my head. "I promised her."

"Yeah, when you were, like, twelve or something. There's got to be a statute of limitations on promises made as a minor."

"Not this one." I shake my head firmly.

Kiko rolls her eyes and lets her head loll back. "I knew you guys kissed back in the day, but this is far more exciting."

My hands go clammy and my toes curl a little. "I'm sorry... you knew what, now?" And if Kiko knows, who else does?

"Oh." She shrugs and flips open her menu. "Sydney told me. By accident. I think El told her once and she let it slip one night over empanadas."

"You mean you got tipsy on margaritas and Sydney blabbed."

"You say tomato, Mia. Anyway, I was wondering if you'd ever fess up to it in the game the other night. It is called *Truth* or Dare, not *Make-up-an-answer-you-feel-comfortable-giving* or Dare. I think we should replay that round."

Julie and Jess pick that moment to arrive at our table, and the best I can do is shoot a warning look to Kiko as if to say "do not say a word," but her face is buried in the menu.

"Sorry we took so long," Jess says, pulling out a chair for Julie, who I swear looks bigger than she did when I saw her two days ago.

Julie grabs a second menu and turns immediately to the back where the desserts are located. "What are you guys talking about?"

"Absolutely nothing." I glance at Kiko who pantomimes zipping her lips closed, which Julie doesn't see but Jess certainly does. She arches an eyebrow at me, but I shake my head.

"What'll you have?" I ask Jess, and once I have her order I drag Kiko to the bar with me to get the drinks and our food ordered. We'll add in Julie's dessert later—she's known for needing fifteen minutes to browse the menu, and we're in no rush.

Kiko orders her hard cider and Jess's beer and promises she won't say anything about me and Elliott for the duration of the evening, once I promise her that I'll tell her about the first kiss on the car ride home.

The bartender—Joel, a guy who graduated a year behind us—finishes mixing my drink and I turn to rejoin my friends. In my periphery, I see him; I do a double take to be sure. Of all places for Elliott to be tonight, of course he's here.

O'Donnell's is, arguably, the best place in town to go for an evening hangout with friends (after all, that's why I'm here, too). But Elliott's not surrounded by a group of guys in their hockey jerseys watching the game. Rather, he's sitting next to a woman with a mess of dark curls and a garnet smile who's resting her chin on her fist and nodding along with something he's saying.

I freeze. My toes tingle and my heart races and I'm stuck here, like a deer in the headlights (which is something we are very used to in the state of Pennsylvania), just staring at the two of them.

"Are you planning to stand all night, or...?" Julie asks.

"Sorry." I slide into the booth, sandwiching Kiko against the wall. She follows my gaze and mutters under her breath.

"Oh, shit."

"What?" Julie leans in to better hear us. As much as she can lean in, anyway, because her bump is already firmly wedged against the table.

Kiko dismisses the line of conversation with a wave of her hand. "So, Jess, how's work going?"

I have no idea what Jess says. I'm fully unfocused, because Elliott's here with someone else and it kills me. And it's my own damn fault, for entertaining this stupid hockey player idea, for standing in front of him yesterday and not telling him that all I want is him, for living in his damn house and not telling him how often—and for how long—I have fantasized about sharing a home with him.

"I'm going to step outside for a moment."

The table goes quiet. I'm pretty sure Jess was mid-sentence in a work story, but I need air.

"Are you okay?" Julie asks. She looks so concerned, even if it's only because it's unlike me to interrupt.

Kiko starts to rise behind me. "Here, I'll come with—"

"I'm fine. I just... I'm fine." I force a smile and venture outside, letting the air bite my skin. It hurts, as it should, and I need it to shock me exactly as it does. I rub my arms to fight the cold and just breathe.

The door opens behind me and I don't need to turn to look to see who it is. It's the same gravelly baritone I've heard every day for the past few weeks and years and in the house and in my dreams. He's laughing, and she's laughing, and I'm alone in the cold.

"Mia?" Elliott interrupts himself mid-goodbye. I sniffle before I turn fully to him and will myself not to break down right here. He turns to his date and gives a platonic-enough "see you tomorrow?" before she nods, inspecting me with a quick glance, and waves.

"What are you doing?" He shrugs out of his jacket and offers it to me; I shake my head. "Seriously. You've got to be freezing."

"I'm fine."

What is it about Millennial women that compels us to "I'm fine" ourselves to death?

"You're literally shivering."

"I'm shaking with rage."

He stares at me, his eyebrow quirked and his lips pursed into a pleading pout, and I take the jacket. "What did my sister do now?"

"Nothing at all." Damn it. This jacket smells like Elliott, all vanilla and earthy.

"So why the rage?"

I look up at him, finally starting to thaw in body temperature if not in attitude. I never imagined I'd be bearing my soul to the love of my life in an unpaved dive-bar parking lot, but I guess I shouldn't be surprised by anything anymore.

"I'm just confused. Like, really fucking confused."

The confusion is mutual, because he cocks his head and furrows his brow. "What happened?"

"*You* happened! Your little date happened! Is this why you were pushing me to meet the hockey guy? So you could start dating..." I don't think I ever got her name. "So you could start dating *her*—" I motion in the general vicinity of the parking lot, "without feeling bad about cutting off our little arrangement?"

Elliott hooks a thumb over his shoulder. "You think that was a date? Me and Darci?" He chuckles, his face relaxes. "We work together."

Like that's ever stopped anyone. "And you dress up like this for all your coworkers?"

"It's jeans and a shirt—"

"At *O'Donnell's*," I shriek, and the argument works against me maybe more than it works for me, because this is not really a great date destination no matter how much you dress up for it.

"We planned on Sunset Diner, but Darci decided she wanted something more relaxed."

The door opens and I stiffen, but it's just Kiko checking on me. "I thought I saw you come out here," she says to Elliott. Then, to me, "You okay?"

I have no idea how I am. Still confused. Still hurt. Still kind of cold. But still one hundred percent a Millennial woman. "I'm fine."

Kiko shifts her gaze to Elliott, then back to me, then to Elliott and me one more time, and says, "Why don't you both go home, and I'll let them know you're not feeling well."

"I think that's a good idea," Elliott says, his eyes locked on mine. The way he searches my face makes me melt a tiny bit.

"I'll grab your stuff." Kiko disappears inside and reemerges moments later with my phone, bag, and coat, which Elliott takes with a muffled "Thanks."

"Sure. Feel better, Mia," she says with a quick touch to my arm.

"Yeah."

I lead the way to Elliott's truck, where he opens my door and cranks up the heat for the drive back to his house. We ride in relative silence with only the sounds of the truck scoring the minutes until he parks in his driveway and kills the engine.

Once we're inside, he revisits the conversation. "I promise, Mia. There was supposed to be a group of us, but everyone else bailed at the last minute. It was *not* a date. Darci's divorce was finalized today, and she just wanted to distract herself with some friends."

Inside, I cringe. How selfish sounding of me; how absolutely off-the-rails I must have seemed.

"And I'm struggling to figure out why it bothered you so much, anyway."

I map my escape route, just in case I need out of this conversation, and lie. "It didn't."

"So that was someone else 'shaking with rage' outside O'Donnell's, then?" He hangs my coat and bag on the hook next to the garage door while I get some distance in the dining room.

"I'm just— I don't understand why you were pushing me away. When I saw you tonight I figured you'd been trying to hook me up with the hockey guy the past few days so you could go on a date and feel, I dunno, less guilty about it? But if it wasn't a date, I don't understand why you're trying so hard to set me up with someone else."

I acknowledge that my voice is growing louder, that my pace is increasing, that my tone is more panicky and intense than it really needs to or should be. But it's nothing compared to the urgent fever pitch of Elliott's own voice when he breaks.

"Because I needed you to be unavailable." It's an admission I don't think he meant to make, if the way he draws back after it comes out is any indication.

The outburst makes my toes sweat, and I'm generally perplexed. "Unavailable? What are you talking about?"

He scrubs a hand down his face before speaking and takes two steps forward, then one step back, like his brain knows he should remain across the expanse of the kitchen and dining room but his body wants to be closer. "If you were unavailable, it wouldn't hurt so badly to look at you and be with you and not actually *be with* you. Because I want you and I know I can't have you, and I thought that maybe if you were seeing someone, even casually, it would make it easier."

CHAPTER 42

now

I WANT YOU AND I know I can't have you.

The words bounce around in my head like a pinball, ricocheting between memories and making shrapnel of truths I've held since I was a teenager.

"You... you what? You *want* me?" I feel ridiculous saying it out loud, but if I misheard him that'll be quite the laugh to share later. After I hide in my room to cry first, of course.

"Has it not been obvious?" His face says *shell-shocked*, but his body says *I need you* as he gravitates toward me.

"No?" I mean, the needy, wanting make-out sessions would have been a clearer clue had he not A) cut them off, and B) pushed this hockey player thing. "Why do you think you can't have me?"

He pauses on the other side of the dining table. "There are so many reasons. One, I know this is temporary. Two, I mean—" he motions to the length of me with a sweep of his hand. "It's you, Mia."

A harsh laugh forces its way through my throat. "What does *that* mean?"

His eyes go soft, locking on mine as his jaw clenches. "It's just—you're *the* Mia Montgomery, and I'm—" he bites his bottom lip and shakes his head as he shifts his gaze to the ceiling. "I'm more broken and damaged than ever, and there's no way you'd ever—"

I can't take it. My heart splinters and shatters just thinking he believes for a second that's true.

I might not have retained everything from thirteen years of public school math classes, but I do know that the shortest distance between two points is a straight line. I lean across the table, reaching for Elliott, cradling the back of his neck in my palm and pulling him toward me. With a bracing knee on the table, I crush my lips to his, feel his hands snake around my waist, pulling me closer until I've crawled completely atop the table and into his embrace.

"Don't you ever say that again, do you understand me?" I scold against his lips. "You are not damaged. You are perfect and you always have been."

Elliott weaves his fingers into my hair and tugs, drawing my head back and exposing my neck to him. He nips and kisses like he's hungry for me. "This is the problem, Mia," he says in the moments when his mouth isn't pressed to me. His breath is hot on my skin. "I don't know how to survive being thousands of miles apart when I know what it's like to be together."

"Hey." I hold his face in my hands and guide him until our eyes meet. "I'm here right now."

The wicked grin he gives me could make me erupt this second. His hands slide down till he cups my ass, and he lifts me off the table, letting my legs wrap around his waist.

I don't know what kind of physical training goes into being a phlebotomist, but the way Elliott carries me, maneuvering through the obstacle course of his living room and up the stairs without so much as a stumble, you'd think he was in his mid-twenties with the upper-body strength of a pommel horse guy.

Elliott goes straight to his room and sits on the edge of the bed. Straddling him like this, I can feel his want, and it feels so good to know he wants me—that he's wanted me for a while, apparently.

He grips my hips and holds me like he doesn't want to let me go, like he's holding fast to something that's already slipped through his fingers.

My head lolls back, my body helpless against this attack of longing, and when Elliott presses a hot, wet kiss to the center of my throat I accidentally sex moan. Loudly. And while it's a faux pas that would've made me apply for witness protection just a few weeks ago, now there's no shame, no embarrassment. Just pure (okay, maybe very impure) pleasure.

"Is this okay?" he asks, still plastering kisses to my skin.

"Did you not hear me just now?" I chuckle, and he chases the vibration with his mouth.

"No, I mean, is this okay? That we're—"

"About to have sex?"

He pulls back and looks up at me, his eyes wide.

"Oh, shit. You weren't thinking of—" I'm already flushed from the making out and the high of hearing him say he wants me, but I feel my cheeks burn now, anyway. "I'm so sorry."

"Mia." He growls a laugh and drops his head, resting against my sternum. He holds me close when I try to peel myself off of him.

"Please let me go suffocate myself with a weighted blanket in peace."

"I wasn't necessarily thinking we'd get there tonight, but is that what you want? To break that rule?" His voice is tender but inquisitive.

This time when I back away he doesn't resist. Instead he watches as I stand and strip out of my sweater before pulling him to his feet, too.

"We can't undo this," he sighs against my lips.

"If you don't want this, we'll stop. But I've never wanted anything more."

Elliott's hands glide along the length of my arms, following them to where my fingers toy with the line of buttons spanning from his chest to his waist. He undoes the top button, his eyes fixed on mine. "Please tell me you're on birth control."

I nod, because even though I'm not having frequent rock-star sex, one truly never knows when the urge will strike, and the benefits of an IUD seemed attractive five years ago when an international tour opportunity across thirteen time zones made maintaining my pill schedule about as easy as passing an A.P. Calc final in third grade.

"And you just bought condoms," I add, working from the bottom button up at a slightly less restrained pace.

He half smiles and squints an eye. "How do you know that?"

"Carla saw you a few weeks ago. Actually, that's what made Julie suggest that I move in with you— to spy on you and maybe babysit you, too."

"How's that working out?" He shrugs out of his shirt and tosses it aside with my sweater.

I bite my lip and rake my hands up his torso, taking in every gentle curve of muscle in a multi-sensory experience. I want to lick him. (Will he think it's weird if I lick him?) Because he'd probably go running if I confessed the whole "I want to run my tongue along every inch of your ridiculously hot body" thing, I interlock my fingers behind his neck and say instead, "I one hundred percent want to do this, if you do."

"Yes. God, Mia, I've wanted this for so long."

In all the times I allowed myself to fantasize about sex with Elliott, I imagined him taking the lead, moving with a confidence I couldn't reciprocate because I felt like everything was forbidden and was therefore so nervous I couldn't fully embrace or enjoy it.

The reality, though?

The reality is that it's perfect.

Our mutual excitement and desire propel us both into a horizontal make-out session with a fair amount of respectful groping, and I'm the one who makes the first move to undress the other.

While I'd love to watch Elliott expertly single-handedly remove his own belt, I have apparently reached the limits of my patience. (Roughly two decades of pining will do that, I guess.)

I unbuckle it for him, unbutton his jeans, slowly pull the zipper down. His breath catches when my knuckles graze him through the thin fabric of his boxers. He groans when my fingertips dance just under the waistband.

I'm intoxicated with the knowledge of having this effect on him, the magic that makes Elliott Bailey moan and gasp and writhe and sigh my name during light foreplay.

But if I'm magic, Elliott's the miraculous and improbable lovechild of Houdini, Copperfield, Siegfried, *and* Roy. Because, holy shit, when he rolls me to my back and hovers over me, giving me ghost kisses so soft and breathy I'm not even sure his lips make physical contact with my skin, I dig my fingernails into his shoulders and beg him for pressure or weight somewhere so I don't float away.

And does the man ever deliver.

He pulls my waist into his, a toned arm under my arched back. With his other hand he inches a bra strap over my shoulder, peeling back the cup to kiss me, gentle but firm. Then he switches hands and repeats on the other side.

"I can't decide if I want to savor this or just rip your clothes off and be absolutely feral with you." Elliott sinks lower, his five-o'clock shadow scratchy on my belly as he nuzzles into me.

"Would it make your decision easier if I told you I will explode if you aren't inside me within the next two minutes?"

Wordlessly he tugs at my leggings, easing himself off the bed to drop them in our growing pile of laundry. He lets his jeans fall at his feet and kicks them to the pile as well, then rounds the bed to the nightstand and takes out a condom before climbing back into bed beside me and pulling a sheet over our nearly-naked bodies.

"I don't know what you like," he says, and it's so adorably and devastatingly vulnerable that I scoot as close to him as I can, trace his jaw with my fingertips, and say, "I like *you*, El."

CHAPTER 43

now

IT HAD TO HAVE been a dream.

Elliott using the word "feral" to describe the way he wanted me.

Elliott surveying my naked body and telling me I'm beautiful.

Elliott's hips rocking into mine while he repeated words like "perfect" and "ohgodyes."

Elliott's forehead pressed to mine as he gasped through a shuddering release.

The way he rolled off of me, lay next to me, held my hand in the moments after, kissed my knuckles.

But I'm here, in his bed, wearing nothing but a T-shirt—*his* T-shirt—because my room was too far away when we got ready for bed last night and he asked me to stay with him. And it wasn't a dream at all.

He tightens his grip around my waist when I try to sit up. "Don't leave me."

The morning light streams through the curtains, soft and filtered, making floating flecks of dust glisten. The whole scene screams perfume commercial, or something equally ethereal.

"I need to hydrate first," I laugh, fighting against the arm draped over me. "Last night was a workout."

"Can we do it again?" He releases me so I can stand and squints up at me with one sleepy eye. "I have the day off."

I roll my eyes but smile. "Once we both brush our teeth, sure."

Elliott beats me to the bathroom and squeezes toothpaste onto my brush while he's already scrubbing.

For the next two minutes our eyes meet in the mirror and I remember every incredible, dirty thing he did with his mouth last night—and again at two a.m.

Okay, we only brush for one minute.

I power off my toothbrush before my time is up, and Elliott spits after I do, a knowing gleam in his eye.

He takes my hand as I try to lead the way back to his bed, spins me toward him, and hoists me onto the vanity.

"Are you hiding condoms in here, too?" I question, giddy with laughter.

He shakes his head and sinks to his knees, nudging my legs apart. "Nope."

Not that he needs the help—he was already hard when we woke up this morning—but he touches himself while he touches and tastes me and it makes me feel so powerful and beautiful and perfect and desirable.

"Will you do me a favor?"

"What?" I'm gripping the edge of the counter, biting back a moan, and honestly he could ask me to do pretty much anything right now and I'd reply with a resounding yes.

"Will you keep my shirt on this time?"

Pleasure rolls through my body. Not just when he takes my hands and leads me back to his rumpled, messy bed, but in the sheer knowledge that he likes to see me in his T-shirt, in knowing he'll wear it once I'm gone and remember what we did while I was wearing it. That is, if I let him keep it.

He's got one hand under my shirt—okay, *his* shirt—and a faceful of my hair as I straddle his hips and suck tiny marks into his pecs and shoulders. If we had to miss out on embarrassing teenage hickeys, I at least deserve some discreetly-placed marks now.

He swats at the nightstand, fumbling for the drawer handle.

Being with Elliott is more intense and magical than I ever imagined. Maybe because he's not the awkward teenager I fell in love with twenty years ago, just learning and discovering with the clumsiness of a beginner, but because he's a man who knows his own body, who uses it with a sureness and a certainty that exudes a quiet confidence that I can't quite get enough of. There's a hardened worldliness to it, like he's given up so much and now he just wants to take, but what he wants to take is me. And I'll freely give myself to him, without hesitation.

"Let me," I say, holding out my hand for the foil packet he's pulled out.

His eyes dance like I just offered him a thousand dollars. And then he watches: he watches while I slip my fingers in his boxers, and while I pull them down far enough to expose his bulge. He watches while I sink down, taking the tip of him in my mouth, then he closes his eyes and groans my name, but he watches again as I tear the wrapper, bites his lip as I roll the condom onto him, guides my hips back over him and teases me for a moment before sinking into me slowly, rhythmically.

We should still be learning each other, but our bodies move easily and naturally together like they were made exactly for this. Exactly for each other. With Elliott controlling the motion, I twist the hem of the T-shirt into a knot at my waist, giving him a better view of where we come together and apparently finding the *turn-Elliott-on-even-more* button.

"Fuck," he says, and I can see him struggle between letting his head fall back onto the pillow with his eyes closed in euphoria, and taking in every second of me taking him.

I let the shirt fall again and lean in to kiss his lips. "Is this okay?" I whisper as my teeth tug on his ear.

He answers with a slow gasp, a restrained "yes." He grips the T-shirt now, wrapping his fist in fabric, slowing and deepening his thrust. "I want you everywhere. I want to make you come in every room of this house. And I'm never washing this shirt again."

I kiss him again, hard, our tongues colliding, and my lips swell from the pressure and his scruff and nothing has ever felt better. Except maybe when he deepens the kiss, his hands splayed, claiming all the real estate of my back, and his pace quickens, quickens, and slows.

He grinds into me in tiny, deliberate circles, and I know that I did that. I turned him on again and again and again last night and this morning.

♫

"Please tell me we can stay like this all day." Elliott strokes my thumb with his and kisses the back of my shoulder.

Freshly showered and recently caffeinated, we're curled up on the couch for a change of scenery and half-watching Psych reruns.

"I have no plans whatsoever. Though it's already noon, so the day's half over."

"Don't ruin it," he jokes, another tender kiss finding its way to my neck.

I have no business wanting him again—not until after dinner, at least—but my entire body responds to that brief touch. What surprises me is that my heart's response is the most pronounced. It does a slow, dramatic somersault behind my ribs, visits my esophagus, and bungee jumps into my stomach before settling back in place like a teenager diving into bed after sneaking back through their window well after curfew.

So, to recap: I'm totally in love with Elliott Brandon Bailey.

See also: I'm totally screwed.

"I still can't believe you're here," he says midway through a commercial for, fittingly, a heart medication.

"You mean you're surprised I'm in your house after you invited me to stay here?"

He shakes his head. "You never told me why you're in the Springs and not in Paris."

Ah, Paris. The City of Love with a siren song so loud my parents must not have been able to hear my hurt when they told me they were moving there.

"Did you know they started hanging out with my parents more, about five years ago? It was kind of crazy to see such different couples occupy the same space. Your parents are really in love, like they never left that newlywed stage, you know? It's really incredible. I wish my parents still had that."

"No, you don't."

He furrows a brow as he tucks my hair behind my ear, but he doesn't say anything.

"Your parents are just as in love. Trust me. But it changes, it grows. They made room in their love for you and Julie, Jess, and Zoe. Now this baby, and even for me. My parents only have room for each other. Literally. Their apartment is barely seven hundred square feet. One bedroom, no full-size couch. I'd have to get a hotel room if I wanted to visit. And I know that because the last—and only—time I was there, they ended up booking a suite at this beautiful, historic hotel a few blocks away and then insisted I stay at their place so I'd be 'more comfortable.'"

"So, they basically used your visit—"

"As an opportunity for a romantic staycation. Yes."

He presses his lips to my forehead and lets them linger there in a long kiss. "I'm so sorry, Mia."

I shrug, because it's been a few years, and it's a reality that I've come to accept from my parents: they are wildly, fantastically in love with each other, and that love doesn't manifest itself in the same way when it comes to me.

"There's always room here, Mia. Anytime you're home, you have a home here."

I know he means well. I know this sweet sentiment is his heart on display, and that he means every word he says. For now.

In reality, though? I know that as soon as I leave town again, and once Zoe finishes senior year and moves off to college, Elliott is going to find someone. He's going to have the time to focus on himself, and he's going to meet someone wonderful, and I don't think they'd love the idea of someone else "having a home" with Elliott. Especially when that someone else has craved him for a lifetime, has tasted his kiss, has become intimately familiar with his body and the way he uses it.

But I say nothing, because I don't want to ruin the moment. Instead, I curl into him, letting him believe his own fantasy, and I kiss him while I still can.

CHAPTER 44

now

WE'RE A LITTLE BIT of a disaster, Elliott and me.

We make dinner, we talk, we laugh. We put on a platonic show for Zoe and Julie and anyone else around us. I push to the back of my mind all the promises I hope for but will never happen.

And then we topple into bed together.

Night after night we sneak around like teenagers, trying to keep the actual teenager from catching us. Sometimes we lie there, blanketed in filtered moonlight, whispering about our day. Sometimes we lie in the dark, saying nothing at all. And sometimes he needs me the way I need him, and I bite his shoulder as he makes me come, and I allow myself—against my better judgment—to imagine any of those scenarios being long-term.

And then, on Friday, I donate blood and I meet the hockey player.

Patrick, the team's social media manager, tracks me down to film a quick PSA for their Instagram stories, introducing me to Mac, the center, two seconds before he commands us to sit on side-by-side stools and then disappears, shaking his head at his phone.

"Mac Bernard," the hockey player says, extending his right arm across his body to shake my hand. "It's great to meet you, Mia."

I smile back, giving his hand a quick, firm squeeze. "You too, Mac."

He's cute and inquisitive and interesting as we make small talk until Patrick returns. Mac's hair is coiffed and gelled, and his navy blue jersey over a pale blue button-down brings out the icy shade of his eyes. He tells me he saw me play when he was in college, during the Flowers' university tour, and asks what I'm working on now. In any other timeline or version of the multiverse, I'd melt a little and make sure we met up for drinks or dinner. But I meet Elliott's eyes as he helps a donor out of their chair, and, sorry, but Mac *who*?

We record our message, encouraging others to take an hour out of their day and donate blood, highlighting how to make appointments at the local donor center or find future drives, and then it's time to answer a litany of questions about my sexual history (which is slightly more exciting now than it was when I donated six months ago) and drug use (which has never been exciting because the answer to everything is "no"), and then they send me out to wait for the next available chair. And of course I wait until Elliott's chair is free again, because I'll take any excuse to be near him.

He smiles when he waves me over, and under the surveillance of a room full of people he finds little ways to activate the butterflies in my chest. His fingers pause as he hands me a nylon glove stuffed with a stress ball. He takes his time cleaning my skin before he inserts the needle, the slow drag of his hand along my forearm basically as good as foreplay.

"You feeling okay?" he asks as he sticks the ends of a few pieces of tape to my armrest.

"Never better."

"You'll feel a little pinch. Did you want me to give you a count-down?"

I shake my head.

"Well, if you want to look away, now's the time to do it."

Normally I would. But normally I don't have the opportunity to soak in Elliott at work, to watch him offer such care and concern to his present donor, and I wouldn't miss a second of it.

"What?" he asks, his brows knitting even as a smile grows on his face.

There's a brief pinch, a slight heat sensation at my inner elbow, and then he's taping tubing to my arm, clicking vials into place, and telling me when to squeeze the ball in my hand.

"Thanks for being here today."

My gaze follows him as he walks to my other side, checking bins and supplies. "Sure. It's been fun."

"Hopefully not too fun?" He rests his hand on the edge of my chair and his eyes flit across the room to where one of his colleagues is helping Mac slide his bandaged arm back into his shirt sleeve, his thin undershirt tight against his torso.

My pinky locks with Elliott's, bringing his attention back to me. "Not nearly as much fun as I'm hoping to have once we're at home."

"You're not supposed to engage in strenuous physical activity for twenty-four hours after donating blood. Didn't you read the educational material?"

"I did. And that's why you were on top, and I just laid here."

It didn't take much time or convincing to end up in Elliott's bed once he got home from work, and now he lazily strokes my arm while my head rests on the spray of coarse hair on his chest.

"Are you ready for the party this weekend?"

He chuckles and kisses the top of my head. "I think you're in clear violation of rule number two, Mia."

Right. The no-talking-about-Julie rule. "I'm not really asking about *her*, per se, but more so about *you* and your readiness level for the event."

He pauses, his knuckles swirling over my shoulder. "What if we told her?" he finally asks.

"About the shower? I thought you wanted it to be a surprise."

"No." He swallows hard. "What if we told Julie and everyone about *us*?"

"Absolutely not." I back away from him so I can meet his eyes, so he can see in mine just how serious I am about this. "Julie can never know. *No one* can know."

"Wow, okay. Point taken."

"El—"

"No, no." He throws his hands up in mock surrender as a smile plays on his lips. "We can't let the world know that Mia Montgomery's got a secret lover."

"Not for free, anyway." I match his playfulness with a jab to his ribcage. "We at least need to try to shop the story around."

"Ah, yes, I can already see the headline." He swipes a hand through the air above us like he's emphasizing a marquee. "Rock Star Mia Montgomery Shacking up with Flannel-Wearing, Phlebotomist Nobody."

"Hey."

If only he could know exactly what I'm thinking, every bit of love for him that I feel, he'd understand the sudden sternness in my voice. But he doesn't. He can't.

Still, he tucks my hair behind my ear as I tell him the simplest truth: "You are not—nor have you ever been—a nobody."

He wraps me in his arms and rests his cheek against my head, and it must be the steady metronome of his heart and the comfort of being tucked against him that lull me to sleep.

♫♪

I'm startled awake in the dark by a frantic whisper, a jostle to my shoulder. "Mia. *Shit*. Wake up, Mia."

"What's wrong?" My sleepiness evaporates under the heat of his panicked tone. The digital clock on the nightstand reads 10:07, and it occurs to me that we never ate dinner tonight, but that doesn't seem like such an emergency that Elliott needs to be pulling on sweatpants in this much of a hurry.

And then I hear it—a clumsy thundering up the stairs—and I think we're being burgled until—

"Dad?"

Elliott wedges himself in the doorway just in time, and I throw the blanket over my head.

"What's up, Zo?"

I can't quite make out what comes next, since I'm focused on not breathing at all. But I know she pauses; I can practically hear the gears turning in her brain.

"You okay, Dad?"

"Of course. Why?"

"You're acting weird. Do you have—" she gasps, then there's whispering, and I have to pee but it's the absolute worst timing, and then a hasty series of apologies is followed by the soft closing of the door and the click of the lock, and a relieved exhale.

I peer out from the covers to see Elliott silently banging his head against the doorframe.

"Holy shit."

"Yeah," he says, rubbing the bridge of his nose. "That was close."

"Does she know—"

"No." He cuts me off with a mumble. "She doesn't know it's you."

I exhale for what feels like the first time since he woke me, relieved, then clamber out of bed and put my own clothing back on.

"Are you leaving? She already knows I'm not alone."

"Yes, but don't you think she'll have some questions if I'm nowhere to be found while you've simultaneously got someone in here?"

Elliott drops himself onto the end of the bed and drags his hands down his face. "You really don't want my kid to think I'm cool, do you?"

"She already thinks you're cool. Trust me."

"Yes, okay, maybe. But I hate lying to her." He takes my hand and weaves his fingers into mine before I can reach for the doorknob. His deep brown eyes go puppy-dog pitiful, and a dramatic pout accompanies them on his face.

"On the bright side, you only have to do it two more weeks."

I won't pretend to be a movie buff, despite our history on the elder Baileys' couch. But I will say that this is one of those record-scratch moments, where someone says something so profoundly stupid that the scene changes course and everyone stops just to stare at whatever idiot said the moronic thing, kind of like Elliott's staring at me now: slack-jawed, incredulous.

"Yeah. That's the bright side."

"You know what I mean," I offer even as my other hand grips the doorknob.

"Sure." He tries for a smile, but it's forced. "Be sneaky out there."

"Of course." I don't have the time or the words to clarify every-thing I'm feeling and exactly what I meant, so I say goodnight, make sure the coast is clear, and slip into the hallway.

I toss and turn, alone in my bed for the first time this week. Falling asleep without Elliott holding me is like falling asleep in a hotel where they only give you sheets and no real blankets, like something crucial is missing.

When Elliott and I first started this arrangement, I was afraid that I was going to be his dirty little secret. But now I've made it sound like he's mine, and I hate it. What's the point, though, in telling everyone if this is just a casual thing?

But then one word sends me spiraling, because Elliott asked if we should tell them about *us*, and I never considered that he might see us as an *us* to tell others about.

♫♩

Bless Zoe Bailey.

Teenagers get a bad rap, but any teenager who plies me with coffee on a Saturday morning is an angel on Earth.

"So, what did you think of Mac?" she asks, passing a finished party favor across the coffee table. The living room has become home base for Julie and Jess's shower tomorrow, and we're surrounded by pastel organza and candies.

I take a long sip of coffee, buying time to think of the right response. "He was nice." (Okay, not a great response, but in my defense the caffeine hasn't really kicked in yet.)

She raises an eyebrow—she's nearly identical to her father when she does that—and repeats, "Nice? Really, Mia? You wrote every song on 'Fields of Stardust' and the best descriptor you can give of Mac Bernard is that he's *nice*?"

"I mean," I reply with a shrug, "we just made that little video together, and that was it. He seems friendly."

Zoe opens a bag of chocolates with lavender wrappers and meticulously divides them into favor bags. Her eyes focus on her work, mostly. But of course she has to also gauge my reaction when she says, "Speaking of friendly. Did you know Dad had someone over last night?"

In unrelated news, teenagers are manipulative weasels who butter you up with coffee before trying to get intel out of you.

"I did." There's really no use in lying about facts she already knows. "But that's really it. It's not like he introduced me or anything. I just heard voices. But cool, I guess."

These teenagers and their damn interrogation tactics. I always ramble when I'm sleepy *or* caffeinated, and when you put the two together...

"Oh." Zoe glances at me in her periphery. "Same. I just didn't realize he was *there* with someone, you know? Like—" she pauses like she's trying to figure out how to put her thoughts into words. "I didn't know he was so close..."

"Are you trying to say that you're surprised your dad's having sex?"

She cringes. "Ew, Mia."

"Sex isn't a four-letter word," I laugh.

"That doesn't mean I need to hear about my dad—" She stops short of finishing her own sentence and shudders. "Gross. I mean, good for him. I'm happy he's getting out there again, but maybe next time he can go to her place? Or at least shut the door if I'm going to be around. Anyway, can we change the topic?"

"Sure."

"Thank God." She finishes another favor. "How's the song writing going?"

And just when I've made it a full hour without thinking of checking for an email from Claudette. "I'm done with what I need to write. Now I'm just waiting to hear from our manager if the rest of the band likes what I did."

Zoe surveys me, confusion shaping her expression. "You sent the songs to your manager? Why not send them to Lily and Jenna directly?"

You know that feeling you get when you have to tell your kid that Santa isn't real? Or when you have a small toilet-side memorial service for the goldfish you won at the county fair's ring toss game, just before you flush his fishy little carcass? That same feeling of dream-squashing dread fills me now.

"So here's the thing about the Flowers."

CHAPTER 45

seventeen years ago

EVERY CITY I'D BEEN in before was small by comparison, but so much harder to navigate. Seriously, who can remember the north-south order of King, Prince, Duke, and Queen Streets, or the east-west order of Mulberry, Chestnut, Orange, Lime, and a dozen other fruits or trees?

No, New York, with its perfect, numbered grid, was simple.

Armed with my old guitar, all the money I'd saved from every birthday and Christmas and my graduation, and two suitcases, I invested in a basement studio apartment. I walked in that first day, proud and ready to take on the city.

It took all of three hours and twenty-four minutes in my apartment to bear witness to a cockroach scurrying across the floor.

Awesome.

But still, I was in a place that provided an opportunity to make music and get noticed, and that was all that mattered.

Okay, there was also the whole *Elliott-and-his-love-child-aren't-here* thing, which was of equal importance.

I found gigs pretty quickly. After all, girls with guitars were a bit of a novelty coming out of the boy band and pop princess era.

One café—a quirky place with a name I never could pronounce—became a favorite for coffee and writing and open mic nights. It didn't pay like busking did, but at least it was a roach-free environment.

"I like your style," I heard one night as I was packing up. "Were those originals?"

Her soft brown hair with chunky blond highlights fell over her shoulders as she reached forward to shake my hand. "Sorry, hi. I'm Sami. Sami Charles."

Sami and I chatted for an hour over coffee, and she told me all about her friends who were shunning Broadway auditions in favor of starting a band, and would I want to meet them?

Shocker: I did. And we hit it off right away.

And Lily and Jenna and I hustled and booked gigs and wrote together, and for a while it was like we were like Josie and the Pussycats: three great friends, happy making music, but feeling like we were destined for so much more. Without the subliminal messages to help us, of course.

And a year after I moved to the city we were tapped to play a huge festival: Making Waves, which was a beachside celebration of indie bands during spring break.

It should have been perfect.

Except I had somehow convinced myself that being with someone would help me get over Elliott, so I'd had a casual fling with this guy Mikey, who was a very chill drummer from another band and who had perfectly spiked frosted tips and a thick pocket chain and who, apparently, had another girlfriend. Which explained why he never wanted to go out together.

And of course all of this came to light at Making Waves when I caught him kissing another woman behind the stage. I felt like Sandy in that scene in Grease where the Pink Ladies orchestrate a run-in with Danny Zuko after the pep rally and she says his name all squeaky and follows it up with the whole "I wish I'd never laid eyes on you" bit, because I totally did all of that. But next to me, Lily scoffed and gasped "Matty?" and Mikey (a.k.a. Matty) pulled his face-sucking lips away from a woman with a rock the size of Rhode Island on her left ring finger and just stared at us.

Realization must have dawned on all the women all at once, because his wife smacked him in the face, Lily cussed him out, and I threw up on Jenna's shoes.

And minutes later we were up on stage playing the best we ever played.

The lore of our pre-show soap opera followed us for years, but so did resentment.

Lily was convinced I'd somehow known we were sleeping with the same asshole, and Jenna just really liked her shoes.

But still, the drama piqued an interest. It drew a crowd.

And we put aside our differences to open for thirty dates on a stadium tour six months later.

CHAPTER 46

now

"SO YOU REALLY CAN'T stand each other?"

I shrug. "We tolerate each other, but we're not like we used to be." I miss that first year together, playing in nursing homes and cafés and bars, just making music and singing about broken hearts. "For a while, when we got the first tour, we were so distracted by success that we overlooked the negatives. But now we're all at such different places. Jenna's married and running a fitness business on the side, Lily's pursuing her passion projects with fashion design and Broadway, and I'm—"

"Writing hit songs even though your bandmates don't appreciate you?"

I meet her gaze over the nearly-finished favors. "Jury's out on whether they're hits or not. I guess time will tell."

"They will be, Mia. And I already made Dad promise to buy me tickets for the next tour for my graduation gift."

♫♪

We get the shower decorations set up just in time; the first few guests arrive twenty minutes before the official start time and help themselves to a seat as Elliott, Zoe, Mrs. Bailey, and I shuttle empty boxes back out to Elliott's truck.

Others filter in, and then Carla, Kiko, and Ali arrive simultaneously, their arms overflowing with elaborately wrapped packages.

Jess and Julie enter to a shout of "Surprise!" because Mrs. Bailey allowed the traditionalists in the room to believe the event itself was a surprise, and Elliott gives her a knowing smile just before he aims a wink at me over her head.

There's mingling and laughing and eating, and the Sunset Diner is overflowing with excitement. So much so that the first time my phone rings I let the call go to voicemail, even though it's Claudette.

And then she calls again. And two more times. And on the fifth call, I figure I should answer.

It's brisk in the parking lot, but not unbearable, and birds sing in the mid-afternoon sun.

"Fina-fucking-ly, Mia," Claudette says before I can even utter a hello.

"Is everyone okay?" I ask on impulse, because Claudette isn't necessarily known for her tactful vocabulary, but this is a greeting like I've never heard from her.

"No." She cusses and takes a steeling breath, exhaling shakily in my ear. It's the same type of sigh she gives when she's rage-shaking and trying to steady her voice.

"Claudette, what happened?" Not that I want to leave the Baileys in the middle of the party, and not that Jenna and Lily are my best friends, but if one of them's on life support somewhere I'll find a plane to get me to them.

"Between you and me, kid? Fuck Lily Asher."

Okay, so no one's dying, then. Claudette's just pissed. "What did she do?"

"She signed a contract for another show, that's what. And she talked to Jenna, and apparently they're teaming up to start their own athleisure brand."

"But the two of them doing side projects is nothing new—"

"It is this time, Mia." She huffs, and her voice softens from its clipped tone. "They want out. They want to kill the Flowers." Before I can say anything else, Claudette adds, "Listen, I'm sorry. I have to go. We'll touch base about contracts and paperwork later. Take care, okay?"

Claudette has never once said 'take care' to end a phone call to me. She's never once sounded so apologetic, so defeated. She really may as well have been attending a funeral, the way she ended the interaction with such polite finality.

The world spins, and I lean against Elliott's truck to brace myself, still staring at my phone.

"There you are! I saw you leave, and—are you okay?" I only realize I'm trembling when Elliott rubs my arms, and he bends to see my face. "What happened?"

I shake my head and swallow back the lump in my throat, but no words come.

"Mia?" He hooks a finger under my chin and tilts my face upward to his, using his thumb to dry the tears on my cheek. "What is it?"

"It's over."

His Adam's apple bobs, and I can't even appreciate that he seems nervous; I can tell from the way he falters and takes a step back that he thinks I mean us. That elusive, mythological *us*. "What?"

"The band... the Flowers... we're just... they quit."

I don't know if he pieces together meaning from any of my stammering, or if all the meaning he derives from it is that I'm devastated. He tucks his arms under mine and pulls me in for the tightest hug of my life, and there's a glimmer here of hope, of comfort, of a different path where the band doesn't matter and the most important thing is this closeness with him, with his arms around my waist and mine around his neck and my tears flowing into his shirt because the best thing about Elliott is that he's never asked or needed me to be anything but myself.

"I'm so sorry," he repeats over and over again. "Whatever you need, we'll figure it out. I'm here, Mia. I have you."

Youthfulness is an excuse, sure, but how vastly different our responses are to the other's worst moments. Elliott finds out he's going to be a father with his ex, whose dad leads the charge to ostracize and alienate him, and I run away. I find out I'm jobless at thirty-five with no useful life skills, and he pulls me in closer.

"I don't deserve you," I choke out.

He kisses the top of my head, long and sweet. "You deserve the world, Mia," he whispers.

When you travel around the country, you're introduced to landmarks and communities shaped by the elements: Tiny mid-western airports with signs guiding you to the tornado shelter. Cities that have rebuilt after catastrophic hurricanes. A state that was formed by volcanoes. Mountain ridges dotted with wind turbines. I've often wondered which element is the most powerful, as one does when riding a bus on a narrow highway through the prairies, and when I finally stood at the South Rim of the Grand Canyon, I knew.

Emotions are a flood. And no matter how strong I thought the dam was that I built to contain them, it's no match for Elliott. His embrace, his growling 'you deserve the world,' his *everything*, may as well be a truckload of C4 molded across the Hoover Dam of my heart.

I tighten my hold around his neck and let the tears fall with no attempt to stop them. "I don't know what I'd do without you, El. I love you so much."

Every muscle in his body tenses, but his grip around my waist loosens as he tries to back out of our hug. "You what?"

Shit. "No! I'm sorry." I pull away and hide the lower half of my face in my hands. Elliott's eyes are as wide as mine feel, and he's unsmiling, frozen in the aftermath of a hug that ended too abruptly. "I didn't—" I didn't think. I didn't mean to say it out loud. I didn't consider that everything changes when you say those words out loud, no matter how long you've lived with them without saying them. I didn't tell him when I first knew, twenty years ago.

And, maybe the biggest mistake of all, I didn't check my surroundings before letting him hold me and kiss me and tell me he has me.

CHAPTER 47

now

"YOU'VE GOT TO BE freaking kidding me."

I don't need to turn my head to recognize Julie's angry voice, but it might be more comforting to see my pissed off best friend than to keep looking at Elliott's pinched brows and set jaw, wondering what's going through his head. Better to dance with the devil you know, and all that.

But of course it's not just Julie glaring at us. Okay, she's the main glarer. Mrs. Bailey looks shell-shocked but not displeased, Jess looks amused, and Zoe... well, Zoe looks hurt.

"You said nothing was happening. You promised," Zoe mutters, her eyes wet and shifting between her dad and me. "So that was you, then, the other night?" she asks, her cold stare landing on me.

I drop my head in a nod, an admission of guilt. "I can explain—" I step toward her, but she shakes her head.

"Don't bother. I wouldn't believe you anyway." Then she storms off, back toward the party.

Julie uses Zoe's exit as her opportunity to express her own seething disappointment. "I let it go before, El, but do you seriously have to sleep your way through all my friends?"

"You have no idea what you're talking about," Elliott snorts.

Jess touches Julie's arm, but Julie shrugs it off to point an accusing finger at her brother. "Bullshit. You and Syd were together *all* the time. I saw her car parked at your place before. And I know you were with her the night she died." Her eyes narrow and her anger turns to the precipice of tears. "Are you the reason, El? Did you fight with her and screw things up like you always do? Are you the reason Sydney's dead?"

"No," he growls next to me. "You are."

"Both of you, stop." Mrs. Bailey takes a step between them, her fingers curled around Julie's shoulder. "You can do this later, but right now, the party—"

"Sorry, Mom, but I've already screwed that up too, so why not just get it all out there?" Elliott's eyes are locked on Julie, and he points a finger right back at her. "You are so obsessed with yourself that you can't even bear for other people to be happy. *That's* why Sydney's dead. Because she was on her way to you. To tell you she was offered a job in Oregon—her dream job—and she was so afraid of hurting you that she was thinking of not taking it. She told me over dinner, and she was sobbing, and I begged her, Jules. I begged her to wait, to let me drive, anything. But she—" His voice catches and he shakes his head, dropping his hand and biting his bottom lip. "She was stubborn."

"Stop it!" Mrs. Bailey yells, which silences everyone. In all the years I've known her, I've never heard her yell. "We're all going back inside, and you can talk about this later. But this is neither the time, nor the place."

Elliott rolls his eyes. "You're right, Mom. We should've done this years ago." He turns to me and asks if he can take me home, and I shake my head *no*, honestly shocked he's speaking to me after the bombshell earlier. "Okay. I'm going to find Zoe, and then I'm out. Enjoy your party, Sis." He storms past her on his way inside, Mrs. Bailey on his heels, hissing a lecture at him.

"Come on, Julie. Let's go back in," Jess pleads, winding their fingers together.

"Not yet," she says. "First I need to understand why my best friend would go behind my back—"

"Because you make it impossible, Jules, to do anything in front of you. Because everyone is so focused on *you* and what *you* want and the rules you set when we were kids that we can't risk openly doing anything that displeases you. Because of *this*, right here, right now. Because you are standing here at a party thrown *for you* by the very people you're berating, and you're surrounded by your wife and people who are here to celebrate you, meanwhile my world just imploded and you don't care about anything except how it affects *you*."

She sniffles and crosses her arms. "I can't believe you would say that to me."

As much as I love Julie, as much as I value our decades-long friendship, I can't keep sacrificing my own sanity to protect her. And today I just don't have it in me to care more about her than I do about me. "Go inside, Jules. Your party awaits."

I lead the way in, unsure if she's following me, uncaring either way. I pass Elliott, whose expression conveys far more compassion than I feel I deserve at present. And then Kiko takes my hand and pulls me aside as Carla and Ali create a diversion to draw attention away from the windows facing the parking lot and the forlorn guest of honor who's standing there.

"What happened out there?" Kiko asks, finding us two chairs at a table in the corner, away from everyone else. "Did I see Elliott kissing you? Does everyone know?"

Right. That happened. Somehow, in the mess of everything that came after, I forgot about that perfect moment. That tender 'we'll figure it out,' that 'I have you' that stitched the hemispheres of my entire world back together when they fractured.

"I told him, Kiko."

"Told him what?" She reads my face and gasps. "Oh! You *told* him, told him. That you—"

"Shh! Keep your voice down!"

"That you love him?" she finishes in a quiet squeal.

I look around, but everyone is up near the dessert table, hugging Julie and Jess as the party winds down. "Yes," I say without whispering, because what's the point? If Elliott knows, why not let everyone else hear it, too?

"What did he say?"

"Well, he didn't say it back, if that's what you're asking."

Kiko presses a finger to her lips. "But you know he does, right? Like, *I* know he does, and we're not even close."

"All I know is that I screwed things up with everyone." I don't bother sharing the catalyst—that awful phone call with Claudette—because what would it matter? Zoe's not talking to me, Julie's just yelling at me, and Elliott knows I love him but probably definitely doesn't love me back.

"How about this—the girls and I stay and help with cleanup, then I take you wherever you need to go. I'm your personal chauffeur for the rest of the day."

I take her up on her offer. Once the guests have gone, I tear down the decorations while the others help Julie and Jess load up their SUV with gifts, putting the overflow packages in Mrs. Bailey's car. Then Jess climbs into the car with her mother-in-law and waves goodbye to Julie, who heads off on her own.

With the group's help, we're cleaned up just moments later, and I send them home with leftover cupcakes and hors d'oeuvres as a thank you.

"Where to?" Kiko asks as we climb into her car, and I don't immediately know how to answer her. "Honey," she says when I pause, and she reaches across the console to hold my hand. "It'll all blow over. I promise. You're gonna be fine."

"Can you take me to the B and B, please?" The irony is not lost on me. If I would've just stayed there in the first place instead of trying to relive some childish memory, none of this would've happened.

"Sure." The pity in her voice is palpable.

We ride in silence until we approach the intersection where Sydney died, and Julie's car is pulled over just off the shoulder. "Change of plans. Can you stop here?"

CHAPTER 48

now

Down the little hill, just in front of the cross, I walk up next to Julie. "Am I interrupting?"

"No," she answers, sniffling. "Looks like I'm getting a two-for-one deal on my apology tour."

I nudge her elbow with mine, because I know she needs it. I know she needs to be reminded that we're friends, and sometimes friends argue. But most importantly friends love each other, and that requires a special kind of honesty. Also importantly, Kiko is still waiting in her car, parked just behind Julie's, in case this blows up spectacularly and I need to make a quick escape.

"I'm sorry for freaking out on you tonight."

It takes everything in me to not reply 'it's fine,' because it's *not* fine that she flipped out. Instead I wait for more.

"The shower was lovely, by the way. Thank you for helping Elliott and my mom plan it."

"Anytime."

She extends a leg in front of her, pressing her toes into the ground, watching as the spongy earth reacts when she moves her foot. "Am I that bad?" she finally asks.

"No," I answer. "You're not *bad*. It's just... I feel like you had this idea for your life for forever, and how we all fit into it. And it's really hard to live up to that, and it's not always what we want."

It's clear from the way she glances up at me sideways that this is news to her.

"Like how you decided that we'd all go to the same college, even though some of us knew that wasn't our path. And you decided we should all go to prom together, even if we wanted to go with an actual date."

"Might I remind you that you *did* go with a date?"

"Right. My first act of rebellion against your carefully laid plan," I note with a wink.

She can't help a snort. "Fair."

"Can I ask you something?"

She cocks her head in inquisitive permission.

"Why did you make the rule about Elliott?"

"What rule?"

"About none of us dating him."

She laughs, her voice brighter than I've heard it all day, and it's refreshing. "I never had a rule about that."

"You absolutely did! When we were thirteen, you were so against me even *liking* him."

"Well, right, because we were thirteen, and I thought boys were gross. Still do, turns out." She shrugs and clasps her hands under her belly. "I mean, I'm also protective of him, so as the years went on—especially after everything with Callie's dad—I wanted to make sure that whoever he was with wouldn't hurt him."

My pulse quickens. Two hours ago I would have been terrified to ask the question, but now I'm just afraid of her answer. Still, I need to know. "Do you think I would hurt him?"

She turns her gaze back to Sydney's cross, and my heart sinks. "Why don't I drive you home," she says. "Can you give me another minute alone here?"

I nod, even though she's not looking at me, and trek back to Kiko's car to get my things.

"Are you okay?" she asks.

"I think so."

When Julie joins us at the cars, Kiko gives her a hug, squeezes my hand, and takes off. Then Julie and I are seated and buckled, but she doesn't start the engine.

"I always knew you were going to leave. Even when I made the college plan, I kind of knew you weren't coming with us. Maybe that's why I made the plan in the first place, to try to tempt you to stay, so you would see how cool it could be if we were all together."

She's avoiding my question about Elliott, which means she's either sure I *would* hurt him and doesn't want to say it or she's sure I *wouldn't* hurt him and feels guilty for making me feel like I couldn't pursue him.

"You talked about me having this plan for my life, and I guess I always have. Maybe it's because I was afraid for so long about how people would respond when I came out. I knew I couldn't control what they said or how they treated me, so if I could at least make sure I had my people around me—" She shakes her head and traces the steering wheel with a shimmering baby-blue fingernail. "Everyone turned their back on Elliott when we were younger, and I was so afraid he'd just run. I knew you were going to get out of here. Can you imagine if you and Elliott were together? He'd have every reason to take off with you, and I... I didn't want to lose both of you."

"Jules, you haven't lost us. Just because I'm not physically here all the time doesn't mean I've left you. Your family is home to me. *You're* home to me. You really can't get rid of me that easily."

She shifts—it's a laborious process, navigating her belly around the wheel and settling into a tolerable position—to turn to face me. "You *left*, Mia. We're lucky if we get to see you once a year."

"There are different ways to leave, you know. You're so concerned about me going to New York or back to California, but you want to talk about losing people? Jules, you're *married*. You're practically four-and-a-half minutes away from having a baby. You just had all these people show up for you."

She rolls her eyes and shakes her head, then turns back to face out the windshield and starts the car. Basically, she's done with this conversation and is ready to get rid of me.

"You don't even make an effort to see your parents," she says as she drives off. "My mom hears it all the time from your mom, that you haven't been to Paris in more than two years."

"Everyone is so obsessed about how often I go or don't go to Paris, or how often I come home," I snap. "But why should I go out of my way to chase down my parents? No one's crossed state lines in the past decade to see me play, and I'm supposed to cross an ocean just to say hi? If I have to come home to see my family, then so do they."

I'm not proud that I've yelled at a pregnant woman twice in one day, but I am proud that I've stood up for myself. Finally.

"Well, I'm sorry you're so disappointed in all of us," Julie says with perfect disdain, her tone even and her hands gripping the wheel as she turns onto Elliott's street. "But you're wrong about one thing."

I swallow back the emotion in my throat. "What's that?"

"Elliott saw shows in three cities last year alone."

CHAPTER 49

now

I BREATHE A SIGH of relief that Zoe's car is gone. I need to talk to her, apologize, explain. But first I have to deal with Elliott and this bombshell from Julie. One crisis at a time.

Maybe it's nothing. Maybe Zoe asked to see the band, and maybe it's just more proof that Elliott's a great dad.

But maybe... maybe it's *everything*.

He's pacing the dining room when I come in, talking on his cell, massaging the back of his neck. He's still in the clothes from the party, his shirt unbuttoned and untucked, and everything about him seems so exhausted.

"I'll call you back," he says into the phone when he sees me standing just inside the door, though I'm pretty sure he hangs up before he finishes the phrase and has his arms around me before he can second guess it in light of the afternoon's accidental admission. But if what I suspect—what I hope—is true, then a blurted confession of love shouldn't faze him.

"Are you okay?" he asks, sliding back to scan my face. "Did you Uber home?"

"No, Jules brought me."

"Oh." He brushes a few stray hairs from my face, but even once they're tucked tenderly behind my ears his fingertips linger in a slow stroke along my cheek, my jaw. Then he clears his throat and backs away, gesturing toward the couch. "I offered to bring you—"

"I know you did. But I figured Zoe would prefer some time away from me." I lower myself onto the sofa, and Elliott takes a seat in his recliner, leaning forward with his elbows on his knees.

He gives a slight nod and wrings his hands. "You just missed her, actually—she went to Callie's for the night. She was upset, but we talked. She'll be fine."

I have no doubt that Zoe will bounce back, that she's probably already over the whole I'm-sleeping-with-her-dad thing, but I know how badly it sucks when people betray you. That hurt doesn't go away quickly.

"Can I ask you something?"

He raises his eyes to meet mine. "Anything."

"How long?"

The corner of his mouth curls upward at the question. "How long for what?"

I take a fortifying breath to push down, down, down all the questions I long to ask him:

How long have you been coming to my shows without telling me?

How long have you known how I feel?

How long have you loved me the way I love you?

Instead I ask the one that's been nagging at me for a week, buried under doubts and fears and a ticking clock, the one that's begging to see the light of day. So I throw it out into the blazing sun and pray we don't get burned.

"The first time we slept together, you said you *wanted this for so long*. And I just need to know—how long is so long?"

He knits his brows and purses his lips before dropping his gaze to his hands, examining each wrinkle and knuckle and cuticle.

"You can tell me it'd been ten minutes or ten years, that you're over it now, that it was an itch you needed to scratch—"

"You're not a fucking *itch*, Mia."

"So *how long*, El? How long have you been coming to shows in secret and how long have you wanted me?"

He snaps his eyes to mine. "You know about the shows?"

I nod. "How long?"

He huffs and rolls his eyes to himself like he's a kid about to admit something that he's afraid he'll be made fun of for. "I've seen every tour but two."

Every tour but two. And I never knew it. For sixteen years, Elliott's been coming to see me play, showing up for me, and I never once knew it—and everything could have been so different if only he'd told me.

"And the other—" My mouth is dry because I'm far too close to the sun. I'm Icarus, my wings are melting, and I give one final surge toward the light before I fall. "How long have you wanted—?"

"You? Us?" He fills in the word when I don't know how to finish my own question. Because now that I think about it, he didn't say he wanted me, only that he wanted 'this,' right before we had sex, and it's entirely possible I've read this whole situation wrong: that he was in a sex drought and I was the rain; that he's such a great friend that he's supported my career from the start; that our friends-with-benefits arrangement and the 'no relationships' rule weren't some elaborate scheme to test-drive something between us, and the whole deal really was all about satiating a physical need.

But then he wets his lips and bites the bottom one. "I don't know, Mia. All I know is that earlier, when you said you loved me? I prayed you meant it the way I do. Because I do. I have. Maybe sixteen years, maybe forever."

Elliott loves me. And he *has* loved me, maybe for as long as I've loved him and maybe longer.

In a perfect world I'd throw myself into his arms or drag him to bed or plead with him to repeat the words a million times until I grew tired of hearing them, which, for the record, would never ever happen. And, for the record, I'm aware that he hasn't actually said the phrase 'I love you,' but I'm not going to argue semantics when he's shown me that he loves me. In arenas and living rooms and high school make-out spots and beds; at fifteen and eighteen and every year "but two" between nineteen and thirty-five, he's shown me.

But it's not a perfect world, and right now the love I have for him is at the center of a whirlwind of a mess that I need to clean up.

I jump to my feet. "Can I borrow your keys?"

He eyes me with suspicion. "I tell you that I love you, and your first instinct is to leave?"

"No." Everything Julie said rushes through my brain. "Leaving is the last thing I want to do. But I have to fix things first. Can I please take your truck?"

He's already sliding his feet into the sneakers he keeps by the door. "I'll drive."

CHAPTER 50

now

Up first: Callie's house.

We make the thirty-minute drive so I can talk to Zoe, even though I fully expect her to slam the door in my face.

"You seem so nervous." Elliott takes my hand, kisses my knuckles, and rests our hands on my jittery leg. "I don't think you have much to worry about with Zo—she was mostly mad at me for, as she put it, 'adding fuel to the fire.' Apparently she's afraid I'm going to do something stupid and be immortalized in song."

It's this—this adorable naïveté—that draws a round of laughter that includes snorting, tears, and silent nostril flaring for a full minute.

"What's so funny?" he asks, a grin spreading on his lips.

"It's just funny how you've been to so many shows and heard all the songs and don't realize every single one's already about you."

His answering chuckle fills the cab of the truck, and it feels so natural and easy to be with him like this, in the mundanity of a normal, settled, *here* life.

"They're not *all* about me," he laughs.

"They pretty much are, I promise."

"Even—"

"Yes. Even *'Touch'*. Written after a visit home, a pretty graphic dream about you, and quality time with a vibrator that had the audacity to run out of battery before I was finished."

"So *'Insatiable'* was a follow-up?"

"No. That one the three of us wrote together after losing at the VMA's and getting drunk on wine coolers in Jenna's hotel room. That one's about a cupcake."

He flicks on his signal and turns into the driveway of a condo complex, and the ease of the last few minutes makes room for a renewed sense of dread.

"Anyway. The whole thing with Zoe is that she flat-out asked me if something was going on between us, and I lied to her. And I kept lying to her, and she deserves better than that."

"I'm here if you need me," he offers with another squeeze of my hand.

Callie opens the door before we can ring the bell and pulls me into an unexpected hug.

"Officially, and in solidarity with Zoe, I'm mad at both of you. But as a fan and a friend? This is awesome. It's about time," she whispers before pulling us in. "She's in her room, angsting. But you can go up," she tells Elliott, who nods and leads me up a set of stairs.

"You ready?"

I shrug. "Does it matter?"

He knocks on the door at the top of the stairs and cracks it open when Zoe calls "yeah?" from within.

"Hey," he says, peering inside through an opening just wide enough for his head to fit through. "I don't know how much time and space you wanted, and feel free to tell me—respectfully—to get lost, but Mia's here, and—"

"No."

Elliott sighs. "Can I come in, at least?"

She must nod, because he slips through the doorway and gently latches it behind him.

I retreat a few steps down, trying not to eavesdrop even though I'm dying to know what they're saying. Callie climbs the stairs with two steaming mugs in each hand.

"I have four hot cocoas, and one of them is spiked. Pick your poison."

"Um... regular, please."

"Works for me." She shrugs and positions a buttercup yellow mug in front of me. "You got this," she says as she passes me and knocks on Zoe's door with her knee.

Elliott opens it wide and lets Callie pass through, then motions for me to come in.

"We'll give you some privacy," Callie says once all the mugs are distributed.

"You can stay, if you want." I wouldn't normally invite an audience to a private conversation, but the way Zoe's eyes widen when Callie and Elliott head for the door tells me she'd rather have them here. "And if it's okay with Zoe, of course."

Callie and Elliott exchange a glance when she says "It's fine," but they stay standing along the wall while I lower myself onto the floor a few feet from Zoe.

"First, thank you. I know I screwed up, but I appreciate that you're willing to talk to me. And second, but more importantly, I'm sorry. And I can try to explain why I lied or answer any questions you have or just go. Whatever you want."

She raises an eyebrow and taps her fingernails against the mug. "I told you it was fine, Mia."

"I know."

"And you lied anyway."

"I did."

"Why?"

Okay, maybe I didn't think through the whole invite-her-parents-to-stay thing, because I don't know what's already out there in the open. But I also know I'm tired of secrets, even if they aren't mine.

"The simplest answer is, at the moment you asked, I didn't think anything else would happen between your dad and me." I can feel Elliott's gaze on me, can feel my face flush, because this apology to Zoe is a confession to her parents, too.

"But something had happened already?"

"Sort of? Nothing serious. Or, at least, we weren't calling it serious."

It also strikes me here and now, at the absolute worst opportunity, that I don't know how open people are with their teenagers about their sex lives or, more generally, how to talk about sex with teenagers.

"Look, I have loved your dad since I was younger than you are now."

Callie stiffens in my periphery, and I know she's crunching the numbers and coming to the same conclusion I reached back then: that Elliott was off limits to me, largely because of her.

"We kissed exactly once, back when I was in high school, but I gave up on the idea that he and I would ever be anything more than friends well before you were born. So when I got back into town for a few weeks and we found ourselves in the same house where we both grew up, watching the same movies, eating the same snacks, I just—I let myself get carried away. But the night before you asked me if something was happening, I had decided it was over." I shrug and inhale as Elliott pushes himself off the wall.

"Why?" he asks, and everyone's attention turns to him. "Why was it over for you?"

"For the same reason your sister doesn't want us to be together. Because you had shown me—" I stop short of mentioning the ring, because I don't want to spoil all the secrets if it had been meant for Callie as I've suspected it had been. "You'd shown me how much it hurt to love someone and watch them leave. And I didn't want that for myself. Not again."

His jaw tenses, and I move on before he can press further.

"And I know it was the wrong choice, but when things... progressed... after that, he even asked if we should tell people, and I said no. I figured I'd be going back to L.A. soon, so what was the point in getting anyone worked up about it?"

"By 'anyone,' she just means Julie, right?" Callie asks Elliott in a mumbled half-whisper.

"Well, that worked out well, didn't it?" Zoe smirks and rolls her eyes. "You could've trusted me to keep the secret."

"She did. We both did," Elliott interjects, but though he's speaking to his daughter, his eyes are on me. "We didn't want to burden you with the guilt of keeping our secret."

"Right," I add. "Because frankly? All the secret keeping sucks."

Maybe Zoe's at her breaking point because she roars at that, and the rest of us relax a little, exchanging nervous glances like we're afraid she'll course-correct back to anger. Instead, once she composes herself, she looks at me, then at her dad, and then back. "So now what?"

Elliott responds. "Now, I mean, you can stay here or come back with us—"

"No, Dad. I'm going to stay here a few more days. But I mean, what's next for you two?" She waves a finger between us. "You love each other, right?"

"Yes," we answer in unison, Elliott firmly and I a little warily, like we're about to get slapped with a huge test that we didn't have a chance to study for.

"Okay," Zoe repeats. "So what's next?"

"Next, we talk to your aunt. And then we talk to each other." He aims a half-smile in my direction, and I wish I felt a fraction of the confidence he exudes in so matter-of-factly stating the next step.

♫♪

You'd think I was about to walk onto a stage in front of a few thousand people the way I go through my 'get hype' ritual: a few jumps in place, rolling my neck, stretching my arms, wiggling my fingers.

Elliott, now seated between his parents after making his own apology to Julie, arches an eyebrow in a way that says 'I'm questioning everything I ever thought I knew about you,' and Mr. Bailey's eyes shift between me and Mrs. Bailey's amused expression in a way that says 'what in the absolute hell have I just witnessed.'

And Jess, the one we figured was most likely to stand guard and prevent me from talking to Julie again, was on her way out when we arrived. "I have craving tacos to buy," she said, zipping her jacket. "If she gets pissed, our paths never crossed. Got it?"

"You sounded ridiculous up there, just so you know," Julie says as a greeting when I make it to the bottom of the stairs. Next to her, she's got a huge bowl of popcorn with candy mixed in, which she doesn't offer to share with me, but at least she pauses the movie she's watching.

I don't give in to her attempt to bait me into an argument. Instead I sit on the far end of the old couch, and I break from my carefully rehearsed script at line one, because it's too easy. "Right there—right where you're sitting right now? That's where I had my first kiss with Elliott. My first real kiss, ever."

As far as openings go, it seems to be an effective attention-getter. She squirms and shifts like she wants to move to a different cushion, but she knows if she does it's admitting defeat.

"And it's right there—" I point to the next cushion over, "that I made a move. Actually, you might remember this. That night you thought I was naked and watching porn?" I shake my head grinning at the memory, knowing it's going to agitate her. "Nope. Second base with Elliott. And there, and there?" I point to the corner cushion and the one on the far left. "It's where we fell asleep together, my very first night back in town."

She curls her feet up next to her and crosses her arms, defiant. Stubborn. Julie. "Your point?"

"Not trying to make a point. Just needed to lay it all out there. Because I'm so tired of lying and hiding and pretending. I love him, Jules. And yes, when I was thirteen, I *did* have a crush on him. When I was fifteen I fell in love, which I only realized when I was sixteen. And at eighteen he broke my heart and no one knew it. And yes, that's why I left then, because I couldn't stand to be here and face him every day. But Jules, I love him. Still. Always. And he apparently loves me, too."

I move a few cushions closer and take her hand in mine. Her face softens, the steely resolve cracking and breaking and revealing the tender friend who hurts just like everyone else behind the hardened façade.

"You are and always will be my very best friend. I am so happy for you now, just like I was when you found Jess, and when you got married, and when you got your Master's, and when you made those really cute clay frogs at your pottery class."

"Kate and Leo-toad," she remembers with a sniffle and a quivering smile.

"Yes! And our friendship is not conditional based on proximity, and it's not conditional based on metrics like how many minutes we spend FaceTiming each week, or how many times we meet up for dinner each year. What is required, though, is that we let each other grow and live, and that we celebrate each other's happiness. And Jules—your brother makes me really, really happy."

She swipes the back of her free hand across her eyes. "But what happens when he breaks your heart again, or when you split up? I can't be in the middle and I can't lose you just because I'm biologically connected to him."

"Slow down, okay?" I laugh. "You're jumping into a future of hypotheticals that we're not ready for yet. Elliott and I haven't even talked about next steps. Hell, I have no idea what's next, with the band breaking up—"

"Wait, what? When? Why?"

"You sound like a reporter covering her bases." She doesn't react to my sad attempt at humor, which I think is a sign that the fight is fizzling and fading. "Earlier today. But it's fine. It's honestly probably for the better. We'll talk about it some other time. I just want to make sure we're okay."

She nods, wriggling her nose with one more sniffle. "Can I say one more thing? And you can think I'm awful, because maybe I am, but it's just something that's nagged at me for a while."

"Sure."

"It hurt," she tells me after a deep breath, "that you weren't here two years ago."

I should have felt this coming, but it catches me off guard. "It doesn't make you sound awful at all."

"No—the awful part is that I was hurt for myself. Like I sat there mourning Syd and throwing a concurrent pity party for myself because I spiraled and thought, '*Would she have come home if this was my funeral? Would I have been enough of a reason for her to come back?*'" Fresh tears spring from her eyes, the kind that gather little by little over time, unassuming, until the dam breaks from the weight and force of them.

"Not coming back for Sydney's funeral is one of my biggest regrets. At the time, I didn't see how I could, and even now I can't deny the challenges associated with trying to make it work within a tour schedule when all the dates are set in stone. But I like to think I showed up to support Syd's family in other ways, and I like to think your stubborn ass will outlive us all."

"And if I don't?" she asks, laughing through the tears.

I wipe a thumb over her cheek, drying it with a gentle stroke. "Then I'll be there to give the eulogy."

CHAPTER 51

now

"SORRY TO INTERRUPT." JESS peeks through the space between wall and railing, catching us mid side-hug as I feel for baby kicks and hiccups.

Julie waves her down from the stairs, and Elliott follows close behind.

The tears are long dry and it's well past eleven, and my stomach growls, taunted by the aroma of queso and chipotle chicken.

"I should head out," I announce as Jess unbags the tacos. I pull Julie in one more time. "We good?" I ask, my cheek smooshed against her temple.

"We're good."

♫♪

Have I mentioned that I love Elliott Bailey? The man gets me. Like, sure, he's a genius in bed. Intuitive, reactive, proactive. Awesome. But even better—at this particular moment in time, anyway—is that he pulls up to the Tacodilla drive through and orders half a dozen tacos with chips and guac.

"Thanks again for your help tonight." I let my head fall onto his shoulder as we wait for our food, and he weaves his fingers into mine.

"I was just the chauffeur. You did the hard part." He turns and kisses the top of my head. "So you guys are definitely good?"

"We are. Thanks for being there."

"Always."

A burly man in a green polo shirt passes a white paper bag and plastic cup to Elliott through the drive through window, and we take off toward home. "I learned some pretty interesting things tonight," he says.

"Really? Like what?" I'm not sure what there was to learn other than I'm an over-sharer with his daughter, and I sip my virgin margarita while I wait for him to say something profound-ish, like he discovered the true meaning of Christmas, or found the exact coordinates for Sasquatch's cave.

But no, he responds with, "I learned that if the vents in my parents' living room floor are open and you're really, really quiet, you can hear a good amount of conversation from my parents' basement. And I learned that my parents think second base is just open-mouth kissing, so you're safe there."

I am absolutely horrified, but honestly? At least I've gotten through the night without anyone asking me if I wrote "Touch" about Elliott.

"Did you learn anything else tonight?"

He tightens his grip on my fingers and brings my hand to his lips. "I learned that I'm the luckiest man on the planet."

♫♩

"So help me, if you sing that song one more time—"

I'm sprawled on the sheets of Elliott's bed, dressed only in an old T-shirt of his, while he brushes his teeth. The house is empty, and tonight would be a great night to challenge him to his "every room in the house" comment from a few nights ago, but I'm thoroughly exhausted and just ready to get some sleep.

"It's just so catchy." He winks from the doorway, brushing his teeth, mumble-singing around the toothbrush when he disappears to the bathroom. The faucet runs and I hear his tired, scratchy voice singing softly, "Oh I get a rush every time you touch me, ohh."

"It's kind of hot," he says, stripping out of his T-shirt and humming a few more bars. "Knowing you wrote that song about me. And why you wrote it."

I peel my eyes off him and roll onto my side, waiting for him to come hold me. "There's more where that came from."

"Oh yeah?" he slides in behind me, drapes an arm around my middle, kisses my shoulder. "What are you thinking?"

"I'm thinking I really want to sleep. But tomorrow, or over the next few days, I want you to do the thing you want to do."

"Hm? What's that?"

Coyly, or as coyly as I can be when I'm so tired I could make Rip Van Winkle's twenty-year slumber look like the blink of an eye, I ask, "*Every* room of this house?"

"Most of them," he breathes, settling more deeply into his ultra-relaxed sleep snuggle position. "Think of the songs you could write."

I laugh, and he laughs, and for right now the songs and the work and the future don't matter. All that matters is that I love Elliott and he loves me, and I am exactly where I've always wanted to be: held in his arms, and in his heart.

CHAPTER 52
now

THE BLISS OF BEING honest, the joy of freely loving and being loved, is short lived. Yes, there's post-breakfast sex. Yes, there's a post- post-breakfast-sex co-shower and some strategic body-wash application techniques. And, yes, we ride hand-in-hand in Elliott's truck to the main strip of Songbird Springs, and we walk hand-in-hand into the coffee shop, and stroll hand-in-hand along the street on a day that feels decidedly *spring*, not just in temperature but in promise and new beginnings.

But of course it can't be that easy. Of *course* my phone rings, and Claudette's face pops up on the screen, and Elliott nods for me to take it.

"I'm here," he says, the abbreviated vow from yesterday: *I'm here, I have you.* He takes my coffee to free up my hands, and I take the call on speaker.

"I've been thinking." Despite her total lack of greeting, Claudette seems happier, more thoughtful, less pissed (and justifiably so) than she was in yesterday's conversation. "Can you get out here on Wednesday?"

"Wednesday?" I glance toward Elliott, who cocks his head and frowns at the phone before looking up at me, and he nods with a shrug. "Um, sure? Everything okay?"

"Great. We're good. Send me your flight details and I'll have a car pick you up."

She ends the call just as abruptly as she began it, and Elliott asks, "What do you think she wants?"

"No clue, but looks like I'm heading back to L.A. on Wednesday."

"I'll come with you. If you want. For moral support."

I shake my head, pocketing my phone and reclaiming my coffee. "You don't have to do that."

"And if I want to?"

Is this what it's like to have someone truly love you? To show up for you when you don't know they're there and to go with you into the unknown?

"I'd love for you to come to L.A.—I can show you around—but I don't want to steal you away from Zoe."

"I'll check in, but she's planning to stay with Callie a few nights, and I'm sure she'd be happy to stay a few extra days. And I've got vacation time I never use. And I want to see your life in L.A." He slides his hand into mine and we continue our walk back to the truck.

Once we're home, he's calling Zoe and I'm booking flights—one way, for now, because Elliott reminds me that I have a life in L.A., one that I don't know that I necessarily want now that I know that maybe I could have—or *do* have—a life here.

♫♩

The car Claudette sent for us swings by my apartment so we can drop off our bags and freshen up after the cross-country flight, and an hour later we're waiting in the lobby at her offices. Elliott comes along for moral support but promises to make himself scarce if Claudette wants this to be a solo meeting.

And it's clear from the moment she struts into the lobby that she's only interested in me.

"Hopefully your time back east has been good, all things considered," she says as she closes her office door.

It has been good, and also awful, and also incredible. "Yes," I agree. "It's been good."

"Sorry to drag you all the way back here, but I wanted to do this in person. Read body language, all that jazz."

I smooth out a wrinkle in my dress but don't otherwise respond.

Claudette wheels her chair under her desk and tents her finger above it. "I hate that the Flowers are done."

My heart sinks because I hate it too, and because I have no idea where she's going with this.

"What you sent me, Mia—I'm excited by it. It's fresh and raw, and I really think it should be out there. Fans will love it. So I was thinking—what if you did it on your own?"

I nearly choke on my own saliva. "Sorry. What?"

"Go solo, Mia. I want to manage you on your own, as a solo act."

"That's such a nice offer, but I don't think—"

"You can, Mia. I know you're going to say you can't do it, but you can. Especially with songs like the ones you sent me. I still have your studio time scheduled next week, and I'll book extra time in a month or two or whenever you can have a full album ready. But only if you want to. If you're not into it, fine. But I wanted to get your thoughts."

My thoughts are everywhere. In disbelief, in excitement, in possibility and hope, in fear, and with the man in the lobby, who would tell me to do it.

"Can I think about it?"

♫♪

Okay, I enjoy having Elliott in my bed as much as I enjoy being in his. But here I have a home-field advantage, and I very much enjoy the surge of confidence that gives me.

"I still think you should do it," he says, panting, gripping my hips, grinding into me.

"Are you trying to get rid of me already?"

"No. God, *yes*, Mia."

"That's not confusing," I say with a laugh, bending to meet his lips, dragging my nails along his side. "Which is it? No, or yes?"

"*Yes*, please keep doing what you're doing. *No*, I don't want to get rid of you."

"Good, because you can't. But maybe we can table this topic till tomorrow? Just enjoy tonight?"

He tilts his head back and pulls me down firmly onto him, moaning my name into my ear, tugging at my hair, as I kiss his neck and come undone. "Only if we can enjoy tomorrow, too."

♫♪

Showing Elliott around L.A. would have been a dream at any point since I moved out here twelve years ago, but today it feels tedious. The city seems like a stranger, like a Tinder date who has matched with someone else when you stepped away to use the bathroom in the middle of dinner, transient and new and quick to move on. Still, we visit all my favorite spots and make it home with a bag of carryout for dinner.

"Have you decided what you're going to do?" Elliott asks over the remnants of his burger.

"Not even close. I think I'm further from a decision now than I was yesterday."

We avoided the difficult conversation all day, distracted by the sights and sounds and hustle and bustle of downtown and the beach, but now, here, there's nowhere to hide from it. And suddenly this giant city seems too small, like if I stay here I'll suffocate, because Elliott has shown me how to breathe again and I'll forget how if he's not around.

"What do you want? Like, perfect world, what would you do?"

In a *perfect* perfect world, I'd climb into bed with Elliott and only get out for holidays. In a perfect world, we'd make up for twenty years of lost time: of lost *I love you*s and lost hand holding and lost small talk. But I'd also miss making music, especially after the last few weeks have opened something in me again. But who's to say that the in-bed-with-Elliott world and the music-making world are both even options?

"What would you do? Not if you were me, but what do *you* want to do? What's your perfect world?"

He clears our trash from the table and drops it in the bin under the sink, his brow pinched in thought. "You can have a great future in music, if that's what you want, Mia. But you can also have a future with me, if that's what you're really asking."

"But how do I have both?" I wonder aloud, the question more rhetorical than answer-seeking.

The sound of a keyboard snaps me out of my daze. Rather, the sound of Elliott playing a keyboard snaps me out of my daze.

"Since when do you play keys?" I ask, because Elliott wasn't exceptionally musical growing up. He has a gentle voice when he sings, low and warm, but I've never seen him with an instrument. And now he's sitting in my living room, playing a familiar melody on my practice keyboard, humming the main melody for "Touch."

He grins, and he looks fifteen again, that familiar spark flashing in his eyes and an indisputable joy filling his smile. "There's so much you don't know about me."

I move to the living room and sit cross legged on the couch next to the keyboard. "So tell me everything."

CHAPTER 53

thirteen years ago // Elliott

SEEING MIA ON STAGE—IN our hometown, of all places—was surreal.

Mia, the shy kid my sister adopted into our family on the first day of kindergarten.

Mia, the tomboy who did not hold back in water balloon fights.

Mia, the one who always knew the right thing to say.

Mia, who wore my hoodie the night before my world changed.

Mia, who seemed to want to kiss me as much as I wanted to kiss her.

Mia, who left. Who broke my heart.

Mia, who'd written songs that I hoped were about me, and some I prayed were not.

Mia, whose absence was profoundly felt, and whose presence again after four years in New York was the reason I ventured out to a town-wide event despite generally trying to avoid the public.

I'd never really struggled with impulse control, but when Julie told me Mia was coming home I found myself at the Ferryton Gallery after work, spending money I didn't really have to buy a ring for someone who might not even love me.

But if she did... If she did love me, she could have come back home and we could have reset the clock to four years prior, and we could have had it all.

I could see why she flirted with Theo Jeffries. His hair didn't look so stupid anymore, and if you removed yourself a degree or two from the whole prom fiasco you could appreciate how he invited Mia in the first place and could understand why he needed to go after his crush when her own heart was broken.

Look, I'm not saying the guy's a saint, because I still hated him a little for breaking Mia's heart. Even if that's what led to her sitting on the couch in my parents' basement and what led to us finally kissing.

But honestly? Theo was always decent. After college graduation he got a job right away teaching music at Hope Middle School in down-town Ferryton, and apparently the kids loved him.

So when I saw him standing in the doorway after Mia's band played I didn't think much of it. Not until I saw Mia—a little tipsy and a lot handsy—slip her arms around his neck and let her body go slack as he snaked his arms around her back. They were laughing, and I could hear bits and pieces of their conversation, and even though mistletoe hung above them they never moved to kiss, which was promising for me.

I took a breath, ready to interrupt their reunion, hopeful to talk to her and rehearsing the whole *"you're the greatest gift"* speech one more time. And then I took one step forward, followed by another, and I could hear more clearly.

"Germany in six months, then Italy and Sweden, Hungary and France, and then who knows?"

"And L.A.'s good?" Theo asked. "You find a place out there?"

"Mhmm," she nodded. "It's little, but it works, you know? And it's *L.A.*! And I couldn't have done it—" she said, and what came after I never heard, because I knew I had to let her go.

From the moment I bought the ring my biggest fear was that Mia would say no. But when I heard about her new life and new opportuni-ties, I was terrified she'd say yes. I knew that Mia was not meant for Friday nights at O'Donnell's and yard work and desk jobs and joint custody and me, and I walked away from Mia and Theo and the party and my dream so that she would pursue hers.

Because Mia was a flower, and she needed to bloom.

And days later, after the new year when everyone had returned to their regularly scheduled lives, I bumped into Theo at the café. And I don't know what came over me, other than I was filled with the profound joy that Mia was pursuing her dreams and the profound grief that I wasn't part of them, but I sat down at his table, uninvited, and asked him a question I hoped would change my life.

"Any chance you offer music lessons to adults?"

CHAPTER 54

now

"So you learned to play the piano for me?"

He nods, still playing.

"And then you just... waited? For a decade?"

"Yep."

"Why?"

He shrugs like he's trying to find words for an answer I should already know. And then the tune changes to something unknown, and he smiles with a puffy exhale. And then... then Elliott sings.

> I hear your voice in my dreams
> singing sweet, meant for me
> on repeat.
> Day and night, time stands still
> but years go by.
> I'm incomplete.
> It's killing me.
>
> Could I have fixed it?
> Would you have let me?
> How did it go so wrong?
> What if I'm only destined
> to tell you I love you
> in my heartbreak song?

In a myriad of ways, Elliott has shown that he loves me. But this? This one's pretty incredible. I dry my cheeks with my sweater sleeve and soak in the fact that while I was writing songs about Elliott, he wrote this one for me. That he learned how to play piano for me. That he loved me for so long.

"Why didn't you tell me?" I ask when he's finished, and I've given up on trying to dry my tears when my sleeve is already saturated with them.

He shrugs and scans the floor between us before meeting my eyes. "I never wanted to intrude on your life. I knew you left for a reason, and I thought for a little while that maybe the reason was me, and I didn't want to impose all the negative on your new life. But if you needed me, or, somehow, *wanted* me in the future, I wanted to be ready." He pulls my hands into his, stroking the back of each with his thumbs. "Because I want you to have the life you've dreamed of, and because I want to be part of it."

"So just to be clear... you want to join the now-non-existent band?"

"To be crystal clear, I want to be wherever you are."

"And what about Zoe?"

"She's moving off to college in a few months."

"And your family?"

"They have each other at home. And they'll still have me, just... wherever you are." He moves from the bench to the seat next to me, our knees touching and hands woven together. "If you want to make music, I want to do it with you. If you think this is a really stupid idea and you want to find actual professionals to work with, that's fine too. But if I can't be your bandmate, please at least let me be a roadie or something—I don't want to miss out on more time with you."

I nod against the fresh wave of emotions that threatens to crush me. "Let's sleep on it and talk through it in the morning. Besides, we need to talk about the whole *you-bought-a-ring-before-we-had-ever-dated* thing."

"What's there to talk about?" His smile relaxes with his body. "Don't we all do crazy things when we're in love?"

Like buying rings. Like learning to play an instrument. Like running away and devoting your life to music.

Like building a thriving career from your heartache.

Like walking away from it all.

Like running toward a future that's unknown and scary and hopeful and bright.

Elliott kisses me, and we sink into the cushions and topple to the floor and love each other in every room of my apartment.

CHAPTER 55

the summer

ELLIOTT KNOWS HOW TO throw a party. Not that the ill-fated baby shower wasn't evidence enough of that—before all the ill-fated stuff started, anyway—but Zoe's eighteenth is a masterpiece. A perfect blend of style and fun and laughter; youthful and joyous, just like her.

And it doesn't hurt that he hired a decent band to perform.

"Hired" is a bit of a stretch, considering we played for free. But we did get to try out some songs that we wrote together, and the reception was great. Which is a good sign, I guess, considering that in six weeks we'll be opening for ten dates of a regional tour.

"So you're really doing it, huh?" Julie sidles up beside me, bounce-rocking from left to right as baby Devon coos in her arms. At just three weeks old he's simultaneously adorable and terrifying, but three weeks ago in Julie's hospital room he was also a little gooey, so this is a decided improvement.

The summer breeze blows across the Baileys' back yard and though most of the extended family has long since gone home, Zoe's friends are committed to a full day of revelry.

"Have you ever played Capture the Flag Water Balloon Tag?" Elliott had asked the kids with a wink and a nod my way, and after some initial skepticism there was an epic battle. Once again, Elliott and I were on opposite sides, and once again his team won, but this time, I did too. Because this time when his arm snaked around my waist I got to fall into it, hold him myself, enjoy it, not have to hide.

Now the sun sets over a gaggle of teenagers on layers of blankets spread across the perfectly manicured lawn, and the sun sets on this chapter.

"We're really doing it."

"You still have a few weeks, you know." Elliott sneaks in behind us, wrapping me in his arms and ducking to rest his chin on my shoulder. "You don't have to get super sappy yet."

Julie rolls her eyes with a grin and readjusts Devon to her other arm. "For the record, I'm always sappy these days. Are we still good for brunch tomorrow?" she asks me.

"Yes," I confirm. "I'll be at your place at eleven."

"We should get going; show starts in an hour," he says with a kiss to my temple. "Meet me at the truck?" I nod as he hugs Julie and kisses the top of Devon's head, then takes off toward the lawn to say goodbye to Zoe, too.

"Promise you'll play at O'Donnell's again when I have the mental fortitude to be apart from my child and can actually have a drink or two to celebrate?"

I laugh along with Julie and envelop her in a hug, careful not to squish the baby. "Just say when, and we'll be there." I mean it, and she knows it. We were in the middle of a recording session when Jess called to tell us Jules was in labor, and we still made it across the country in time to greet our little nephew as he entered the world. Elliott's official nephew, my honorary one.

"I'll be fine." We both know this, too. Because Julie has always been fine, even when she didn't know it, and because she knows that even when we're not right here, we're still there for her.

"Eleven o'clock. See you then." With a little wave and a smile that matches hers, I take off for Elliott's truck.

♫♩

"Maybe this was a mistake."

We're almost at O'Donnell's, and there's a bead of sweat along his hairline that I'm guessing is not a result of the mild temperature outside.

"It's normal to be nervous, but it's just doing what you've been doing. What *we've* been doing."

"Well, not *everything* we've been doing."

I hang my arm out the window, letting it surf the evening air. "Are you having second thoughts? Regretting the decision to join me?"

He finds my other hand on my thigh and takes it in his own. "Babe, I have a lot of regrets in life, but none of them involve spending extra time with you."

When I talked to Claudette two months ago about my decision, she initially—understandably—resisted. "It's untested, Mia. They know nothing about him."

"They know a lot, actually," I argued. "Because I've been singing about him for years."

That was enough to convince her to at least hear us, and she praised the chemistry. "That could be your band name—The Chemistry, The Alchemy... something like that."

"Or—" We'd already laughed about it in bed the night prior, half-dressed in a tangle of limbs and linens. "What if we just call ourselves Neon?"

She thought for a moment, nodding along as she considered it. "It's elemental, it sort of ties back to the idea of The Fluorescent Flowers for some recognition... it could work." And then it was a whirlwind of studio time, auditions to round out the band, traveling for interviews, writing sessions, rehearsals... but for the next two weeks we get to relax here before going back to L.A. and finishing tour prep.

First up, though, is an hour at O'Donnell's, which lets us test which songs from our setlist are best received by the crowd so we can narrow things down for a five-song set for the tour.

Elliott pulls into the lot and kills the engine, then stares out the windshield at the concrete wall ahead of him. I know these nerves, this doubt, and I brush a thumb over his cheek. "You're going to be great. I have you, too, you know."

He presses a kiss to the inside of my wrist and smiles. "Let's do it."

The familiar faces in the bar make it almost easy to play and sing: from Kiko's wine-buzzed dancing to Carla's wide-smiled head bopping to Elliott's friend Darci's on-beat clapping, there's a comfort here that lets us focus on the joy of music and the excitement of making it—doing anything, really—together.

I used to imagine how nice it would be to come home from work and have Elliott hold open the door and take my coat and kiss me, still in the doorway, welcoming me home. But honestly? Having him with me on stage, feet away, gazing at me with the same love and adoration I've felt for him for more than half a lifetime? Knowing the near future means walking with him, hand-in-hand, into a tour bus or whatever hotel room we're staying in? Knowing that *home* is a relative term; knowing that *home* is where Elliott is?

It's better than anything I could ever have imagined.

CHAPTER 56

eleven months later

"I CAN'T BELIEVE HE'S already one." It's at least the tenth time I've said it, but it's true. Somehow, Devon went from this tiny, fragile thing to a nearly toddling toddler with bulbous cheeks and chunky leg rolls. All that to say, I'm happy to hold him now, and snuggling him at his party was a highlight. "It's just gone by so fast."

"Get ready, because each year seems to pass faster than the one before it." Elliott turns up the radio and hums along to the song—*our* song—before lacing his fingers into mine. "Are you up for a detour?"

I feel like life has been one giant detour to this moment, like we took the long way around to becoming an us, and if I can spend two decades on one detour, why not spend two hours on another? "Sure. What do you have in mind?"

And that's how we find ourselves in the bed of his truck at Swallow's Ridge, my head on his chest, gazing out at the sunset. "I wrote a song here," I confess. "When I thought you loved someone else and could never love me."

"I wrote you letters here. Telling you how much I missed you. How I felt."

I twist to look at him, resting my chin on my hand over his heart. "I never got letters."

"I never sent them." He kisses the top of my head and traces invisible words on my arm. Words that feel like *love* and *forever*. "I figured you were busy with the guy you wrote about in *Touch*."

"And now?"

"Now," he says, tilting my chin and bending forward to meet my lips with his, "now I want you to be very busy with the guy you wrote about in *Touch*."

We scramble, laughing, back into the truck, and as soon as we're home I turn to go upstairs. But Elliott has other ideas and hoists me over his shoulder to carry me down the stairs to our basement—which is now half music room and half home theater, complete with a familiar wraparound couch we just had to take when his parents replaced it with something more comfortable. Framed in a large shadow box above the TV is an old, loved, plush neon daisy.

Elliott pulls me onto his lap and weaves his hands into my hair, and the hesitation from our very first kiss is replaced with the urgency of someone who missed too much already, the need to never let go.

"You guys had better be decent!" Julie's voice calls from the stairs.

We are, but we're not, and I can feel Elliott's want below me. Oh, the joys of your family having keys to your home so they can house sit when you're on tour.

Still, Julie descends with a bag of pre-made chocolatey popcorn. Jess is right behind her with a travel game console and controllers, then Ali, Kiko, and Carla with wine and glasses. "Mom and Dad have Devon for their traditional grandchild birthday sleepover," Julie announces with a grin, plopping onto the cushion next to ours. "So I decided I'd kick all your asses one more time before I get the best sleep I've had in eighteen months."

Jess sets up the game and the tournament starts, and everyone's just as into the competition as we ever were.

I soak it all in during a bye round for me, catching Kiko's eye across the room as she does the same. She raises a glass and smiles, and between Grand Prix races Elliott kisses my jaw and whispers 'I love you' into my skin, followed by a growled promise of what we're going to do when everyone leaves.

The basement is filled with shrieking laughter and conversation, memories and plans, sounds of family and friendship and history and wholeness. All on the cushions of a decades-old sofa that's seen us through it all. All exactly as I've ever wanted it to be.

God, this couch.

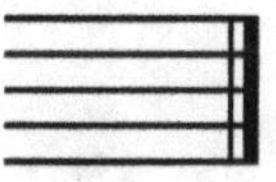

ACKNOWLEDGEMENTS

It's 1:04 A.M. and I have to wake up at 6 for work. But I also just realized I never typed this page, and I really want to get it done because I presently feel just sentimental enough to do it without sobbing.

This book is my heart and soul. It's my childhood, my memories, and my friendships, all jumbled into this particular assortment of letters.

The idea started, maybe, with a crush on my friend's brother. Rather, with the moment my mom informed both my friend and her brother (and his wife) about said crush. This story is born not in that crush, but in the memories of a wrap-around couch, in popcorn and chocolate chips, in Center Stage and Nintendo, in seventh-grade English classrooms and eighth-grade trauma, in friendship and growing up.

I almost didn't finish this book. At forty thousand words, more than halfway done, I walked away. It was hard and painful and I was terrified no one would like it if I went just a *little* deeper with my subject matter. But just like Mia, I'm so glad I came back. I'm beyond proud of this story.

Truthfully, none of it would have been possible without Jeff, who is the absolute best husband and partner a person could ever hope to have. Who encourages me and supports me always, even when I make it very hard to do so. Thank you for letting me rest my head on your chest to figure out how to describe the first Swallows Ridge scene.

Also, my mom, who frequently asks when she's getting the next book but then deals me in for another card game when I really should be writing. Mom, you're an incredible cheerleader and friend, and I love you.

I'm forever grateful for all the early readers and supporters of my work: Darci, Kayla, Laura, and my ARC readers!

For RJ, who formats and edits like a champ.

And for Alexandra, who crafts such lovely covers.

For my friends and original Couchies: thank you. You're blessings.

To the local indie bookstores who have supported me (Aaron's, Cupboard Maker, and my beloved Pocket Books), thank you for taking a chance on me. (Please please please support your local independent bookstores!)

Thanks to my family for putting up with my constant talking about writing (despite my lack of actually doing it), and for showing up in so many ways to support me.

L & Z, my good eggs... you bring me so much joy and laughter. I'm immensely proud of you both and hope you make your dreams happen. Love you, bruh, and wuv iz tiz.

And to *you*—thank you for picking up *Band Mates*. Thank you for giving me a chance and investing your time and energy into these characters and this story. I'd write no matter what, but it's so much better knowing you're out there reading it.

A FINAL NOTE

Did you know:

- Every 2 seconds, someone in the U.S. needs blood and/or platelets.

- Approximately 29,000 units of red blood cells are needed daily in the U.S.

As someone who strongly dislikes needles and is generally a wimp (but has one tattoo regardless), I will say that blood donation is an easy and relatively painless way to help save lives. The donation process takes about an hour of your day, and you get free things (my favorites are Famous Amos cookies and Oatmeal Creme Pies, but we've also gotten free T-shirts, beanies, movie tickets, and more). Please consider donating to help save lives!

ALSO BY MEGAN

Coffee Dates
Ship Mates